MURDER AT THE MASQUERADE

A Harlowe & Fitch Historical Mystery

ELIZABETH ROSE

OLIVERHEBERBOOKS

A Note to My Readers:

Dear Readers,

The **_Harlowe & Fitch Historical Mystery Series_** is ongoing, and the main mystery has been solved at this point, though a new murder always awaits. While every installment can be read as a stand-alone, it is advised, and also ideal, to start from the beginning with **_Murder at Mablethorpe Castle_**, Book 1, and to read them in order. If not, there could be surprises ruined along the way.

Welcome to the world of Harlowe & Fitch, where investigations into murders in Mablethorpe and the surrounding areas are underway. A headstrong noblewoman searching for justice, and a stealthy sheriff trying to secure the safety of his town, team up to uncover that which is hidden but needs to be brought to the surface.

Elizabeth Rose

Chapter One

Grimsthorpe Manor, England, Late 1300s

Lord Daniel Lovelle, lord of Grimsthorpe Manor, pulled his wife, Lady Amelia Lovelle, into the solar, pushing her up against the wall, kissing her hard.

"Daniel, stop it!" Amelia turned her head and tried to push him away. For a man twenty years her senior, he was determined, and never seemed to stop trying. Even if it never worked. "We're in the midst of a masquerade, celebrating the betrothal of Lady Vivienne Harlowe and Sheriff Zachariah Fitch, unless you've forgotten." Her mask covered her eyes and the upper part of her face, leaving her mouth free so she could speak, eat, and drink. Her abundance of fake blonde hair was propped high atop her head, curly tendrils cascading down her shoulders to her exposed cleavage. Her costume for the gathering tonight was that of a milkmaid.

"We have time, Amelia. Sheriff Fitch and his betrothed have yet to arrive," he said in a low, gravelly voice. His beard scratched at her neck as he nibbled behind her ear, trying to excite her. Unfortunately, all it did was repel her instead. She never should have agreed to marry him. The past two months of being his wife hadn't ended her troubles but only made more.

Daniel pulled at her bodice next, trying to reach inside. When she pushed him away he had the look of lust in his eyes. He always had that look...just not the means to see things through.

Dressed in his musician costume, her husband looked ridiculous in his parti-colored hose, and his actions were naught but appalling. Short curls of graying hair on his chest peeked out from his partially untied tunic, and the sight did nothing to make her want him. He wore a cord around his neck that hung down, holding a small flute. Black horsehair made up his head covering, the lot of it falling halfway down his back and sticking out in all directions. He also wore a headpiece made from paper and wax that was in the shape of a lute. The tall neck of the lute stuck out in a silly manner to one side, strapped as it was atop his head. Every time he turned his head, he almost hit someone or something with the blasted thing. "It'll work this time, I promise."

"Daniel, I've heard that before. You know it won't." She let out a long sigh.

"This time will be different, I swear. I have an amulet that will make things better." He reached into the top of his braies and pulled out a stone attached to a cord around his waist. He held up the amulet to show it to her. Her jaw dropped when she realized it was in the shape of male genitalia.

"What is that!" she gasped, not believing her eyes. "And where on earth did you get it?"

"It doesn't matter. All that should concern you is that tonight will be different from all the other times."

"Nay!" she scolded, pushing him away. "What is the matter with you? We are hosting an important celebration for these people, just as you promised your good friend, Lord Mablethorpe, since he is not able to host such an affair himself just now."

"I think the masquerade can wait. Really." He waggled his eyebrows, glancing down at his breeches. "It'll be any moment now I'm sure."

Amelia wrinkled her nose and shook her head in disgust. "Take a moment and compose yourself, Daniel. Then return to the party and act in a proper manner. In the way that is expected of a nobleman." She pushed him away and hiked her bodice back up, then proceeded to shake out her skirt. That done, she made her way across the room and yanked open the door. In her hurry to leave, she almost knocked into a hefty woman dressed like an alewife.

"Oh, I'm sorry, my lady," said the masked woman in a hoarse voice. She curtsied, holding her beefy hand atop the wimple that covered her head as she kept her face pointed at the floor. The corridor was filled with guests since it led directly to the great hall where the party was to take place. She noticed a man dressed like Robin Hood, with a short green velvet tunic and a hat and red plume on his head, standing in the shadows. Several women dressed like dancers were flirting with a couple of men who looked like nobles, all of them wearing masks and cloaks covered in feathers. There were even people dressed up like animals...these, too, masked to conceal their identity, of course. One man even had antlers atop his head. The costumes were elaborate and expensive. Everyone loved a masquerade. It was fun to cavort about, flirt, and act silly without anyone ever knowing who they were. The costumes were all grand, except for the figure at the end of the corridor wearing a long, black hooded cloak and carrying a scythe. He was obviously Death. An odd choice for such a joyous event as this.

"It's all right," Amelia told the woman. "No harm done." She glanced up and down the corridor. Torches on the stone walls were lit and burning brightly, the smoke filling the area. "Nay, no more torches!" she shouted, seeing a servant boy lighting one further down the corridor. "I told you, it's too smoky. Not to mention, it is dangerous with all these ornate costumes. Page, find some oil lanterns to replace these at once," she called to a young boy standing there in awe, watching the masked guests walk by. "I've ordered fewer torches this night. The keep is lit well enough."

"Aye, my lady." The boy, dressed in naught more than rags and bare feet, ran off to find the oil lamps as told.

The open flames of burning torches made Amelia uneasy. Her husband always wanted to use them for better lighting, assuring her that they were safe. She felt otherwise, believing that torches belonged outdoors, not inside a manor. Everyone knew that! She glanced back at the closed door of the solar, hoping her husband wouldn't be long. Amelia needed him to be with her when she greeted their guests of honor. She had never met Lady Vivienne or Sheriff Fitch before, and felt very nervous, still being a new bride. She didn't want to seem like a bad hostess. When she looked back down the corridor, the man dressed like Death had disappeared and for that she was glad. Because that was the last thing she needed to see tonight.

Lord Daniel Lovelle poured himself a drink of whisky, trying to quell his anger. All he wanted was to be able to perform his husbandly duties. But for years now, things weren't working out the way they should. His new bride was young and beautiful, but seemed to want nothing to do with him since he couldn't satisfy her the way she desired. He thought tonight would be different, but Amelia had never given him a fair chance. He ripped the amulet off the cord around his waist, holding it in his palm and staring at it blankly. Mayhap it really held no power, after all. He heard the door open behind him and quickly thrust the amulet in a secret pouch he had sewn into his cloak. A smile spread across his face as he poured himself a drink. Perhaps all hope wasn't lost, after all.

"I had hoped you'd return, Amelia," he chuckled, bringing the cup to his mouth to take a drink as he turned around. When he realized the person who had entered the room was not his wife, he stopped in mid-motion. "Who are you?" he ground out. "You don't belong in here. This is my private solar. How dare you enter without being invited inside the room."

Heavy footsteps resounded as the person came toward him.

"God's eyes, put down that torch! Don't you know how dangerous that is around all these costumes?" As the intruder approached him, he turned to place his cup on the table. That's when something hit him in the head, his headpiece knocking against something. Then he felt choked and as if he couldn't breathe. Dizziness overcame him and his knees buckled. He clutched his throat as his body hit the floor. He gasped for air. All he could see as he fought for his life were flames shooting up all around him. The fire burned him as his head covering went up in smoke, the wax and paper of his costume making him naught but a living torch and he was not able to do anything about it. Daniel tried to cry out, but could no longer talk, see, or hardly even breathe. Smoke filled the room as well as his lungs. Still, he fought for his life, trying to make out the person behind the mask, someone who was now choking him using something wrapped around Daniel's throat. But it was too late. This night had taken a horrendous turn. When his eyes drifted shut from lack of air, he realized this was a situation from which he would never be able to return.

THE MASQUERADE BALL at Grimsthorpe Manor was going to be a true delight, thought Lady Vivienne Harlowe as the cool evening air hit her face as they traveled in the wagon to the celebration. She had never felt so alive. Or so pretty. She had been anticipating this event for the past month, ever since she'd learned that the masked ball was being given in her and Zachariah's honor.

Vivienne's Uncle Gilbert and Aunt Ellen Irvine were her guardians ever since the death of her parents. They'd lost their three children to death through the years and considered Vivienne no less than their own daughter. They did everything for her, always wanting her to have the best. They even put up with her not-so-ladylike ways of wielding a sword and even wearing breeches on occasion. The ball would have been held at her home, Mablethorpe Castle, but since her uncle was still ill and healing, it was decided that the celebration should be held somewhere else. For now, he needed rest and quiet, most especially, time to fully regain his strength.

The clip-clop of the horse's hooves echoed off the brick road leading up to the door of Grimsthorpe Manor. This was the home of Lord Daniel Lovelle and his new bride, Lady Amelia. Lord Lovelle was friends with her uncle, although Vivienne didn't really know him. Her uncle had told her that Lord Lovelle was also favored by the King.

The King. Vivienne's hand went to her chest, where she wore a jeweled ring of King Edward's, hidden safely under her clothes. It had been her mother's dying wish to give it to her. With her last breath, her mother told Vivienne that it was the King's ring and that King Edward was her birth father. Vivienne actually had a chance recently to meet Edward, but it hadn't been a long enough visit for her to truly get to know the man who'd sired her. A crazy thought filled her head then, or mayhap it was a wish, she wasn't sure. But she found herself wondering if perhaps her father...King Edward, would be here at the Masquerade Ball to help her celebrate her betrothal as well. Anxiety filled her, and as quickly, she shook away the thought and dropped her hand to her side. The King had more important things to do than to be here to greet his bastard daughter. Why had she ever had that thought? Why did it even matter? She'd been raised by Abiathar Harlowe, who had been married to her mother, Flanie. Vivienne had a father, and didn't need King Edward to step in and be one now. Or did she? After all, her mother and Abiathar were both dead after being murdered on the road seven years ago.

"This is beautiful!" she exclaimed, releasing a deep cleansing breath, taking in the sight in the setting sun. Her guard, Richard, stopped the horse and wagon directly in front of the manor. Sheriff Zachariah Fitch, her betrothed, sat on the bench seat next to her, looking ever so handsome in his costume portraying Robin Hood.

Grimsthorpe Manor was nothing like a small manor house at all. Nay, it was more like a small version of a castle and much more elaborate too. A long brick road led up to the manor and through the gate that opened up to an inner courtyard. Rose gardens and pruned trees made to look like animals lined the walkway and filled large spaces in front of the keep. The holding itself was a fortress, stoutly secured with its two stories and four square towers, one on each corner, rising up to kiss the sky. The towers were like tall soldiers guarding over the place. The property's eyes and strength. The entire estate was mayhap only about a third of the size of Mablethorpe Castle, but still impressive, grand, and very intriguing, indeed. Vivienne couldn't wait to see more.

"Move quickly, Vivienne, a storm is approaching and we are about to get wet." Zachariah jumped from the wagon and held out his arms to help her dismount. Dressed as a Greek goddess,

Vivienne felt like a queen tonight. Over her fine linen chemise, she wore a long gown created from gold silk that was pleated and fell to the ground and even trailed behind her. Her large triangular sleeves, or tippets, were just as long, and fluttered in the breeze as she walked. Over one shoulder was a long, white wispy veil that she chose to wear around her neck and down her back, rather than attached to the laurel wreath crown on her head. Although it was custom for a noblewoman to wear her hair plaited, Vivienne's long blonde tresses tumbled loose tonight because she felt as if braids were too inhibiting for a goddess.

Just as her soft, velvet slippers touched the ground, thunder rumbled and shook the air. The sky looked ominous now, and threatening. Not at all what she wanted to see at a celebration that was supposed to be uplifting and fun. A cool breeze blew in, causing her to wrap her arms around herself for warmth.

"Here's your cloak, my lady." Zachariah draped her long purple woolen cloak lined in ermine fur around her shoulders.

"Zachariah, I didn't think...this isn't a proper cloak for a goddess!" She now wished she'd had enough foresight to have a goddess cloak designed for the evening, in case there was a turn in the weather. While the days were still warm, it was autumn now, and soon the winter winds and snow would cover the land and the plants would die and turn brown. It wasn't at all what she liked, but it was a part of nature.

"Mayhap not," said Zachariah. "But it is the cloak of a lady, and protection enough to keep her dry since we're about to be soaked." He looked up at the darkening sky when he spoke. "Be glad for its comfort."

"I am," she admitted, drawing the cloak more securely about her. Sure enough, as if to prove Zachariah's words, rain started to fall, hitting against them. It made a tinkling sound as it struck the metal hoods of the lanterns on high poles that lined the walkway leading to the stairs of the keep. The flames jumped and flickered in the wind, casting shadows on the stone courtyard as the lanterns swung back and forth on their tall poles, each long line of them seeming as silent, unbending sentinels in the wind. A sudden shudder wracked Vivienne's body. Not because of the weather, but because that dreadful churning in her stomach had just returned. And that was never a good thing at all.

"Oh no," she said, holding her palm against her belly as she accepted the sheriff's proffered arm to escort her inside.

"We need to get going, Vivienne. The sky is about to open up," the sheriff told her in a low voice from her side as they started to walk. She stole a quick glance at him, glad he'd chosen to dress as Robin Hood tonight. He looked strikingly handsome, wearing a short green tunic and pointed hat with a long red plume attached to it. He wore tight hose instead of breeches, and had complained to Vivienne earlier that he felt too exposed without actual trews, even if it was considered stylish. She told him she liked the costume, and that his mask would conceal his identity so he need not feel embarrassed.

"Wait," she said, stopping once again, her stomach tightening. "Something doesn't feel right," she told him, recognizing the signs. In the past, every time something bad was about to happen, her stomach had felt this way.

"Doesn't feel right?" the sheriff repeated her words. "Could it be because rain is hitting us like sharp arrows and you're standing here like your feet are frozen to the ground?" There was no hiding the irritation in his voice.

Vivienne heard a slight sound coming from the back of the wagon and she turned to look, since it'd caught her interest.

Zachariah looked down at her hand on her belly.

"Oh, nay, Vivienne. Please don't tell me your stomach is churning." He shook his head, knowing exactly what that meant. "Can't I have just one night with nothing bad happening?"

"I can't help it, Zachariah. It's not like I want to feel this way, it just happens."

"So just push that feeling away right now. We cannot afford any trouble. This is a masquerade ball in our honor. A lot of planning and expense has happened in preparation and nothing is going to ruin our happiness tonight. Do you hear me? Absolutely nothing, I say."

"I truly wish I could agree to that—however, I can't help feeling that something bad is about to happen. I hope I'm wrong, but I'm usually not." Beyond all hope, Vivienne wanted to be wrong about this. After all, tonight was special and a true celebration in their honor. But sadly, her churning stomach always meant that trouble followed them, and sometimes even a murder was on the way.

"Did you want me to wait for you, Lady Vivienne?" Richard, Vivienne's castle guard, who was acting as their driver tonight since her uncle insisted on the guard's protection, looked down from the bench seat of the cart.

"There's no need to stay," the sheriff told him. "I'm here with Lady Vivienne. Just return to Mablethorpe Castle and come back to collect us at midnight."

"Aye," said Richard with a nod, starting to turn the horse and cart. The rain began to fall faster.

"Nay, wait!" cried Vivienne with her hand in the air. "Richard, I'd prefer if you'd stable the horse and wait for us here in Grimsthorpe."

"What?" Zachariah looked at her in surprise. His expression told her that he was highly insulted.

"Are you sure, my lady?" asked Richard. The guard's eyes flashed over to the sheriff and then back to her again. "After all, you do have Sheriff Fitch with you for protection."

"I know. But I have a feeling I might need your services tonight as well, and want you near."

"As you wish," said Richard, turning the wagon and heading for the stable.

"Come along," growled Zachariah, taking her by the arm and all but pulling her down the walkway that led to the keep.

"You're upset with me, aren't you?" she asked.

"Nay." He couldn't look at her when he spoke. "Yes. Oh hell, I don't know. I just thought that now that we're betrothed and about to be married, you'd have enough trust in me that you'd know I'd protect you and that you don't need your damned castle guard."

"I do know that."

"Then why did you ask the guard to wait as well?" They continued forward to the keep as they spoke.

"Because, I saw movement under the hay in the back of the wagon as I dismounted."

"Movement?" Zachariah stopped for a second to look at her, not even seeming to notice the rain anymore that was making his plume soggy. His hand slowly rested on the hilt of the sword he wore at his side. "Are you saying someone is hiding in the wagon?" His gaze trailed back to the cart as Richard drove it to the stables.

"Yes, I believe so. And I thought I heard a slight whimper too."

"Whimper? Like crying? Of a...baby?" The sheriff craned his neck to see through the rain, trying to focus on the wagon now.

"Nay. Like a dog."

"Oh hell no!" Zachariah threw his hands in the air. "Martin is in the wagon with Grunt, isn't he?" he spat, speaking of Vivienne's seven-year-old son and her bloodhound. "If so, that is even more reason for Richard to leave and take them back to Mablethorpe Castle anon."

"I'd normally agree with that, Sheriff, but since my stomach is churning and I know trouble awaits us tonight, I want to keep my son close to me. Or at least close to Richard so he can protect him."

The sky opened up then and rain poured down, causing everyone who was still outside to dash for cover.

"Pick up your skirts and run, Vivienne, or we're going to spend the evening wringing water out of our clothes and looking like drowned rats."

"Let's go." Vivienne lifted her hood over her head, picked up the hem of her gown, and then, with Zachariah's hand still on her arm, they ran for the keep and entered through the opened door just as the downpour turned into an all-out squall.

"Good evening. Will you join us in the great hall from some spiced mead?" came a woman's voice as Vivienne lowered her hood. Wearing the mask, she had to turn her head fully to see who was speaking.

To her surprise, she saw a woman in a milkmaid's costume standing there at the door and greeting guests. "Lady Lovelle? Is that...you?" asked Vivienne, never having met the woman, but figuring she held the elegance of a noblewoman, so it must be.

The milkmaid raised her mask to show her eyes, perusing Vivienne from head to foot. "Are you Lady Vivienne Harlowe by any chance?" she asked curiously.

"Yes. Yes, I am." Vivienne quickly lifted her mask too and smiled. Then she put it back in place, resuming her anonymity once again. "And this is my betrothed, Sheriff Zachariah Fitch." She motioned with her hand to the sheriff. He was looking down, pulling on his tunic, and trying to wring out some water. The red plume on his hat dangled to the side like a limp fish from being so wet. She elbowed him in the side and his head jerked up.

"Yes. Hello. My lady," he said, with a deep bow. Unfortunately, dipping his head so low sent a stream of water pouring out of the rim of his cap and onto his foot, causing Vivienne to raise her hand to her mouth to hold back her giggle.

The lady of the castle nodded. "Yes, I saw you here earlier, Sheriff," said the woman.

"Me?" Zachariah's hand slapped against his chest. "Nay, my lady. I assure you it was not me. We've only just arrived."

"Nay, I'm certain of it." She cocked her head and peered at him from the corner of her eye. "I am sure I saw you in the corridor outside my husband's solar just recently."

"That couldn't be," said Vivienne with a smile. "As the sheriff said, we've only just arrived."

"Oh. I see. My mistake." Lady Lovelle replaced her mask, looking quite confused.

"Thank you for this wonderful opportunity," said Vivienne.

"My pleasure," answered the woman. "Please follow me to the great hall."

"Will Lord Lovelle be joining us too?" she asked, as they walked behind Lady Lovelle and entered into the highly decorated room with its vast ceiling. "Your husband is a good friend of my uncle, and I'd like to thank him personally as well for hosting this celebration in our honor."

Vivienne stopped, taking a moment to drink in the beautiful surroundings. Sconces on every wall held burning candles that were surely made from beeswax since from where she was standing she could smell the scent of cinnamon and roses. The hall was lit up with a soft glow. Around her was a crowd of people all looking so magical in their costumes and masks. Even if she knew someone here, which she didn't, she wouldn't recognize them tonight. The guests all wore elaborate costumes, some of the women's headpieces even taller than their hair that was braided and coiled at the tops of their heads. The men looked elegant as well. There were magical-looking beings, some dressed as knights and ladies in their best clothing, and still other guests who were dressed as commoners or even animals. One thing was for sure by all the smiles, everyone was having fun. It was truly an exciting sight to see.

All the guests were laughing and talking and drinking, while musicians played cheery music. The long trestle tables were covered with silken cloths of silver and gold that actually matched Vivienne's costume. Such finery was silly and wasteful, in her opinion, although certainly eye-catching and pretty. Still, the cloths would be ruined with stains and grease by the end of the night.

"The table coverings match my outfit," she commented.

"Yes, on purpose," said Lady Lovelle. "You uncle told my husband what you and Sheriff Fitch would be wearing, and we were sure to go to extremes to make everything about this night the best we could for you."

"Well, thank you. So much," said Vivienne, never having felt this pampered or special.

"May I take your cloak, my lady?" A servant girl stood there with her arms outstretched.

"Allow me," said Zachariah, lifting the cloak from around Vivienne's shoulders and handing it to the young girl.

"Mary, don't drag the cloak on the ground," called out Lady Lovelle after the girl. "It's so hard to find good help," said Lady Lovelle in apology. "I hope you like the flowers. They all came from the many gardens on the grounds."

"Oh, I do! And the garden I saw in front was breathtaking." Vivienne looked around at all the flowers of so many kinds that decorated the great hall.

Atop every table stood a vase that held bouquets of purple

Michaelmas daisies, or asters, mixed with bright orange and gold marigolds. In the corners of the room were large vats holding late blooming roses of pink and white that trailed down the sides of the earthenware vessels, woven in with dark green ivy. That only made Vivienne's stomach churn more since ivy indoors was considered bad luck and a harbinger of misfortune. But Vivienne wasn't about to tell that to Lady Lovelle, since she didn't want to seem ungrateful. Vivienne's favorite flowers took her interest next. They were the colorful chrysanthemums that were placed in an indoor tiered fountain in a corner of the room. Instead of water inside the fountain, there were thick bunches of chrysanthemums that burst forth like little suns, filling the air with their sweet, powerful scent.

There were even wire cages hanging from the ceiling beams that held foxglove, late-blooming violets, and what smelled to her to be apple mint. It was breathtaking, indeed. No expense spared. And all in her honor. Vivienne was impressed, and felt so special that she didn't want this good feeling to end. But as soon as the thought crossed her mind, that gnawing at her gut got even stronger, making her feel as if she would retch.

"My husband was momentarily distracted, but will be with you soon," Lady Lovelle reported. "Please, feel free to roam the great hall and mingle with the guests. There are servers to bring you spiced wine and warm mead, and fruit hand-pies to hold you over until the meal is served."

"Thank you," said Vivienne. "This is wonderful. Thank you so much."

"What is going on over there?" asked Zachariah, nodding with his head to indicate something across the room.

Vivienne looked up to see a crowd of people standing around a small table that looked to be covered in a dark cloth with suns and moons painted on it. A young woman who appeared about twenty years of age or so, was seated there and she had cards spread out on the table.

"Oh, that's my silly husband's doing," said Lady Lovelle, with a disgruntled expression on her face. "He hired a woman to tell fortunes. I think such things are the work of the devil and didn't want her here, but he insisted on her inclusion, saying that you'd like having her here, Lady Vivienne."

"Really?" she asked, not sure if she should feel insulted or pleased by the way the lady of the castle said that. Either way, Vivienne was curious and did feel quite intrigued. "I think it was a nice gesture."

"Thank you, Lady Lovelle," said the sheriff. as another guest struck up a new conversation with the lady of the castle and took her attention. "Vivienne, let's find some drinks and mayhap something to eat," said Zachariah. "I'm hungry."

"You go on, I'll wait for you over there," said Vivienne, her eyes fixed on the small table. "I want to see what that fortune-teller is doing."

"I'm sure whatever it is, it is only some silly nonsense, so don't get swept up into any of her so-called predictions," he warned her.

"I'll be fine," she responded, walking straight to the table as Zachariah went to hunt down food and drinks. Vivienne stopped directly in front of the mysterious woman, as everyone seemed to move aside when she approached. It must be how much she looked like a goddess, because in costume and wearing a mask, no one should know who she was.

Slowly, the entertainer's attention turned upward and locked on Vivienne. "Can I read the cards for you? My lady?" asked the girl.

"My lady, did you say?" asked Vivienne with a slight giggle. "What makes you think that I'm a noblewoman and not a commoner?"

"The cards told me." She scooped up the cards as the onlookers laughed and walked away, leaving just Vivienne there with her.

"You are Lady Vivienne Harlowe for whom this celebration was meant." The woman told her, and didn't ask.

"Yes, that's right. But don't say that too loudly. After all, this is a masquerade, and our identities are supposed to be kept a secret."

"Of course." With her eyes turned downward, she mixed the cards and placed them in a pile in front of Vivienne. She then used the fingers of one hand to fan them out atop the table.

"What are you doing?" asked Vivienne curiously, never having encountered anything like this before.

"Choose a card. I will read your fortune."

"Me? Oh no, I don't think so." Why was her body shaking?

"Why not? Are you afraid of what you might discover?" This woman had no fear in saying what she felt. Vivienne wasn't sure she liked that.

Vivienne's hand went back to her clenched stomach and her gaze swept the great hall. She wished Zachariah would hurry back, because part of her *was* afraid. Scared, that is, of what she might find out since her stomach was so upset. But Vivienne wasn't one to ever turn down a challenge. Neither was she about to walk away before she at least chose a card. This opportunity might never happen again and she couldn't let it just pass her by.

"Well, all right," she said, her hand shaking as she slowly reached out and picked a card, sliding it facedown across the table. "What is your name?" she asked, trying to make small talk.

"I am Morgana. I am here today not only by request of Lord Lovelle, but also as a favor to the King."

"The King?" That surprised Vivienne, since King Edward

was superstitious and she didn't think he'd have anything to do with having fortunes told. "Do you know King Edward?"

"Yes, of course. I am his card reader." Her face remained stone-like and there was no expression at all in her voice. "You know him too."

"That's right. I do." Vivienne cleared her throat. "I...I actually met King Edward just recently." She had almost told Morgana that she was the King's bastard, but stopped herself for some reason. It wasn't a secret anymore, but something made Vivienne want to stay quiet about that connection right now.

"I know. You are the king's bastard."

So she did know, after all. So much for discretion.

"I am," she admitted softly.

Morgana continued to fuss with her cards. "As am I." The girl peeked at the card that Vivienne had handed her, but didn't turn it over. Her eyes widened and then turned almost to slits.

"You are?" asked Vivienne anxiously. "Do you mean that you are the king's bastard too? Really?" she asked, excited to possibly meet another of her half-siblings.

"We are half-sisters, my lady. It shouldn't surprise you, since the King has many bastard children."

"I know that. But I never thought I'd be meeting one of my half-siblings tonight."

"I did."

"You did?"

"Of course."

"How did you know? Oh, the King must have told you."

"Even before King Edward asked me to come here, my cards told me I'd be meeting you, Lady Vivienne."

"So King Edward asked you to be here? I thought it was of Lord Lovelle's doing."

"Where do you think Lord Lovelle got the idea?" She slowly looked up, her green eyes that reminded Vivienne of a cat, staring into her as if she could see right through her. Vivienne had never seen anything like it. "I...I don't know what to say."

"Vivienne? I brought you spiced wine, since I couldn't find any mead." Zachariah walked up and put the goblet in her hand.

"Zachariah, this is Morgana. And you'll never believe it, but she is a bastard of King Edward as well. That means we are half-sisters."

Zachariah moaned and lifted his cup to his mouth and took a drink.

"She had me draw a card and is about to tell me my fortune," continued Vivienne.

"Vivienne, I don't like this," said Zachariah. "You are too gullible sometimes. You shouldn't believe a word that someone like her tells you. She doesn't really know your future, no matter what she says."

"Zachariah, that was rude," Vivienne retorted.

Morgana shook her head and put her hand over the card which was still not turned over. "Perhaps he's right, my lady. It would be best for you to enjoy this celebration and not be distracted with your future or concerned with my readings at all."

"Thank you," said Zachariah, sounding relieved. "I couldn't agree with you more. Come, Vivienne, we will dance." Zachariah said, and started to pull her away but Vivienne refused to leave.

"Nay." She slipped out of his grip. "I am not going anywhere until Morgana shows me the card I chose and explains to me what it means."

"It's just all silly nonsense," growled the sheriff. "I urge you to walk away right now."

"Nay, I won't do that, and you can't make me," Vivienne protested, her stomach churning more than ever now. "Let me see my card," she said to Morgana. "Turn it over," she commanded, holding her breath.

"If you insist, my lady." Morgana flipped the card over and Vivienne's jaw dropped. She heard air hiss out from between Zachariah's teeth. Mayhap she shouldn't have been so stubborn. Truth was, she should have walked away after all, just like Zachariah wanted. Vivienne didn't need to ask the meaning of the painting depicted on her chosen card, because it was more than clear. It was the image of the Grim Reaper, in a long black cloak with his hood covering his head. Beady little red eyes stared out from under the hood, but nothing else about his face could be seen. The Grim Reaper stood over a grave while clutching a scythe with his long bony fingers. All around him was a storm with jagged lightning and eerie black shadows coming out of the clouds.

"That means...death, doesn't it?" Vivienne all but whispered. Her mouth felt so dry that she could barely speak.

"It does, my lady," was Morgana's answer.

"Whose death?" Vivienne asked, her heart now beating so hard that she thought it would pop right out of her chest. The sound of it filled her ears like ancient drumming.

"It is not clear who, but there is no denying the fact that before the evening is over, someone will have died." Morgana pushed the card back into the pile, still showing no emotion at all.

"Stop it!" shouted Zachariah. "Right now. I don't like this game you play. You are purposely trying to ruin our evening by upsetting my betrothed, and I will not allow it. I'll have a word with Lady Lovelle about sending you away."

"Nay, Zachariah, don't do that." Vivienne nervously gripped his arm and looked back at Morgana who was putting her cards away into a purple velvet bag with a black leather drawstring. "Morgana, are your card readings ever wrong?" By the rood, she hoped the girl would say yes.

"Not usually, but I suppose it could happen," was her calm answer.

"See? That's what happened. It's all a mistake," Zachariah said, trying to soothe Vivienne.

"However, I don't need the cards to tell me, since I already know it will happen," continued Morgana.

"What does that mean?" asked Zachariah, but Morgana didn't have a chance to answer before a scream was heard at the other end of the hall.

"My lady!" cried a chambermaid. "There is a fire in Lord Lovelle's solar and he is lying on the floor. I think he's dead!"

Chapter Two

Chaos emerged as the attendees of the party started screaming and running to and fro. The acrid smell of smoke started to taint the air, and the threat of the manor house going up in flames was more than real.

"Go outside, now!" Zachariah shouted into the panicked crowd, then ripped off his mask and threw it to the floor. "Listen, all of you! Bring buckets of water and make a chain," he yelled at them as he took off at a run for the burning solar.

Vivienne glanced over to the table that the card-reader had occupied, but she had taken her things and was gone. Frantically, Vivienne scanned the surging swell of guests pushing and shoving to get out, and that's when she spied Morgana weaving her way through the crowd, heading out the door to the courtyard. Thankfully, it seemed the rain had let up. Vivienne picked up her skirts and hurried after her, determined not to let her leave.

"Morgana, wait!" she yelled, running after the girl. She had to push through the crowd, and almost fell, but managed to exit the keep. Once outside, she saw her heading for the stables and hurried down the stone steps in pursuit. "Morgana, wait up. I want to talk to you," she called out, but the girl didn't stop or even turn around, and Vivienne wasn't even sure that she'd heard her.

"My lady, what is all the commotion?" Richard ran up to join her, his sword clutched in his hand. Right behind him was her young son, Martin, his little friend, Mouse, and her dog, Grunt.

"Mother? Did I hear there is a fire inside?" asked Martin, as the two young boys ran to her side. Grunt barked, adding to all the noise and chaos.

"Martin, what are you and Mouse doing here?" she scolded. "And why did you bring Grunt?"

"I'm sorry," said Martin, hanging his head. "But Mouse and I have never seen a masquerade ball before and we were curious."

"That's right," said the dark-haired little boy that everyone called Mouse. He was an orphan who had befriended her son. Vivienne's heart had gone out to him, and she took Mouse as her ward since he was so young and all alone. "We like the costumes." Grunt barked some more.

"This was not a good idea at all." She pulled the boys close to her, not wanting them to get trampled in the frenzy. Her gaze shot over to the stables, but she could no longer see Morgana. Her opportunity had passed and she'd no longer be able to speak with her half-sister again tonight.

"I should like to help put out the fire, but I won't leave you." Richard slipped his sword back into his sheath.

"A man is dead," she told him.

"Is it another murder?" asked Mouse with wide eyes, looking up at her.

"God's teeth, I hope not," Vivienne answered, releasing a deep breath and looking back at the keep. Her hand went to her stomach again, and that told her that indeed, another murder had taken place. Still, she prayed that somehow she was wrong. "Richard, please help put out the fire. I'll watch the children."

"But, my lady," said Richard, with concern showing on his brow. "If it is indeed another murder, I should stay and protect you and the children instead."

"I'll protect her." Martin reached to his side for his wooden sword that he used in training to someday become a squire. "Oh, no. I forgot my sword back at the castle."

Grunt continued to bark.

"Grunt will protect us," said Mouse, kneeling down and hugging the barking dog.

"It'll be fine, Richard," Vivienne insisted. "Just please help put out the flames before the manor house is gone. This place is too beautiful to lose it. Now hurry."

"I will, my lady," Richard answered, taking off at a run.

"Mother, we can help put out the fire too," said Martin, always wanting to do his part to help, no matter what the situation.

"Nay, Martin. You two are little and would just get in the way. We'll wait for the sheriff to tell us it is safe before we enter the keep."

"Keep bringing buckets of water—we've almost put out the fire," shouted Zachariah, using a blanket from the bed in the solar, beating down the remaining flames. The curtains had caught afire, and by the looks of it, so did Lord Lovelle's costume, but the damage was thankfully minimal otherwise.

"Daniel!" cried Lady Lovelle, stopping in the doorway, her hand going to her mouth as she spied her half-burned husband's body lying on the floor.

"Someone, get her out of here," shouted Zachariah, taking

the blanket he'd been using and running over to cover the dead man's body to keep it from his wife's sight.

"I've got her," called out a tall man with dark hair, who seemed to work there. He looked to be a few years older than Lady Lovelle.

"Jerome," cried Lady Lovelle, running to the man and hiding her face against the man's chest.

"Who are you?" asked Zachariah.

"I am Jerome. Lord and Lady Lovelle's steward," said the man, still trying to calm the lady of the castle. "Is that...Lord Lovelle?" He looked down to the dead man on the floor.

"It is, I'm afraid," answered Zachariah.

"Sheriff, I'm here to help." Richard rushed into the room, coughing from the smoke.

"Thank you, Richard, but you are too late. The fire, thank goodness was caught in time, but I'm afraid Lord Lovelle didn't fare as well." Zachariah got down on his knees and pulled back the blanket to expose the body and check for signs of life. Sadly, Lord Lovelle had not survived. "He's dead," Zachariah announced.

"What do you think happened?" Richard kneeled down next to him, shaking his head as he stared at the body.

"I don't know yet." Zachariah moved Lord Lovelle's frayed and half-burned collar aside, spying signs of strangulation through the charred remains. A red rope-like burn colored what was left of the skin on his neck. "Can someone fetch the town sheriff, please?" he called out.

"He should be here already," said Lady Lovelle through her weeping. "He was invited to the party as he seems to always be here at the manor."

"What happened?" A short, burly man who was quite overweight, walked into the room. His hair was mussed and his tunic untied. He wore parti-colored hose and was covered with a dark cloak, his girth sadly preventing the cloak from properly closing, so revealing his gaping tunic and multi-colored hose. There were remnants of paint on his face, and Zachariah surmised that he must have been clothed as perhaps a jester, although he didn't see a hat.

"Oh, Sheriff, I'm so glad you're here," cried Lady Lovelle, running to the man's side. "Daniel has died. And someone started a fire."

"I'm here now, my lady." The Sheriff of Grimsthorpe put his arm around her shoulders. "You have nothing to worry about. You know your protection is my first concern."

"Yes, Sheriff, I know that. You always take good care of me, and for that I am ever grateful," answered Lady Lovelle with a sniffle.

"We need to find out if anyone saw anything." Zachariah covered the corpse back up and stood.

"Who are you?" Grimsthorpe's sheriff walked over to glare at Zachariah, causing Richard to jump up and stand next to Zachariah with his hand on the hilt of his sword.

"Richard, it's fine," Zachariah said softly and then put his attention back on the town sheriff. "I'm Sheriff Zachariah Fitch from Mablethorpe," he said. "This Masquerade is in honor of my betrothal to Lady Vivienne Harlowe."

"Oh, yes. Of course." The sheriff reached out to shake hands. "I am Ludwig Shireman. Sheriff of Grimsthorpe."

Zachariah shook the man's hand, which was covered in soot.

"Sorry about that." Ludwig smiled and wiped his palm on his tunic. "I've been helping to put out the fire." Zachariah hadn't remembered seeing him helping, but he supposed he could have been fetching water from the well down the line.

"This is Richard, Mablethorpe's castle guard," Zachariah told the man, nodding at Richard.

"And I am Lady Vivienne, Sheriff Fitch's betrothed." Vivienne swept into the room like the goddess she was dressed to be. Martin and Mouse plodded along behind her, with Grunt bringing up the rear.

"My lady," said Ludwig, looking down at the boys. "What are children doing here? I thought this was an adult masquerade only."

"This is my son, Martin, and my ward, Mouse." Vivienne pulled the boys to her, keeping her hands on their shoulders. The dog barked. "And my bloodhound, Grunt. They sneaked into the wagon, since the boys had never experienced a masquerade before and were curious to see the costumes and festivities."

"This is no place for children," growled Sheriff Grimsthorpe. "They'll have to leave."

"I agree," said Zachariah. "They can't be here."

"Why?" Martin boldly spoke up. "We've seen dead people before, if that's what's worrying you. Dead people don't bother us at all."

"Martin, hush!" Vivienne scolded.

"Was he murdered too, just like my brother?" asked Mouse, his big, brown eyes drinking in the dead man at their feet.

"Murder?" asked Ludwig with a chuckle. "Nay, boy, he obviously died in a fire."

Zachariah cleared his throat.

"What is it, Zachariah?" asked Vivienne.

"Sheriff Grimsthorpe, I'm sorry to tell you that this man was strangled before he, as well as the room, was set on fire."

"So he *was* murdered!" exclaimed Martin, taking a step toward the body, but Vivienne quickly yanked him back to her.

"That can't possibly be," said Grimsthorpe's sheriff. "And just call me Ludwig, Sheriff Fitch. Everyone does."

"Well then, Ludwig, check for yourself if you don't believe me." Zachariah uncovered the corpse and held out his arm.

"There are obviously marks of strangulation around the man's neck. His lips are blue, as well as his fingertips and behind his ears. Or what's left of them, anyway. That shows oxygen deprivation."

"How can you see anything through his charred remains?" Ludwig made a face and leaned over to look closer. "I really can't tell anything at all."

"This needs to be thoroughly investigated," instructed Zachariah. "You need to call in the coroner right away."

"Nay. Can't do that." Ludwig stood up and smoothed back his graying hair, which only made the bald spot atop his head even more prominent.

"Why not?" asked Vivienne.

"Because Grimsthorpe doesn't have a coroner," said Lady Lovelle, still weeping. The steward held her once again, giving her a kerchief to dry her eyes.

"Then call in the physician," suggested Vivienne. "He will confirm Sheriff Fitch's statement."

"The physician is out of town right now, but should return by tomorrow," said Lady Lovelle.

"What about your deputy, Ludwig?" asked Sheriff Fitch. "He should be here to help you investigate, not to mention help move the body."

"He...died. About a week ago. I haven't had time to replace him yet. I am training a new man named Rodger, even though I'm not sure he has what it takes to be in law enforcement."

"Then I'd be more than happy to help you," said Zachariah.

"Me too," Vivienne quickly added.

"You?" Ludwig made a face at Vivienne.

"My mother helps Sheriff Fitch with investigating murders all the time," said little Martin.

"So does Grunt," added Mouse, proudly petting the dog on the head.

"I'll take your help, Sheriff Fitch, but I won't have a lady helping me do my job," grunted Ludwig.

"The more eyes on the situation the better," remarked Vivienne.

"Nay," spat Ludwig, causing Vivienne to frown.

"Excuse us a moment," Zachariah told the others, pulling Vivienne to the side to talk to her in private. "Vivienne, you can't expect others to accept you being a part of investigating murders. Mayhap it would be better this time if you stayed away and just let me handle this with Grimsthorpe's sheriff."

"Zachariah, you know we agreed that even though we will be married soon, that I would continue to help you investigate murders."

"Yes, but things are different in Mablethorpe, sweetheart. Everyone knows and accepts your ways there. But here in Grimsthorpe, no one is going to agree to let a lady do a man's job."

"Hmph!" Vivienne's arms crossed over her chest and she glared at him.

"Is there something you want to say?" he asked.

"Yes. If you don't let me help, I won't tell you about how Morgana told me someone would die tonight before it even happened."

"The card-reader said that?" Lady Lovelle rushed over, having overheard their conversation. "I knew she'd be trouble. She must have done this. She killed my husband, I know it."

"Now, Lady Lovelle, please don't jump to conclusions before we've even found any clues," instructed Zachariah.

"Then find some clues," said Lady Lovelle. "Lady Vivienne, I want you and Sheriff Fitch to stay here at the manor and help to investigate my husband's death."

"See?" Vivienne looked over at Zachariah and raised a brow. "Not everyone rejects a woman's help."

Zachariah just groaned.

"We'd be happy to do that, Lady Lovelle," she answered. "Isn't that right, Sheriff Fitch?"

"That's correct," Zachariah said under his breath, not liking this idea at all, but knowing now that the lady of the manor had requested their services, that he couldn't turn her down. Not after all she went through to plan and carry out a masquerade ball in their honor. "Lady Lovelle, since it seems as if your husband might have been murdered, it is important to stop the guests from leaving until I can question them first."

"So *you* can question them?" asked Ludwig.

"So *we* can do so," Zachariah quickly corrected himself.

"Yes, the guests must be stopped from leaving," Ludwig quickly agreed. "Until the killer can be found."

"MARTIN, I'm sorry but it is best if Richard takes you and Mouse back to the castle," Vivienne explained a little later. "I cannot take the chance of anything happening to either of you while there is a killer on the loose." The boys were standing in the courtyard with Vivienne and Grunt. Richard had just brought the wagon and was sitting in the driver's seat waiting for them.

"I'll protect them with my life, and return them to Mablethorpe at once, my lady," said Richard. The horse whinnied and yanked its head to the side, seeming to be in a hurry to leave. Richard had to hold tightly to the reins and Vivienne wasn't sure the horse wasn't about to run, just to get out of there. Animals could always pick up on trouble.

"Thank you, Richard."

"I'll let your aunt and uncle know what happened tonight and tell them that you'll be staying here for a day or two to assist with the investigation."

"Yes. We'll send for you once the investigation is over," Vivienne told him.

"Come on, Grunt," said Martin, taking the dog by the collar and trying to pull him to the wagon, but the hound wouldn't go.

"Leave Grunt here," Vivienne instructed. "He's been an asset to solving murders in the past and we might need his help."

"Can't we please stay too?" asked Martin, releasing the dog's collar. Grunt ran over and sat down right at Vivienne's side.

"Please?" said Mouse in his soft voice.

"Nay, now don't ask again. And do not try to sneak back or you both will be punished for a long time to come," Vivienne warned the young boys. "I think you'd both better sit up front with Richard so he can keep a close eye on you."

"Fine," said Mouse, climbing up to sit on the bench next to Richard.

"Goodbye, Mother," said Martin, giving her a quick hug and following suit. He looked ever so sad staring at her from the seat of the wagon. Mouse was next to him doing the same, but said nothing.

"I'll return to Mablethorpe soon, I promise." Vivienne walked over and kissed each of the boys on the head.

As they started away, Zachariah emerged from the keep and ran after the wagon. Richard stopped for a minute while they spoke, and then Richard left.

"What did you say to Richard?" she asked Zachariah, walking over to join him.

"I just asked him to have my brother bring back some different clothes for me." Zachariah made a face and held out the ends of his long tunic. "After all, if I'm going to be investigating a murder, I'm going to need to be comfortable, not to mention taken seriously. I ought to be wearing a pair of breeches."

Vivienne giggled. "I suppose I should have asked Richard to have my handmaid pack me a bag as well. I won't be able to get away with being a goddess for long, I suppose."

Zachariah put his arms around her waist and pulled her to him, giving her a quick kiss on the lips. "You'll always be a goddess to me, Vivienne."

"So...you want me to stay dressed like this?" She held out her arms to her sides. "It might be days or weeks before we solve this murder."

"Don't worry. I told Richard to have some clothes sent back for you as well."

Grunt barked and took off running toward the stables.

"I wonder where he is going?" asked Zachariah.

"I don't know, but it's almost as if he's seen someone or knows something. Come on, let's find out." She picked up her gown and ran to the stables, with Zachariah right on her heels. When she got inside, she saw Grunt at the foot of a ladder. He was looking up to the hay loft and barking loudly. "I think someone might be up there," she whispered to Zachariah.

"I'll find out." With his sword strapped to his side—part of his Robin Hood costume, even though Vivienne told him he was supposed to have a bow and arrows—he climbed the ladder, disappearing up into the hay loft. Vivienne stood with Grunt, watching from below.

"Is someone up there?" she called up to him, but only silence answered her. "Zachariah? Did you hear me?" She was getting ready to climb the ladder herself when his head appeared over the ladder's top.

"Grunt was right." He pulled someone over to him, and she saw a woman scowling.

"Morgana? Are you hiding up there?" she asked. "Whatever for?"

"I'm not hiding. This is where Lord and Lady Lovelle told

me to sleep," Morgana answered. The two of them started down the ladder.

"Why didn't they give you a room inside the manor?" asked Vivienne.

"Why would they?" she answered, reaching the bottom of the ladder. "I'm just a bastard, and I do the work of the devil, don't you know?"

"I'm sure no one said that." Vivienne tried to console her newly-discovered half-sister.

"It's what Lady Lovelle said, word for word."

"She did?" asked Vivienne, reaching out and picking strands of straw from Morgana's long black hair. "I'm sorry to hear that."

"She didn't want me here. It was only Lord Lovelle who welcomed me when I arrived." Morgana fussed with the cloth bag hanging over her shoulder that held her cards and whatever else she possessed.

"Lady Vivienne told me that you predicted someone would die tonight," Zachariah said, as he reached the bottom of the ladder and joined them.

"That's right." Morgana bit her lip and looked to the ground.

"How did you know that?" asked the sheriff. "Did you perhaps overhear someone talking?"

"Nay. It's not like that." This question for some reason upset the young woman. She also didn't seem to want to explain.

"Well, was it in the cards? Is that what told you?" asked Vivienne, trying to come to her sibling's aid.

"Partially."

"Then, what's the other part?" asked Zachariah.

"I just...know things. That's all there is to say."

"Can you read minds, perhaps?" asked Vivienne. "I heard that some people can really do that."

"Nay! Of course not. I don't know or use magic. I'm not a witch!"

"I'm not so sure about that since you knew of the death before it happened," said the sheriff. "How do you explain that if you're not a witch and didn't overhear anything?"

Morgana let out a deep sigh. "Yes, it is true that I told you it would happen, but I had nothing to do with Lord Lovelle's death, I swear."

"I still don't understand. How did you know someone would die tonight?" Vivienne truly wanted to get to know her sister better and what skills she might have. No matter how strange or mysterious things seemed.

"I don't know how it happens. Not really. It just does." Morgana seemed almost as shaken as Vivienne felt right now.

"Sheriff Fitch?" The steward came to the door of the stables.

"Yes?" answered Zachariah.

"My name is Jerome. I am the castle steward."

"Yes, I know. I saw you inside Lord Lovelle's solar helping to comfort Lady Lovelle," he answered.

"Sheriff Ludwig has sent me to find you. He said to tell you that the body of Lord Lovelle has been moved."

"Moved? Where did he put it?"

"The corpse is laid out in the undercroft for now to keep it cool."

"Doesn't the physician have somewhere better to keep it?" asked Zachariah.

"Nay. The physician has a small one-room office in town and he lives there with his family. Sheriff Ludwig felt it would be better to keep Lord Lovelle's body here for now, until the questioning is over."

"Yes, I suppose that would be a good idea."

"When exactly will the physician return?" asked Vivienne. Grunt was with them and wandered over to sniff Jerome's leg.

"Actually, he has just returned to Grimsthorpe. He got back early."

"Then let's go talk to him," said Vivienne, starting for the door.

"Wait, Vivienne," said Zachariah. "The undercroft is no place for a lady. And certainly not one dressed like a goddess. Your fine costume will be ruined. You should stay here with Morgana."

"Why?" asked Vivienne. "I can see that Morgana has nothing more to say, so I feel my presence is needed in the undercroft instead."

"I've told you everything," agreed Morgana.

"Except how you knew someone would die," answered Zachariah.

"I've told you everything that I can for now," Morgana corrected her statement.

"Fine," grumbled Zachariah. "I can see Lady Vivienne isn't going to give up, so she'll come with me. But Morgana, you are not free to leave yet."

"I am expected back at King Edward's palace soon," explained Morgana.

"Then we'll send a missive and let him know you're here and for a good reason," Zachariah replied.

"And what reason is that?" She glared at him. "I told you I had nothing to do with the murder."

"That's right," added Vivienne. "Morgana was with me when the murder occurred."

"We don't know exactly when the murder occurred yet," Zachariah pointed out. "So stay here in the stables until I call for you again, Morgana." Zachariah left before either Morgana or Vivienne could protest. Vivienne hurriedly followed.

"Vivienne, I don't like that woman," Zachariah spoke under his breath as they headed to the keep, right behind Jerome.

"Well, I do." Vivienne smiled. "I see a lot of myself in her. I have a feeling she's going to do good things in life someday."

"How can you say that when you don't even know her? And what good could a damned witchy-woman possibly do?"

Vivienne stopped and looked directly into his eyes when she answered. "I can't tell you how I know she will do some wonderful things, but I assure you that she will. I feel it in my heart, I guess."

"Now you're sounding a lot like the witch," he complained.

"Her name is Morgana, and she is my half-sister." Vivienne pushed back her shoulders and stood a bit straighter. "We have the same blood, Sheriff. And I am telling you right now that Morgana is not only innocent, but I have a feeling that in the future she is going to be a strong asset in solving murders."

"And if you're wrong?" he asked, not looking at all pleased by her words.

"I'm not wrong and you know it."

"Do I?"

"Zachariah, she's...family," she told him.

Zachariah groaned. "Please don't say the word *family*."

"Why not?"

"Because every time you do, another person ends up living with me, and my house is already overcrowded."

"Did you mean to say *our* house? After all, we'll be married soon."

"We'll discuss this at another time, Vivienne."

Vivienne knew he'd said that because they'd never finalized if they'd be living in town or at the castle once they were wed. He was the sheriff and needed to live in town. But she was a noble and needed to live at the castle. Not sure what would happen or what they would do, she just smiled and answered in the kindest tone that she could.

"Yes, we'll have to discuss our living arrangements soon.

However, right now we have work to do. There is a dead man in the undercroft and a killer on the loose. Let's go find the person who ruined our betrothal celebration, because we need something good to happen in our lives. And I assure you that I am not willing to let every single special occasion be ruined by another murder."

Chapter Three

Zachariah ducked and walked through the door that led down the stairs to the undercroft of Grimsthorpe Manor. Jerome, the quiet steward, led the way. Vivienne was right behind Zachariah, and he held out his hand to help steady her while descending the steep stairs in her long goddess gown. Grunt pushed his way around them and made it to the undercroft first, where he proceeded to sniff around, probably looking for food.

There were tallow candles lit in jars, creating enough light to see the half-burned body of Lord Lovelle lying atop a thick board that was propped up between two barrels that probably contained apples. Ludwig was standing next to the body. Another man stood beside him, and was of average size, and looked to be about Zachariah's age of twenty-six. He had thinning hair, a short beard, and a long mustache that curled up on the ends. Zachariah assumed this must be the physician.

"We're here," he announced, causing the sheriff to turn around and the man with the mustache to look up.

"This is the town's physician, Sigbald Leach," Jerome introduced them. "And you already know Sheriff Ludwig."

"Sigbald, this is Sheriff Zachariah Fitch from Mablethorpe and his betrothed, Lady Vivienne Harlowe," Ludwig said, taking over the conversation.

"My lady," said the physician with a slight nod, still studying the body and not bothering to even look up to acknowledge them. "The masquerade was for the two of you."

"Yes, that's correct," said Vivienne. "And I can only say that I'm sorry things turned out this way, and that we didn't even get a chance to enjoy it."

"Mmph," snorted Sigbald, finally looking up at that comment. His bushy brows shot out in all directions and were in dire need of trimming. And while his mustache was very long, his beard was cut short with jagged ends, as if he'd used a dull knife to do it. This was an odd-looking man indeed.

"Sigbald, can you tell us what you've discovered?" asked Zachariah.

"Well, my guess is that he died of smoke inhalation by the blue tinge to him." The clothes were still on Lord Lovelle, probably since the corpse was fragile, and there were enough holes burned into the clothing to see the dead man's skin without removing his attire.

"The blue tinge means lack of oxygen," Vivienne spoke up, causing him to scowl at her.

"Does she really need to be down here?" asked the physician.

"I always assist Sheriff Fitch on murder investigations," Vivienne answered. "Even if I am a woman."

"Murder?" The physician shook his head. "Nay, this man died from smoke inhalation and from being on fire. No one could live through these bad burns. The fire almost consumed him."

Vivienne continued. "We think that is what the murderer was trying to do. Consume his body by flame before anyone could notice the real reason he died. It's just a good thing Sheriff Fitch moved quickly and managed to put the fire out fast. It was a stupid thing for the killer to do, since the entire manor could have been lost."

"I can't do my work with all this chatting." Sigbald threw his hands in the air.

"Vivienne, please. Let me," said Zachariah, with his hand on her wrist. She looked over at him and slowly nodded. "What about the red marks around his neck?" asked Zachariah. "It seems to me that he might have been strangled first and then lit on fire and burned."

"Yes, I see the marks," said Vivienne, walking closer and staring down at the body, as gruesome as it was to look at the corpse.

"Sheriff Ludwig, I don't feel as if a lady should be staring at this corpse, since it is so badly burned," said the physician in a soft voice.

"I've seen worse," said Vivienne, continuing to examine the body. "A woman with her face chewed up by rats and her eyeballs gone is much more horrifying than this, I assure you."

"Sigbald, do you feel as if it could have been murder?" asked Zachariah.

"Nay, it's not likely," said the physician, checking over the body a little more and then covering him up with a sheet.

"And why not?" asked Vivienne, crossing her arms over her chest.

"Lord Lovelle was liked by everyone, that's why." Sigbald collected up his things and put his instruments back into his bag. "I'm certain no one would have a reason to want to kill him."

"I agree with Sigbald," said Ludwig. "This was most likely just an accident and nothing more. Lord Lovelle was drinking and probably knocked into a candle and it started the fire."

"If that were true, why wouldn't he have run from the room?" asked Vivienne.

"Mayhap he tried, but tripped and fell," said Ludwig. "After all, we did find him on the floor."

"Yes," answered Sigbald. "That could be how he got the marks on his throat. Something most likely fell atop him."

"Those burns were too bad to be started by just a candle," said Zachariah. "It was most likely a torch that started the fire in his solar."

"Lord Lovelle did like lighting torches inside the keep," Jerome spoke up. "Even though Lady Lovelle always told him it was dangerous and that he should keep lit torches outside only."

"There you go," said Ludwig with a shrug. "The man caused his own death it seems."

"Well, I'll be going now, since I've yet to be back to town since I returned," said Sigbald. "My family will be waiting for me."

"Thank you, Sigbald," said Ludwig. "Will you order him a coffin so we can bury his body on the morrow?"

"Of course, Sheriff."

"Wait," said Zachariah, holding up his hand. "You're just going to call this an accident and let it go at that? You're not even going to try to investigate in case it was a murder?"

"Like Sigbald said, Sheriff Fitch, everyone liked Lord Lovelle," stated Ludwig. "There is no reason to think anyone wanted him dead."

"That is true," said Jerome. "He was a hard man to dislike. Lord Lovelle was always kind to everyone."

"What about the proof?" asked Vivienne. She yanked back the sheet and pointed to the dead man's neck. Or what was left of it. "Sheriff Fitch and I can clearly see strangulation marks around his neck. You can't just ignore that."

"Mayhap it was from something he was wearing," said

Ludwig. "Does anyone know exactly what kind of costume he was dressed in?"

"I do," said Jerome. "Lord Lovelle was dressed like a musician, with a long headpiece sticking out to the side. He also wore a cord around his neck that held a flute."

"It makes sense then. I'm sure that when he fell, the cord must have tightened and choked him," said Ludwig.

"That very well could be what happened," said Sigbald, no longer looking at the body. "I've seen some crazier things in my time."

"I don't see a cord," said Vivienne, looking back at the corpse.

"It most likely burned up in the fire that partially consumed his body," said Sigbald. "Well, there is nothing more I can do here so I'll be on my way."

"Nay, there is nothing else that any of us can do," agreed Ludwig. "It's been a long night and I, for one, wouldn't mind getting a little shut-eye."

"I'll see you all out," said Jerome, leading the party up the stairs. Sigbald headed up the stairs after him, but Vivienne and Zachariah didn't move.

Ludwig stopped and looked back at Zachariah and Vivienne. "Are you coming?"

"Not yet," said Vivienne. "We want to have another look at the body first." Grunt wandered over and plopped down at her feet.

"Fine, but there's nothing more to see," said Ludwig.

"If you don't mind, Sheriff Grimsthorpe, we'd like to stay here a few more minutes," said Zachariah.

"Suit yourself," said Ludwig. "Just be sure to blow out the candles when you leave so another fire won't break out."

"Of course," said Zachariah with a nod. Once they heard the door close, he looked back at Vivienne. "I've never seen anyone so lazy as the lot of them. They all just want to throw the man in the ground and not even consider the fact that he might have been murdered because it would mean work on their end if they had to actually investigate."

"We have to stop the funeral from happening tomorrow," stated Vivienne. "At least until we can try to find some clues."

"I agree. We'll have to work fast. Mayhap you can talk to Lady Lovelle and convince her that it is in her best interest to prolong the funeral until we can safely rule out the fact it might have been a murder."

"There is no *might have been* about it." Vivienne picked up one of the dead man's hands and looked under his nails. "It looks to me as if he'd been fighting for his life."

"What did you find?" Zachariah peered over her shoulder.

"It's hard to tell since he is so badly burned, but doesn't it look to you as if he has black fibers under his fingernails? And it's not soot."

"It does. You're right. I wonder if it was from the cord he wore."

"It makes sense. Mayhap someone choked him with part of his own costume. And when he fell down unconscious, they lit him on fire."

Zachariah leaned closer and sniffed. "I can't be positive, but he almost seems to smell like whisky."

"Yes, he does." Vivienne slipped a shoe off Lord Lovelle's foot and took a big sniff. "I think you're right. What do you think, Grunt?" She held out the shoe to the dog.

"Vivienne, don't be silly."

"Nay, Grunt loves whisky. If he smells the scent he'll try to lick the shoe." Sure enough, the dog sniffed the shoe and then his tongue shot out and he tried to lap at it and Vivienne quickly pulled it away. "That's enough, Grunt. Thank you." Vivienne put the shoe next to the body and pulled the sheet over him again. "I think the smell of the smoke, or mayhap looking at the corpse is making me feel ill."

"Then let's get out of here. We have guests to question, and knowing Ludwig, he probably already decided to send everyone home just so he could get a good night's sleep. I've never seen anyone as lazy as him."

Vivienne made her way to the stairs with Grunt while Zachariah blew out the candles. It became dark in there, and for some reason, it frightened her. Mayhap it was because it was a small, underground enclosed space that they shared with a corpse. Or it might have something to do with the fact she thought she saw something move from the corner of her eye, but then it was gone.

"Hold my hand, Zachariah," she told him, as they headed up the stairs.

"I should have brought one of the candles for light instead of blowing them all out. I'm sorry. I'll go back and relight one."

"Nay. Let's just get out of here. Something about this place makes me jittery. All I've wanted to do since we arrived in Grimsthorpe was just to relax, but that has yet to happen."

"LADY LOVELLE, can you tell us where your husband was when we arrived and he wasn't there to greet us?" Zachariah had been given a room by Lady Lovelle to spend the night and where he could question people. Vivienne was given a bedchamber to use as well. Since the sheriff and physician told Lady Lovelle that nothing was amiss, they'd had to secretly call her to Zachariah's room to question her in private.

"I don't understand," said Lady Lovelle, fidgeting atop the chair. Vivienne watched from across the room and Grunt sniffed around the floor.

"Why wasn't your husband with you?" Vivienne walked over to join them.

"He had some business to take care of, and said he'd join me soon." She looked like she was keeping something from them, and Zachariah realized he would have to try to draw it out of her.

"Was there an argument between you? Or perhaps your marriage was in trouble?" he asked, getting a surprised reaction from Lady Lovelle.

"Nay!" she gasped, being overly dramatic as she held her hand to her chest. "My husband and I are...*were* still newly-weds. If you know what I mean. We were in his solar together, but the party was starting so I went ahead of him, and as you know he never showed up."

"That does nothing to answer the sheriff's question," said Vivienne. "Why wasn't he with you? Please explain in detail."

"Did he perhaps stay behind to...take care of other matters?" asked Zachariah, watching the woman's cheeks blush, knowing that he was on to something now.

"He just needed time to relax before joining the party."

"I don't understand," said Vivienne.

"Vivienne." Zachariah cleared his throat. "I think what Lady Lovelle is trying to say, without actually coming out and saying it, is that her husband was amorous and it wasn't the proper time to act like newlyweds since the party was starting."

"Oooooh." Now Vivienne's cheeks blushed. She sat down on a chair and Grunt rushed over to her. She reached out to pet the dog behind his ears. It was the craziest thing, but it actually looked as if Grunt was smiling.

"So when you left the solar, was there anyone else there with your husband?" asked the sheriff.

"Nay! Of course not. Why would anyone else be there at a time like that? We were the only ones in the room." Lady

Lovelle pulled a kerchief out of her pouch and dabbed at her face.

"What about out in the corridor?" asked Vivienne. "Did you see anyone there who might have entered his room after you left?"

"Well, yes, there were many of our guests out in the corridor. But Sheriff, why are you asking me all these questions? Sheriff Ludwig and the physician told me my husband's death was nothing more than an unfortunate accident."

"Yes. However, we're not convinced of that," he told her.

"What do you mean?" asked the woman, slowly lowering her hand cloth to her lap.

"Lady Lovelle, we have reason to think that someone murdered your husband," Vivienne explained.

"Murder? Nay. That's absurd! Everyone liked Daniel. Who would want to kill him? And why?"

"That is what we want to find out," Zachariah continued. "Now, try to remember. Whom did you see out in the corridor?"

"Well, let me think." Lady Lovelle put her hand to her mouth, and her eyes looked upward and to the side as she seemed to be recalling something. "I bumped into a big alewife as I left the room. Or someone dressed as an alewife, I mean. And I saw you, Sheriff Fitch, in your Robin Hood costume at the end of the corridor."

"It wasn't me. I already told you that."

"My lady, I'm sure someone just had the same costume as Sheriff Fitch," Vivienne politely explained.

"Perhaps." Lady Lovelle sighed. "Since everyone was in costume and had masks, I don't know who any of them were. I saw some people dressed like knights and noblewomen. And dancing girls too. Some were even dressed up as animals or magical creatures."

"Did any of them stand out to you for any reason?"

Zachariah stood up and paced the room. Grunt followed with his tail wagging.

"How so?" asked the woman.

"Did anyone seem uneasy?" asked Vivienne. "Or as if they were watching you?"

Lady Lovelle shuddered and looked to the floor. She wrapped her arms around herself.

"What is it?" asked Vivienne. "Please, you need to tell us everything if we have any chance at all of catching the murderer."

"It's probably nothing," said Lady Lovelle. "But I did see someone at the end of the corridor who looked like—"

"Like what?" Vivienne got off the chair and stood. "You must tell us."

"He...or she...was dressed like...Death."

"Death?" Zachariah chuckled. "Surely, no one knows what Death looks like."

"I do," said Vivienne, barely moving. Her arms wrapped around herself. "He wears a black long cloak with a hood that covers his face. And he carries a scythe like the Grim Reaper."

"Yes!" Lady Lovelle jumped from her chair. "I thought I'd just imagined him, but you've seen him too?"

"Not actually as a physical person," said Vivienne, and Zachariah knew she was talking about the card she'd chosen from the fortune-teller. "But I will say, I have a pretty good idea what Death looks like, and I don't care for him at all."

Chapter Four

"I don't know what we're going to do," Zachariah told Vivienne later that night. They had questioned a few dozen people, but were still no closer to getting any real answers. Since everyone had been in costume when the murder occurred, no one could identify anyone, so it did them no good at all. "The funeral will be tomorrow, and I don't see how we can stop it. I've managed to detain all the guests, but they are getting restless. Plus, Lady Lovelle isn't convinced her husband was murdered, and she wants his body buried as soon as possible."

"I think we need to recreate what happened." Vivienne was lying back on Zachariah's bed, petting Grunt who had curled up on her lap.

"How so?"

"If I can convince Lady Lovelle that we should have the masquerade ball tomorrow after all, mayhap that would buy us some time."

"Yes, it would. Good idea," said Zachariah with his hand to his chin. "Everyone feels cheated not to have had the opportunity to enjoy the masquerade, so this will be the perfect answer.

Plus, it'll give us a chance to see all the costumes so we can look for those people in the corridor that Lady Lovelle mentioned."

"I'll go to her and convince her at once." Vivienne had just gotten off the bed when there was a knock at the door and it opened slowly and someone poked their head into the room.

"Zachariah? Are you in here?"

"Isaac!" Vivienne cried out and ran over to give the sheriff's brother a big hug, happy to see him. Isaac had once left his family to be a mercenary, but lately had returned home to Mablethorpe. He was now Zachariah's deputy, and doing a great job helping to investigate murders.

"I'm here too, my lady." Maleine, Vivienne's sixteen-year-old handmaid, peeked out from behind Isaac's tall form. When Maleine lost both of her parents, Vivienne decided to bring her to the castle to work for her. When Vivienne discovered how observant the girl was, she decided to let her help in investigations too. Maleine had proven more than once now to be a great asset to them. Both Maleine and Isaac carried long, strapped canvas bags over their shoulders. The bags looked to be stuffed full.

"Maleine! I've missed you. Come on in, both of you." Vivienne pulled them into the room and closed the door behind them. Grunt stood up on the bed, shook himself, and then barked, wanting attention too.

"Oh, hello Grunt." Maleine put down her bag and ran over to pet the dog. "Martin really misses you."

"What on earth are you two doing here?" asked Zachariah.

"Richard told us what happened." Isaac pushed the bag he held into Zachariah's hands. "Here. I brought you some clothes so you can get out of that silly costume that makes you look like a fairy."

"Say that again and I'll introduce you to my fist," grumbled Zachariah. "And just so you know, my costume was Vivienne's idea, not mine." He looked down to the costume which in his opinion did look a bit feminine. Yes, he was most anxious to get back into his own clothes again.

"Now, now, it's a great costume, no matter how much Isaac mocks it," said Vivienne, looking over at him and throwing him a kiss. Love did funny things to people. Like making him wear a costume that his betrothed chose for him, even though he felt as if he didn't want to be caught dead wearing it.

"I brought clothes for you as well, my lady," Maleine told Vivienne from the bed.

"Egads, what all did you pack?" asked Zachariah, testing the weight of the bag that Isaac had given him, feeling how heavy it was. "There's got to be enough in here to last me six months. I only need one change of clothes Isaac, not everything in my entire wardrobe."

"Well, I wasn't sure how long you'd be here," said Isaac in his defense. He walked over to a side table that held a flagon of ale and two cups, and poured himself a drink. "Plus, I had to pack clothes for me too. I even brought along a costume, and I hope I'll be able to wear it. It's a good one. Nothing like that feminine costume of yours."

"Isaac, stop it," said Zachariah in a warning voice, since Isaac was poking fun at his Robin Hood costume once again.

"Oh, you will have a chance to wear it, Isaac, so it is a good thing you brought it," Vivienne interrupted.

"Really?" Isaac looked up with a huge grin on his face. "So we didn't miss the masquerade ball after all? I figured by now it was probably over."

"Nay, it was interrupted by the murder and never had a chance to happen," Vivienne explained. "Actually, I was just about to go find Lady Lovelle and try to convince her to go ahead with the masquerade ball tomorrow, after all, as was origi-nally planned. I think since she spent so much money on the event, and went to such great extremes to decorate and make it special, that she will agree with me."

"Even though her husband just died?" asked Isaac.

"Well, when I tell her this is a way for us to seek out her husband's murderer, it should make her decision easy."

"Oh, so she knows her husband was murdered and didn't just accidentally die." Isaac took a swig of wine.

"We haven't convinced her yet that it was a murder, but I'm sure that if anyone can do so, it is Vivienne," said Zachariah.

"Oh, good!" Maleine clasped her hands together in excitement. "Because I brought a costume as well, and I hope you'll let me attend the masquerade ball too, my lady."

"Of course you can. You both can," said Vivienne. "I don't see a problem with that at all."

"Now wait a minute." Zachariah dropped the bag to the floor, shaking his head. "Why would you two even think you're going to stay here in Grimsthorpe at all? I just asked for our clothes to be dropped off, not to send visitors. Isaac, you and Maleine will ride back to the castle with Richard tonight, and return to Mablethorpe at once."

"Too late." Isaac plopped down on a stool with his cup cradled in his hands. "I told Richard to leave. He's already gone and won't be back until we send a missive asking him to return."

"You simpkin, why would you do that?" asked Zachariah through gritted teeth. "Isaac, you are my deputy now and are supposed to be watching over the town during my absence. You can hardly do that from here, and it is too risky to leave it unguarded."

"Calm down, Brother, the town won't be unguarded," Isaac assured him, reaching over for the flagon and refilling his cup since he had already drained it dry. "Everything is taken care of, thanks to me."

"I'm afraid to even ask what that means." Zachariah didn't

always agree with his reckless younger brother's ideas. He wished Isaac could be more sensible, like him.

"Constable Dorson returned for a few days to pack up some things that his family left behind in their urgency to move," Isaac explained. "I took the liberty of asking him to stay in town for a few days, and he has agreed to do so and help us out until we catch the murderer here in Grimsthorpe."

"Nay. I can't expect Emery to do that," protested Zachariah, talking about his past constable who had recently taken the job as sheriff in another town, wanting his family to get away from all the murders that had been occurring in Mablethorpe lately. Emery felt as if Mablethorpe was no longer safe for his wife and three children and had taken measures to protect them. Zachariah couldn't blame him, he supposed, since there had been a lot of local murders lately. However, he didn't agree that the town of Mablethorpe was no longer safe. Still, since Emery had the chance of being promoted to sheriff somewhere else, Zachariah was happy for him to start a new life elsewhere.

"Adrian is there assisting him, and so is Wymond," Maleine spoke up, talking about Vivienne's sixteen-year-old brother, and Maleine's boyfriend who was the same age.

"Oh, no," said Vivienne, worry flashing across her face. "I really wish Adrian would stay at the castle where he is safe. I just found him again after so many years of thinking he was dead, and I don't want anything to happen to him again."

"I agree," said the sheriff. "Hearing that those two are assisting the constable doesn't make me feel any better at all. Adrian is a noble and should be at the castle, like Vivienne said. And Wymond doesn't have any experience with the law."

"Wymond has learned a lot about the backstreets and places like Rotten Row from his days as being the Pied Piper's assistant," Maleine answered, referring to the boy's days of helping a rat catcher.

"Wrong side of the law," mumbled Zachariah. "And like I said...it does nothing at all to instill confidence in me."

"What about Martin and Starah?" asked Vivienne with a waver in her voice. "Who is watching over the children?"

"Lord and Lady Mablethorpe are keeping a close eye on Martin. The sheriff's sister, Cassandra, is watching over Starah, now that she lives with Sheriff Fitch," Maleine told them.

"I don't know if I truly trust my sister to watch my daughter," said Zachariah. He had just made amends with Cassandra for leaving after the death of their parents, to become a Winchester Goose in the outskirts of London. But his sister having been a prostitute, legalized or not, wasn't something that Zachariah could ever accept. Cassandra, even reformed, he was sure, was still going to be a bad influence on his seven-year-old daughter for many years to come. And now that his daughter's old nursemaid, Nairnie, had gone back home to her family, there was no one to keep any of them in line anymore.

"Well, I trust Cassandra totally," Vivienne told him. "And since Starah will be my daughter soon as well, I say that it's fine and we have nothing to worry about at all. Starah idolizes Cassandra and won't give her any trouble."

"It's the fact that Starah likes Cassandra so much that worries me," he said under his breath.

"I, for one, am actually glad that Isaac and Maleine are here," Vivienne continued talking. "Now we will have more help in solving the murder and will get results much faster."

"I don't need help." Zachariah was still against this idea.

"The more eyes the better," Isaac told him, taking another drink of wine.

"That's right," agreed Vivienne. "If we work together, we might even be able to solve this murder before Lord Lovelle's body is ever put in the ground."

"So, what do you say, Brother?" Isaac looked up, waiting for his answer. "Will you accept our help, or have you already got a sheriff and deputy here in Grimsthorpe assisting you?"

"Believe me, the sheriff here is no help at all," said Vivienne, blowing air from her mouth in a disgusted manner. "And he doesn't even have a deputy at the moment. Just a man in training."

"Oh, like I was in training, before I got my promotion to deputy." Isaac got up and stretched. "Got any food around here?"

"Isaac, stop thinking about your stomach," grumbled Zachariah.

"I'll go speak to Lady Lovelle right now about going ahead with the masquerade tomorrow after all," said Vivienne, heading for the door.

"Do you think Lady Lovelle will really agree to it?" asked Maleine. "After all, she's in mourning after just losing her husband and must be very upset."

"I don't know," said Vivienne in thought. "The weird thing is that I don't get the feeling that Lady Lovelle is really in much mourning at all. Her tears seem fake to me. But either way, letting the masquerade party continue will get her mind off her troubles I suppose, now that she has no husband and her future is uncertain at this point. Come with me, Maleine," said Vivienne, picking up the bag of her clothes. "We'll drop this off in our room, and then go see the lady of the castle before she goes to sleep. You'll also have to tell me what kind of costume you came up with, because I can't wait to see it."

"Oh, my lady, my costume is not nearly as good as yours of course, but Lady Mablethorpe helped me obtain one on such short notice. Come, Grunt," Maleine called to the hound as she walked out the door with Vivienne, chatting like crazy, the way all women did that always drove Zachariah crazy. Grunt ran out of the room after them.

"Well, shall we go down to the kitchen and look for something to eat?" Isaac was headed to the door as well, but Zachariah stopped him.

"Isaac, wait."

"What is it?" Isaac stood with one hand on the door.

"Close the door. I don't want anyone to hear us."

"All right." Isaac did as told, and turned around. "What takes your concern?" He crossed his arms over his chest.

"Now that Vivienne and I are betrothed and about to be married, I am having a difficult time accepting the fact that she's still assisting me with investigating murders."

"Really? Did you tell her that?"

"Nay. But neither does it matter. She's never going to give it up. She has been very clear about that!"

"Do you really want her to stop assisting you? I mean, face it, she's good at it."

"I'm not...really sure. I mean, part of me wants to keep her away from any potential danger, and at all times have her where I know she'll be safe."

"Of course. That's understandable. Although, I feel as if Lady Vivienne can take care of herself. Most of the time."

"I suppose she has proven that to me—however, she's going to be my wife soon. And hopefully someday we'll add to our family with more children."

"I see. Go on." Isaac cocked his head and was actually being very attentive, which was a first for him.

Zachariah continued. "Another part of me doesn't want to even suggest that Vivienne change. After all, I do love her for who she is, and the last thing I want is to change her."

"Then don't. The answer is simple. Let her continue being who she wants to be. Now let's go find something to eat." Isaac once more reached for the door.

"That's easy for you to say, but things are a little more complicated now."

"What does that mean?" Isaac's hand stilled on the door, and he looked back over his shoulder in question.

"A fortune-teller read Vivienne's cards tonight."

"And?" Isaac raised a brow.

"Vivienne chose the death card."

Isaac lowered his hand and slowly took a few steps toward Zachariah. "Brother, since when do you believe in fortune-telling, or anything that has to do with that kind of nonsense? You've always been too sensible for that. That kind of stuff is all fake and you know it. It's created to control and scare people, nothing more. Besides, you barely even believe in superstitions."

"I know. But something about this woman seemed...concerning."

"How so?"

"I'm not sure. She predicted that someone would die tonight, and then someone did."

"Oooh, so you're saying you think she is the one who murdered Lord Lovelle?"

"Mayhap. Or perhaps she can really see into the future. And if so, I don't like the fact that Vivienne drew the death card. I don't like it one damned bit!"

"Perhaps Vivienne drew that card, and all it meant was that Lord Lovelle was about to be murdered."

"Do you really think so?"

"I honestly have no idea." Isaac shrugged. "But if you believe it, then mayhap you'll stop all your silly worrying that is probably for nothing, and I can get something to eat. Now come on. If we wait any longer, the kitchen will be closed and all the food will be gone."

"I suppose you're right, and I am just being foolish. I am sure it doesn't mean anything at all." Zachariah followed his brother out the door. But all the while he was still not able to shake the feeling that there was something about the mysterious woman named Morgana, other than being Vivienne's half-sister, that was going to play a huge part in both of their lives sometime very soon.

"LADY LOVELLE, the sheriff and I believe that the masquerade should continue as planned, and on the morrow," Vivienne told the lady of the castle as she and Maleine spoke to her in her private chamber. Lady Lovelle's handmaid, Ester, was there, and they'd just met her. Ester had helped the lady of the castle change into her nightclothes, and was now turning down the covers on her bed. She was a tall woman with wide shoulders and dark hair wound up in a knot and tucked under her wimple with just a few strands sticking out. From the back she looked more like a man. She was probably a good two decades older than Vivienne, with dark circles under her eyes and a deep crease on her forehead. Vivienne wondered why Lady Lovelle hadn't chosen a younger woman to be her handmaid. One like Maleine, who could move faster and who was more her own age.

"The sheriff? Which sheriff?" Lady Lovelle stood looking out the window, dabbing her eyes with a hand cloth. "If Sheriff Ludwig thinks it's a good idea, then yes, by all means we'll do it."

"Nay, I am speaking of Sheriff Zachariah Fitch from Mablethorpe," said Vivienne, exchanging worried glances with Maleine. She wasn't sure she could talk Lady Lovelle into this if the Sheriff of Grimsthorpe didn't agree with the idea. Sheriff Grimsthorpe seemed to be very protective of Lady Lovelle and she in return seemed to live by whatever he told her to do. It made Vivienne wonder if Lady Lovelle had acted the same way with her husband.

"Well, what does Sheriff Ludwig say about this?" Her blue eyes glanced over to Vivienne, more with curiosity than grief.

"He doesn't know about the idea. Yet. But of course, he'll be informed," she answered. "Since it was so late, and we hadn't talked to you about it yet, we haven't told him."

"I don't know if it's a good idea." Lady Lovelle sighed and closed the shutter. "After all, my husband just died and I am in mourning. It might not be proper."

"A masquerade ball might help you ease your mind," Maleine spoke up. "Since we know how hard this must all be for you. We are thinking of your benefit, of course."

"Well, thank you," said Lady Lovelle.

"My lady, you need your rest," said the handmaid. "Perhaps your guests should leave now since it is time for bed?"

Vivienne found the handmaid overstepping her boundaries, but said nothing about it.

"Just a minute, Ester," said Lady Lovelle raising her hand up in the air. "Lady Vivienne, do you and Sheriff Fitch really think my husband was murdered? Because Sheriff Ludwig said it was an unfortunate accident and nothing more."

"Yes, we do believe it was murder," answered Vivienne, feeling nervous but trying to sound confident at the same time, even though she wasn't completely sure. "It would be a good way for us to possibly replay the events of tonight and help us to find your husband's killer."

"I don't know." Lady Lovelle walked over and held on to the bedpost while Ester picked up a boar's bristle brush and ran it though Lady Lovelle's unbound hair. "Sheriff Ludwig believes we should bury Daniel first thing in the morning, and that might be the best."

"Excuse me, my lady," said Maleine. "But there might be

more clues that Lady Vivienne and Sheriff Fitch have not found yet. Once the body is buried, there is no hope in finding something important that might have been overlooked."

"You seem to know a lot about this for just being a handmaid." Lady Lovelle looked down her nose at Maleine, causing Maleine to lower her eyes to the floor. "And you are very imprudent."

"I'm sorry. I've spoken out of turn, my lady, and I ask your forgiveness," said Maleine in a soft voice.

"My lady, it is time for bed," said Ester, making Vivienne wonder why the lady of the castle didn't reprimand her own handmaid for speaking so boldly.

"Maleine is not just my handmaid, but an important asset in solving crime," Vivienne stuck up for the girl. "She knows how you feel losing someone close to you and is only trying to help."

"How could she possibly know how I feel?" asked Lady Lovelle, letting her own handmaid help her into the bed.

Vivienne reached out and rested her hand on Maleine's shoulder. "Maleine's mother was murdered and she lost her father as well, just recently. She is no stranger to grief, I assure you."

"Oh. I see." That seemed to shut her up. Even so, she turned again to Maleine. "So," she began, pinning the girl with a stare, "did you help in finding your mother's murderer then?"

Maleine's eyes shot up to Vivienne in a silent plead for help.

"That case is solved," said Vivienne, wanting to put an end to this discussion.

"Well? Who was it?" Lady Lovelle persisted.

"We cannot discuss prior cases, I'm afraid, but I will say that you cannot discount the fact that your husband's murderer could be anyone," Vivienne told her. "It could even be someone close to you. Someone that you'd never suspect." Vivienne hoped this would put just enough fear into the woman to have her agree to continuing with the masquerade.

"I never thought of that." Lady Lovelle sniffled and once again dabbed at her eyes as her handmaid tucked in the covers around her. "Well, I suppose it couldn't hurt to continue with the masquerade. After all, I was really looking forward to the party and have spent so much money as well as time planning it. I am sure Daniel would want me to see it through. And I don't want to disappoint my guests, since they didn't get what they came for. What will they think of me if they leave and don't get the masquerade ball that was promised? The enjoyment and pleasure? I am sure most of them spent a lot of money on their costumes. It would be a shame to disappoint them."

"Then you'll do it?" asked Maleine, with hope in her voice.

"Without having Sheriff Ludwig's approval?" added Vivienne, knowing there was no way she or anyone could talk the lazy sheriff into furthering the investigation.

"Why not?" Lady Lovelle smiled and straightened her back.

"My lady, do you that is a wise decision?" asked Ester, glaring at Vivienne and Maleine. "This is a sad time in your life."

"Yes," Lady Lovelle answered. "And funerals are so sad too, but a party makes everyone feel happy. The masquerade will take place as promised. I'll go out to the great hall right now and make the announcement." She threw back the covers and put her feet on the floor. Ester ran around the bed to help her.

"That would be wonderful," said Vivienne with a sigh of relief. "Of course, you'll have to find lodging for all the guests for the night, because we really can't allow anyone to leave until we've been able to question them all. And it is late and dark and not safe for them to travel."

"That won't be a problem. Grimsthorpe Manor has plenty

of room." The woman's eyes seemed to sparkle with excitement now. "This will make my guests happy and I won't lose their respect, after all. Ester, bring me my gown."

"Yes, my lady." Ester sighed and went back to the wardrobe to get Lady Lovelle's clothes.

"What will you tell your sheriff? About your husband's burial?" asked Vivienne.

"Don't worry about Ludwig." Lady Lovelle waved a dismissive hand through the air. "He'll do whatever I say. He has to, since I am lady of the castle. I'll tell him the funeral will have to be postponed until after the masquerade. After all, Lady Vivienne, this is supposed to be a happy time, celebrating your betrothal to Sheriff Fitch. For sure, I don't want to disappoint either of you."

"Well, thank you, Lady Lovelle. You are so kind," Vivienne answered, getting up and heading to the door with Maleine following.

"Besides," said Lady Lovelle, getting out of bed. "I'm sure you'd like one more chance to help solve a murder before you have to give up investigating forever."

"Oh, I'm not giving up anything," said Vivienne. "I will continue to help Zachariah solve murders, even after we are married."

Lady Lovelle had a look of surprise as well as a half-smile on her face. "You don't really think your husband will allow that, do you?"

"Of course, he will," said Vivienne. "Zachariah and I have already talked it over. He agreed that nothing will change regarding us doing murder investigations together, even after we are wed."

"And what if you become pregnant? Do you really believe your husband would allow you to join him in dangerous situations then?"

"Well...yes," said Vivienne, suddenly not feeling so confident anymore since she and Zachariah hadn't discussed that possibility at all.

"You'd want to put your baby at risk?" asked Lady Lovelle. "And to cause excessive worry for your husband for your own safety as well? I can't understand that. What kind of wife and mother does that?"

"I'm not yet a wife, but I am already a mother," she pointed out to the woman, feeling her words creating sudden doubt within her.

"Oh, yes, that's right. Your son is the boy who sneaked into the wagon without you even realizing it. You really need to keep a closer eye on your child. After all, like you said, there might be a killer on the loose." Lady Lovelle turned and lifted her arms, waiting for her handmaid to undress her. Vivienne slowly turned and walked out the door with Maleine, realizing that what the woman said was true, and not knowing how to respond to her valid criticism.

"Don't fret, my lady," said Maleine, putting her hand on Vivienne's arm to comfort her as she closed the door behind them. "Lady Lovelle doesn't realize how different you are from most noblewomen. And how different Martin is from most children."

"True," Vivienne said with a slight nod. "But she is right when she says most mothers wouldn't let their children get anywhere near a murder scene. Or even think of purposely letting their children be in the line of danger. Mayhap I do need to change my ways. Perhaps I am being too careless, perhaps even reckless." Her hand went to her belly which was upset once again. She hadn't thought about being pregnant while proceeding with her work. Yet such a consideration changed everything.

"Don't let Lady Lovelle upset you with her words," said

Maleine. "She doesn't have children, so she has no idea what it's like to even be a mother. You are a wonderful mother to Martin, and you take excellent care of Mouse, as well, so don't let anyone convince you otherwise."

"Thank you, Maleine, but she does make a good point. I would never want anything to happen to Martin, Mouse, or to any children that the sheriff and I might have someday together. I can't take the chance of losing anyone I love. Family is so important to me."

"Nothing like that will ever happen again! The sheriff will see to it. So please, don't let that woman's words distress you, my lady. After all, she doesn't even seem very sad that her husband is dead and was probably murdered, so she is no shining example of a good wife. She seems more concerned with the grandness of the masquerade ball and what others might think of her if they aren't treated to a night of lavish entertainment, as promised."

"You're right about that, Maleine." Vivienne was impressed by how the girl could often see things that slipped right past her. "We need to find out more about her relationship with her husband, because things might not be what they seem."

Maleine leaned over and whispered. "Do you think she had something to do with her husband's death?"

"I don't know yet," said Vivienne. "But until we're sure she is not guilty, she, as well as everyone, will remain a suspect. Just like Sheriff Fitch always says, expect the unexpected and don't let emotions get in the way of any investigating because that will only cloud your judgment."

"Then let's go to the great hall and start investigating. We will watch the expressions of the guests as Lady Lovelle tells them the new plan." Maleine headed down the corridor. Vivienne slowly followed, not able to push away the guilt inside her now, after everything Lady Lovelle had to say about being a good wife and mother. As much as she loved investigating murders with Zachariah, the last thing she ever wanted to be called was a bad wife and an uncaring mother!

Chapter Five

"Just look at her flirting with all the men! I can't believe it." Maleine stood with Vivienne the next day as the masquerade ball was in full operation. While the guests seemed hesitant at first, hearing about the mysterious way Lord Lovelle had died, the promise of food, dancing, music, and carousing was enough to keep them at the castle.

"Lady Lovelle does seem to be enjoying herself," commented Vivienne, fully dressed in her goddess costume and wearing her mask. Lady Lovelle glided around the room, doing her best to charm everyone, especially the men.

"She doesn't even know who she's flirting with and neither does she seem to care." Maleine lowered her stick mask to take a better look across the great hall. She was dressed all in black, portraying a cat. She had fake ears on her head, a long tail, and whiskers painted around her nose.

Vivienne felt a hand on her shoulder and turned and screamed. Maleine looked up and screamed as well. Standing there was a tall person wearing a long black cloak, tall boots up to their knees, long leather gloves, a leather wide-brimmed black hat, and the scariest part being the mask, which looked like a bird with big eyes and a long, curved beak.

"Take it easy," came a low male voice. The man picked up the beak mask to expose his face. "It's just me. Isaac."

"You frightened us," said Vivienne. "Why are you dressed the way the doctors were during the plague? You look so frightening."

"Good. That's what I was going for," chuckled Isaac. "Actually, the town physician of Mablethorpe is the one who lent it to me."

"You look too horrifying dressed all in black like that," scolded Maleine.

"Well, what about you? You're all in black too," Isaac answered. "What are you supposed to be?"

"She's a cat, silly!" said Vivienne.

"She looks more like a rat to me."

"Isaac, that's not nice," said Vivienne.

"Lady Mablethorpe helped me make the costume," Maleine told them, raising one hand to straighten the ears attached to a band going around her head. "It was actually Starah's idea since she wanted me to look like her cat, Midnight."

"Did I hear my daughter's name mentioned?" Zachariah walked up and made a face when he saw Isaac. "Egads, Brother, did you really think that costume was appropriate when we've just had a death at the castle?"

"Aye. That makes it even more appropriate in my mind." Isaac replaced his mask.

"Sometimes I wonder about you," said Zachariah. "I hope I didn't make the wrong decision in making you my deputy."

"I'm the perfect man for the job, and you know it," came his muffled reply from behind the mask. His head moved when he spoke, causing the bird beak to move as well, and Vivienne couldn't help but shudder.

"Zachariah, Maleine was just saying the Lady Lovelle doesn't seem very sad, with her husband just dying." Vivienne put her attention on her betrothed instead of his brother.

"I asked around," said Zachariah. "It seems her husband was a good twenty years older than her. She also has a reputation for always having eyes for the men."

"I wonder why they even got married," commented Maleine.

"Mayhap because every older man wants to spend his time in bed with a younger woman?" Isaac spoke from beneath his mask.

"Isaac, keep such talk to yourself," warned Zachariah.

Isaac picked up the mask again. "It could be a clue. After all, we haven't yet ruled out that the woman didn't kill her own husband because she wanted someone younger."

"Or that the whole reason she married Lord Lovelle was to inherit what he owned once he passed away," added Maleine.

"You both actually make good points," said Zachariah with a slight nod. "We need to consider everything. Now circulate and talk to everyone. There has to be someone who saw the murderer enter Lord Lovelle's solar yesterday."

"Lady Lovelle said she knocked into a big woman dressed as an alewife," Vivienne told them. "I'm going to look for her here, as well as someone else dressed like Robin Hood." Once she said it, she realized that the sheriff's costume had changed since yesterday. He still wore the upper part, but now instead of just hose, he donned a green pair of breeches. "You changed your costume. Why?"

"I felt too exposed," Zachariah answered. "Besides, I never liked the damned thing to begin with."

"Because you looked like a girl?" said Isaac, once again sounding muffled.

"I said to keep your comments to yourself, please." Zachariah scowled at his brother.

"Well, I liked the costume and that is why I chose it for you." Vivienne crossed her arms over her chest. "But if you want to change it, then so be it."

"Vivienne, I am working and need to feel comfortable and able to focus."

ZACHARIAH KNEW that Vivienne wouldn't be happy with his change to his costume, but he didn't care. He couldn't concentrate on the investigation when he felt as if everyone was staring at his back end. "I think we should split up. Vivienne, you and Maleine mingle with the guests and see what you can learn. Focus on the males since it is unlikely a female could strangle a full-grown man and then set him on fire without being stopped."

"That's not true." Vivienne still scowled at him, but now for an entirely different reason. "After all, if the killer was a big woman like the one Lady Lovelle knocked into in the corridor yesterday, she would most likely be strong. It is very possible she could have pulled off such a murder."

"Especially if Lord Lovelle was taken by surprise, or was well in his cups," added Maleine. Grunt ran up just then, as if the hound knew they were talking about whisky.

"Vivienne, why didn't you keep Grunt in your room? He shouldn't be out here at the masquerade," Zachariah told her. "He'll only be too distracting."

"Grunt didn't want to stay there all alone." Vivienne reached down and petted her dog on his head. "Besides, he is a bloodhound and has proven in the past to be helpful in the investigations."

"Then take him with you. He'll be your protection. Isaac

and I are going to go back down to the undercroft to look at the body again in case there is something we missed."

"What? We are?" Isaac quickly lifted his mask. "I thought I'd be able to mingle with the ladies a little. To get information, of course."

"Well, think again," grumbled Zachariah. "We need to use this time to our advantage. There might not be another opportunity to view the corpse before Sheriff Ludwig throws it in the ground and it's covered up forever, along with the secret of who killed him."

"Did I hear my name mentioned?" At that moment Ludwig walked up with a companion at his side.

"Ludwig," said Zachariah with a nod. He almost laughed aloud at what the man was wearing. He was dressed in chain mail with a sword at his side, probably trying to look like a knight. He had on a metal helm, and just a black mask over his eyes. It wasn't enough to hide his identity or his big belly from anyone. "Who is your friend?" Zachariah asked about the person next to him. It looked to be a man. He was smaller in stature, thin, and dressed like a stag, including a headpiece with horns and all.

"This is my deputy-in-training, Rodger. Although, I thought we were all supposed to stay anonymous."

"True." Zachariah was about to introduce the others with him, but decided not to do so after that comment.

"Do you really think you're going to find a murderer?" Ludwig chuckled. "I assure you, Lord Lovelle's death was an accident and nothing else."

"Why would you say that?" asked Vivienne.

"We just came up from the undercroft and everything regarding the body looked like nothing but an accident," Rodger spoke up.

"You were down there just now?" Zachariah felt like he'd

already lost his advantage. If the sheriff was at all involved in the killing, he probably removed any piece of evidence that they might have missed.

"Yes, Sheriff Fitch. I am Sheriff of Grimsthorpe, and it is my job to check on things and people and make sure everything and everyone is safe. Now if you'll excuse me, I see Lady Lovelle and want to offer her my condolences once again and to see if she needs anything at all."

"Of course." Zachariah nodded. Rodger stood there awkwardly for a moment and then hurried away after the sheriff.

"Zachariah," said Vivienne. "Didn't Lady Lovelle tell us she saw someone dressed like a stag with horns on his headpiece when she exited her husband's solar yesterday?"

"Yes, she did," he answered. "It was most likely Rodger, since I've yet to see anyone else dressed in a similar fashion."

"I haven't seen another Robin Hood yet either," said Vivienne.

"What about the person dressed like the Grim Reaper?" asked Maleine. "We haven't seen him anywhere."

"What? There's someone else dressed like the breath of death besides me?" Isaac sounded more than disappointed.

"Lady Vivienne. Sheriff Fitch," called out Lady Lovelle. "We'd like you two to have the first dance." She waved at them from across the great hall. Ludwig was with her, and Zachariah couldn't help but wonder if it was his idea to keep them from investigating.

"Of course," he called back, holding out his arm to Vivienne. "Shall we dance, my lady?"

"Yes. I'd love too, Sheriff." Vivienne's smile always seemed to warm him. He thought she was the most beautiful woman, even when she wasn't dressed like a goddess. However, her costume of a goddess seemed so fitting because that is how he always saw her in his eyes. They walked out to the center of the great hall with everyone standing around and watching their every move.

"So much for keeping anonymous," he remarked, taking her into his arms as the music started. They bowed to each other and started the dance and for a few minutes all his worries seemed to subside as he focused on the beautiful woman who would very soon be his wife.

"This is nice," she told him. "We are actually having a moment just for us."

"I agree." He spun her around and they continued to dance. "Even if our 'for us' moment is being watched by so many prying eyes at the moment." Thankfully it wasn't long before everyone else joined in on the dance floor. He even saw Maleine and Isaac dancing together, which made him think that none of the other women wanted to even come near Isaac when he was dressed in that awful costume.

"Our wedding is in a few weeks, and that will probably be the next time we dance." He felt compelled to say that for some reason.

"Yes, that's right." Vivienne seemed more quiet than normal today, and that was unusual for her. She was always chatting about something or another. Zachariah couldn't help but feel that something was bothering her.

"You...still want to marry me, don't you?" He held his breath, waiting for her answer. God's eyes, he didn't even know what he'd do or say if she told him no.

"What?" Her eyes opened wide and she stepped on his foot.

"Ouch!" He released her and grabbed his foot, hopping on one leg.

"Oh, I'm sorry," she apologized. "It's just that your question was so unexpected that it startled me. I'm sorry if I hurt you."

"I'm all right." He rubbed his toes clad in the soft shoe, and then continued to dance. "Vivienne, is something bothering you?"

"Of course."

"There is?" Now he stopped dancing and his eyes opened wide, afraid to ask but having to know. "What is it?"

"Zachariah, there is a killer on the loose and we basically have no clues as to who murdered the victim, or why. That is bothering me immensely."

"Oh, that. Of course." Once again they were dancing. "But, I meant...is there something besides the murder bothering you?"

"Like what?"

"Like...us. Getting married, mayhap."

"Zachariah!" Now Vivienne stopped dancing and she let go of him. "Please don't tell me you are having second thoughts about our wedding."

"Nay! Of course not. Not at all. It's just that you seem so quiet and that's not like you. So, I was afraid you were starting to have doubts."

"I just...have a lot on my mind." She flashed him a smile that seemed fake to him. "Let's try to focus on the fact that this celebration is for us since we are the guests of honor."

"Yes. Let's." But when they started to dance again, Vivienne gasped. "What is it?" he asked her.

"I just saw a very large woman."

"The one dressed like an alewife?" He turned around to see whom Vivienne was talking about. Sure enough, there was a large, beefy woman standing near the kitchen, clapping her hands to the music. "That one is dressed like a—a fairy. I think. I can't really tell. All I know is that the costume looks nothing like that of an alewife."

"True. But mayhap she's changed her costume from yesterday. Mayhap she doesn't want to be recognized if someone might have seen her. Or mayhap her costume got ruined with blood or mayhap burned by the fire when she killed Lord Lovelle."

"That's a lot of mayhaps."

"I'm going over there to find out. I'll take Maleine with me." Vivienne hurried away to get Maleine, and together they crossed the great hall, heading for the large woman.

"Give me that, you little thief!" came a woman's voice, making Zachariah spin around, sure he would see a thief stealing from a lady. Instead, he saw nothing of the kind. But he did spy Grunt over by the fortune-teller. The hound had his front two paws up on her table and he had something in his mouth. Morgana was holding on to the other end, trying to get the item back.

"I knew that dog was only going to cause trouble." Zachariah hurried over to the table, but by the time he dodged the guests and made it there, Isaac had arrived there first.

"I'm Isaac. What's your name?" Isaac whipped off his bird-like mask with the long beak and tucked it under his arm.

"Her name is Morgana and she's Vivienne's half-sister," Zachariah told him, grabbing Grunt by the collar and pulling him down to the floor. "What have you got there, you little thief?" He gently took something from the dog's mouth. It was a long brown cord. "Is this yours?" he asked, holding it up.

"Yes, it's my belt." Morgana went to take it from him, but Zachariah quickly pulled it away. "Lord Lovelle was strangled with a cord around the neck. Did you know that?"

"Why would you think I'd know that?" asked Morgana. "Because you believe that someone like me should have the ability to read your mind? Or is it because you are saying you think I'm the killer, Sheriff?"

"Yes, what are you saying, Zachariah? You shouldn't assume things that are not true," said Isaac with a scowl, taking the girl's side. It was obvious he wanted to flirt with her, and didn't want her in a bad mood because of what was just said.

"I'm just making a comment," Zachariah told her, handing her back the cord. "Lord Lovelle wore a very similar cord around his neck with a small panpipe attached to it, in case you didn't know."

She tied the cord around her waist, not looking at the men at all. Morgana wasn't dressed in a costume. Or at least Zachariah didn't think so, even if he wasn't exactly sure. She wore a brightly-colored blue and orange dress with a full skirt. A long headscarf covered her ebony black hair with a knot tied on the side, with the rest falling over one shoulder. The headscarf was yellow and hung all the way down to her waist.

"Lord Lovelle's cord was black not brown. And it wasn't a panpipe, but a small flute," she told him.

"How do you know that?" asked Zachariah, becoming suspicious.

"I know because I saw him yesterday when I gave him his card reading before the masquerade started."

"You gave him a card reading?" Zachariah found this an interesting bit of information.

"Card reading? Nice." Isaac nodded. "Can you give me one?" He leaned one hand on the table, bending closer to her. She backed away. Grunt snooped around under the table.

"Where did you give Lord Lovelle his reading? Was it here?" Zachariah needed to know more.

"Nay, he wanted it in private so I went to his solar like he requested."

"You did?" both Zachariah and Isaac said together.

"It's not what you're thinking. I mean, nothing happened between us."

"So, do you think that Lord Lovelle wanted to...get intimate with you?" asked Isaac.

"Him? Intimate?" Morgana wrinkled her nose. "Of course not."

"So what did his card reading say?" asked Zachariah.

"I never had a chance to do it because Lady Lovelle walked in, and he told me to leave as soon as he saw her."

"Why didn't you tell me this yesterday?" asked Zachariah, feeling angry with the woman. "And why didn't Lady Lovelle mention that you were in her husband's private solar previous to his demise?"

"Lady Lovelle asked me not to say anything about being there. She said she didn't want gossip starting right before the masquerade because it wouldn't bode well for them."

"Did his wife seem angry with him?" asked the sheriff. "I mean, that she found you in the room?"

"Of course she was. Wouldn't you be angry if you were her and walked into a room to see your spouse with another woman?"

"I...I suppose so. I hadn't really thought about it," he said. "Until now." Suddenly, Zachariah's mind was filled with visions of men going after Vivienne, since she looked so fetching dressed like a goddess. Jealousy reared its ugly head. He didn't like having thoughts like this at all. But now, thanks to the witch, he had another worry to add to his list.

"So how about reading my cards?" Isaac asked Morgana once again. "I'd like to know my fortune regarding love. And money."

"Since Lady Lovelle is paying me to be here, I have to read the cards for anyone who asks." Morgana sighed and sat down behind her table, shuffling her big cards that had objects, places, and people painted on them. Grunt reached up from under the table and rested his head on her lap.

"What do you want?" she said to the dog. "I don't have anything for dogs. Now, go away."

"Come here, Grunt." Zachariah reached around the table and pulled the dog away. When he did, he noticed that Morgana's bag was open. Sticking out of the top he saw a pouch made of velvet that had an L stitched on it.

"Choose three cards," said Morgana, fanning out the deck.

"Let me see." Isaac's hand wavered above the cards, and he moved it back and forth but didn't choose any.

"Hurry up, Isaac!" spat Zachariah. "We have work to do."

"I don't know which ones to choose."

"It doesn't matter," said Zachariah. "You were the one who said this is all nonsense, so why should you even care?"

"You said that?" Morgana's big green eyes looked up at Isaac.

"I meant it was nonsense for my brother. Not me."

"Then choose your cards," she challenged him.

"You choose for me," Isaac told Morgana, and lowered his hand. "You can do that, can't you?"

"I can." She answered with no form of emotion in her voice at all. Morgana used two fingers to push three cards forward and then collected up the rest.

"Ah, I can't wait to see them." Isaac reached out to turn them over, but Morgana's hand shot out and she slapped him away.

"Ow! What did you do that for?" Isaac, like a whining baby, rubbed his hand.

"You asked me to do it for you, so let me finish my job."

"Like you should be doing yours," Zachariah told Isaac under his breath.

Morgana flipped over the first card. "This is your past," she told him. On the card was the painting of a man not paying attention and about to step off a cliff, with a dog at his feet.

"Hey, that looks like me," said Isaac, seeming happy about it. "What is that card called?"

"The Fool," she answered.

Zachariah burst out laughing and Grunt barked happily thinking it was a game. "Yep, that's you all right, Isaac."

"I am not a fool!" Isaac retorted. "I was a mercenary," he told Morgana.

"Same thing." Zachariah grinned and looked the other way.

"The Fool means new beginnings, innocence, and taking a leap of faith into the unknown," she explained.

"Yes, that's right." Isaac stood up taller and smiled. "That is me after all. I just started my new job as deputy sheriff of Mablethorpe."

"However..."

"What? There's more?" Isaac's head snapped around to face her again.

"Your card was reversed."

"So? Does it make a difference?" asked Isaac, seeming to become a little concerned.

"Yes," she answered. "Reversed, it means something totally different."

"Please, tell us what that is." Zachariah was enjoying seeing Isaac squirm or he would have stopped this nonsense by now.

"It means, being naive, reckless, and having a lack of foresight," explained Morgana.

"Now, *that's* my brother exactly," said Zachariah with even a wider smile. "Mayhap there is something to this card-reading stuff after all."

"Never mind. Show me the second card and tell me what that means," Isaac said, trying to hurry it along and to stop talking about The Fool.

Morgana flipped over the middle card. It was a woman with dark hair dressed in a robe with a hood. She wore a tall headdress.

"She kind of looks like you, Morgana." Isaac tried to flirt, but Morgana was not falling for his games.

"This is the high priestess. She basically tells you to slow down, look inward, stop doubting yourself, and quit over-thinking things. Instead, trust your gut instincts, even when everything points in a different direction."

"Slow down? Stop over-thinking things?" blurted out Zachariah. "If Isaac slowed down any more, he'd be dead. And believe me when I say he never thinks before acting. That is part of his problem."

"Hush, Zachariah!" Isaac frowned. "Let Morgana tell me my future, not you."

"The last card is the card of the future and that yet to come." Morgana flipped it over and when Isaac saw it, he got a glint in his eye.

"Two naked people. I like it already!" Isaac grinned from ear to ear.

"It's The Lovers card," she told him.

"So...I guess it is looking good that I'll be finding myself a lover soon?"

Morgana shook her head with her eyes half closed.

"No? But it's not reversed!" Isaac slapped his hand on the table in frustration. His action only caused the card to jump and managed to scare the dog. Grunt ran across the great hall and in the direction of Vivienne.

"The Lovers card represents relationship, connection, and deep passion," she told him.

"Like I said...I'm going to find a girl to bed. I guess I am lucky after all."

"Isaac, stop acting like an ass," hissed Zachariah, embarrassed by his brother's words and actions.

"It could represent romance, or mayhap just self-love," Morgana continued.

"What? Nay! No self-love." Isaac swished his hand through the air and Zachariah chuckled.

"It also means commitment."

"Oh, hell no," said Isaac. "I'm not getting rooked into marrying anyone. I've had enough. Let's go, Zachariah."

"Nay. Just wait and let her finish." Zachariah, grabbed his brother by the arm and made him stay a little longer. Once again, Zachariah was enjoying his brother's discomfort. He figured Isaac deserved this after having poked fun at Zachariah's costume, telling him it was feminine in nature.

"The Lovers card is a crossroads," Morgana told him.

"Oh, so does that mean I'll be going somewhere?" asked Isaac.

"When I say crossroads, I mean more like heart verses head. It's all about making a decision, and finding the right path. That could be with your soul mate, or mayhap not. It's really hard to say."

"I don't know what a soul mate is, and neither do I care to know. I don't believe any of this nonsense, just like my brother said...it's stupid," complained Isaac.

"Now wait a moment. I never called what Morgana does *stupid*." Zachariah raised up his hands, hoping not to be cursed by the witchy-woman.

"Excuse me, but I'm going to go find a nice physical woman to dance with." Isaac left, leaving Zachariah standing there alone with Morgana.

"Did you want a reading too, Sheriff?" She pushed Isaac's chosen cards into the deck.

"Nay. Not for me. However, I do want to know one thing."

"What's that?"

"If someone pulls the death card...what exactly does that mean?"

"Oh, like the card that Lady Vivienne pulled? You're afraid she's going to die?" The woman was too smart for her own good.

"I didn't say that. I'm just asking off the top of my head. Just curious, that's all."

"I thought you didn't believe in any of this and thought it to be nothing but nonsense."

"Never mind. Thanks anyway." Zachariah started to walk away, but stopped when he heard what she had to say.

"The death card seldom means actual death."

"Really?" He turned around to face her, feeling somewhat relieved. "So what does it mean then?"

"It's all about endings."

"Endings? Like...with a relationship?" This wasn't making him feel any better.

"Possibly. It's all about letting go. Shedding the old to make room for the new."

"Oh. I see." Damn, this wasn't sounding good regarding his upcoming commitment of being married to Vivienne. And with Vivienne's mood lately, he was wondering if she was regretting having agreed to marry him even if she wouldn't admit it.

"It's the ending of one cycle and the beginning of a new one," Morgana continued.

"I see." His mouth felt dry and he had to wet his lips by pressing them together.

"Don't worry, Sheriff Fitch. Lady Vivienne is not going to leave you." Morgana smiled for the first time. He wasn't sure if it was because she was enjoying watching him squirm, or that she was genuinely trying to be pleasant. Or trying to ease his worries.

"Nay? How can you be sure?"

"Don't doubt yourself," she told him, pushing her deck of cards into a velvet bag. "If you feel that you're not good enough for my half-sister, then you will live the rest of your life in doubt and there will always be problems between you."

"Doubt, you say? What doubt? What do you mean?" He was starting to wonder if perhaps she could really read his thoughts after all.

"Lady Vivienne loves you, Sheriff. I can see that without having to consult my cards. Listen to your heart and not your head. Your head is only going to get you in trouble."

"Now that's an interesting thing to say," he mumbled, thinking how he always told Vivienne to listen to her head and not her heart when it came to their work with solving murders. "Thank you. I think."

He walked away feeling a sense of relief that Vivienne wasn't about to die. But at the same time he now felt more confused than ever. What could that Death card have in store for his wife-to-be, and how was he a part of all of it as well?

Chapter Six

"Excuse me, but who are you?" Vivienne asked the hefty woman standing by the door that led to the kitchen. The woman wore a costume that looked like a meld between a bug and possibly something magical, since she had wings made of paper attached to her back. She wore purple hose and a frilly tunic that almost looked to be shredded on the ends. In her hand she held a stick with a paper star on the end.

"Who am I? Who are you?" asked the woman, eying up Vivienne and then Maleine.

"This is Lady Vivienne," Maleine blurted out before Vivienne could stop her. "The masquerade is in her honor."

"Oh, pardon me, my lady." The woman tried to curtsy and almost fell down. Vivienne noticed the scent of whisky on her.

"Is that the costume you were wearing yesterday?" asked Vivienne, and suddenly the woman became still and quiet.

"Please don't tell Lady Lovelle," begged the woman. "I wasn't invited to the masquerade. I'm just the laundress, Gunora. I should go back to work. I'll be going now."

"Nay, wait," called out Vivienne. "Were you here yesterday too?"

"I work here at the castle. I'm always here, my lady."

"Were you in the corridor by Lord Lovelle's room yesterday?" Maleine wanted to know.

"Yes, but so were many others. Why are you asking? Does this have something to do with his death?"

"Did you wear the costume of an alewife yesterday?" Vivienne asked, watching the woman's face grow ashen.

"Why do you ask?"

"Please, just answer the question. It is important that you tell me the truth."

The washerwoman hesitated, looked around, and then finally answered. "I was going to be an alewife, that is true. However, my costume...disappeared. When I couldn't find it, I decided to stay away. Then I heard the masquerade resumed so I had to come up with this quickly, even though it isn't the best by far."

"So, you're saying you never wore the alewife costume at all?" asked Vivienne.

"Well...nay. Not really. Why do you ask?"

"Lady Lovelle bumped into someone who looked like you wearing an alewife costume yesterday," said Maleine.

"Well, it wasn't me." Her hand flew to her chest. "Now, can I go, my lady? I don't want Lady Lovelle to punish me."

"Did you see anyone else about your size wearing the costume?" Vivienne asked, hoping not to insult the woman. Unfortunately, she did.

Gunora's eyes narrowed to slits and her mouth turned down into a frown. "There are many women my size, and we're not all thin as a wisp like the nobles, all frail and dainty. It is because we have to work for a living!"

"Never mind. Thank you, and you may go." Vivienne figured it wasn't worth angering the woman any further. "Oh, one more thing," she called out as Gunora started to walk away. "Did you see anyone dressed like Robin Hood?"

"You mean, the sheriff? Yes. He's right over there." She nodded with her head to where Zachariah was standing.

"Besides him. A different Robin Hood," explained Vivienne.

"Nay, I can't say that I did. Why? Did you lose one?"

"How about the Grim Reaper?" asked Maleine quickly.

"I did see someone lurking about the corridor wearing a long black cloak and hood," admitted the woman.

"Was he holding a scythe?" Vivienne was finally getting some answers.

"Mayhap. I'm not sure. I don't pay much attention when I have laundry to do."

"Whose laundry do you wash?" asked Vivienne.

"Just about everyone's in the castle. Why? Do you need your clothes cleaned too, my lady?"

"Nay," said Vivienne. "I was just wondering if you happened to notice that anyone had clothes that possibly didn't belong to them."

"I don't know what you mean." The woman seemed scared.

"Anything out of the ordinary," she said, trying to explain what she meant.

"Nay."

"Will you tell me if you remember anything or do see something suspicious?"

"I don't ever see anything," said the woman, curtsying quickly and turning and running into the kitchen.

"I think she is hiding something from us," said Maleine. "She seemed way too scared."

"I think so too," Vivienne agreed. "Oh, there's Zachariah. It looks like he's heading to the undercroft. I'm going to go catch up with him and help him investigate the corpse some more." Grunt kept nuzzling her and barking. "Maleine will you please put Grunt back in our room? He is proving to be a distraction, just like Zachariah said he'd be."

"Of course, my lady." Maleine took Grunt by the collar and had a hard time pulling him away from Vivienne. The dog was acting quite odd.

Vivienne saw the flash of the red feather atop Zachariah's hat as he turned a corner. She picked up the hem of her goddess gown and hurried to try to catch up with him. "Sheriff? Wait for me, Zachariah," she called out. There were a lot of people and much noise and he didn't seem to hear her.

"It's so hard to move fast in this gown," she complained, heading for the undercroft. When she got near the entrance, she saw the flash of green as Zachariah closed the door leading to the undercroft, having just gone inside. "He moves too fast for me."

Slowly pulling open the door, she peered down the dark stairway, seeing a lone candle lighting up the area around the corpse that was still laid out on the board going across two barrels. The air stank from the body which was already decomposing. Vivienne covered her nose with her hand, wondering how Zachariah could do this work and never seemed affected by it.

She slowly made her way down the stairs, not wanting to take her hand away from her nose to call out to Zachariah. As she descended, she could see him standing with his back toward her, leaning over the body, inspecting something. Just as she got to the bottom of the stairs, she realized something. Zachariah was no longer wearing breeches. Instead, he was dressed again in just the long tunic and hose. She was about to say that she was glad he'd changed, when the man turned around, first noticing her. He had a knife in his hand and headed toward her. That's when she realized he wasn't as tall as Zachariah, and that he wasn't really her betrothed at all.

"Stop! Who are you?" she screamed as the man lunged forward. Vivienne grabbed his arm with two hands, trying to wrangle the knife away from him, but he was too strong. So she did the only thing she could. She bit the man hard on the fore-arm. So hard that she drew blood.

"Mmmph!" he mumbled, pushing her to the ground and bounding up the stairs with the knife still in his hand. She heard the door slam, leaving her there alone with the corpse. Her heart beat so wildly, she wasn't sure it wouldn't jump right out of her chest. Thankfully, the imposter left the lit candle, or she'd be sitting in the dark with a dead man.

In the dark.

That thought was horrifying to her for some reason. It only seemed to make things worse, but right now even in the light of the candle, they were pretty bad, she had to admit.

She heard the door squeak open, and saw a flash of a green costume at the top of the stairs. Realizing the intruder was returning to hurt or possibly kill her, she quickly crawled to the side and hid behind one of the barrels that held up the charred body of Lord Lovelle.

The intruder had to realize she was still down here, and her hiding place wouldn't protect her for long. Still, she didn't know just what to do and needed a moment to think and come up with a plan. Damn, she hadn't even brought her dagger with her. Now she wished she had also taken Grunt down here with her. What had she been thinking?

Heavy footsteps echoed on the stairs, and then she heard muffled voices. It sounded like two men talking but she couldn't make out what they were saying since they were speaking so softly. Then the talking and the footsteps stopped, and her heart almost stilled as well. She stayed unmoving and silent, closing her eyes and praying not to be discovered. However, Vivienne knew there was no way to get out of here now. There was only one exit, she was wearing a long gown and couldn't run, and the intruder she had just bitten knew that she was still down here since she hadn't had the time yet to leave.

To her horror, she felt someone grip her hard on the arm and pull her up to her feet.

"Who are you and what are you doing here?" came a deep shout. "Vivienne?"

Her eyes slowly opened to find Zachariah standing there in his Robin Hood costume gripping her by the arm. Isaac was with him, wearing his costume, but he was no longer wearing the mask.

"Zachariah!" She fell into his arms, hugging him and never wanting to let him go. Her heart still beat in her throat from having encountered the intruder, not to mention hiding right next to a rotten corpse.

"Sweetheart, why did you come down here without me? What were you thinking?"

"I thought I was following you down here, but it turned out to be the other Robin Hood."

"The other one? So there really is someone with a costume just like mine?"

"Yes," she answered, her body shaking. "He attacked me with a knife, but I bit him on the forearm and he ran away." The tangy metal taste of blood was still on her tongue.

"Vivienne, I don't like this. Every time I turn around, your life seems to be in danger."

"Well, I don't like it either," she retorted. "It's not like I purposely look for trouble."

"Nay. Trouble just follows you wherever you go."

"And murder and death too. Don't forget that part," added Isaac.

"I can't stop thinking about the Death card I drew in Morgana's reading. Mayhap I was supposed to die down here today." This was all starting to become too real for Vivienne.

"Nay. That's nonsense and I don't want to hear another word about it." Zachariah pushed her stray curls of hair behind her ear. "You are not going to die."

"How do you know that?"

"Because he asked Morgana and she said that is not what the card meant," Isaac supplied the information.

ZACHARIAH COULD HAVE HIT his brother for telling that to Vivienne. He'd confided in him in secret, but Isaac didn't know the meaning of being discreet. Zachariah had been worried, but the last thing he wanted was for Vivienne to know that. It would only add to her own concern.

"You did what?" Vivienne pushed away from him and blinked several times. "You said you didn't believe in fortune telling. So you really do, and thought I was going to die?"

"Nay, that's not it at all."

"Then what was it? Tell me the truth why you asked Morgana about it."

"I only asked her for your sake," he answered. "I could see something was troubling you and I wanted you to have peace of mind."

"And if she would have said that, yes, I was going to die, would you have told me then? Or would you have even told me at all?"

"Well...that's not the point, sweetheart. What is important is that you are not going to die and that is not what the card meant at all. It just meant change, nothing more."

"Either way, I don't think I like card readings," she told him. "I'm never going to do one again."

"If you don't like your reading, you should have heard what she had to say about me," chimed in Isaac. "I'm never getting another one again either."

"What did she say about you, Isaac?" Vivienne wanted to know.

"That he's been reckless and a fool, will have to make a choice and commitment, and might find his soul mate, that's all," Zachariah answered for him.

"Well, that doesn't sound so bad." Vivienne wiped a stray tear from her cheek.

"Not to you, mayhap," grumbled Isaac, pulling back the sheet on the body. "Zachariah, I thought you said there were strangulation marks on the body. I don't see any."

"What are you saying?" Zachariah hurried over to the table with the corpse. "They are right there." He pointed and looked down, but didn't see them anymore. "Nay. That's impossible. They can't be gone."

"Well, I don't see them. Mayhap you just imagined them," said his brother.

"Nay, he didn't. I saw them too." Vivienne hurried over and peered around Zachariah. "I don't see them now either."

"Something is odd here." Zachariah leaned over to inspect what was left of Lord Lovelle's neck a little closer. Then he reached out and touched the area, and rubbed his fingers together. "Someone has put something over the marks, trying to hide them."

"What is it?" asked Isaac.

"I'm not sure. Mayhap flour?" Zachariah inspected the powdery substance on his fingers, taking a sniff.

"Let me see," said Vivienne, inspecting his fingers. "Nay, I think that is chalk." Vivienne reached out and touched the substance on his fingers. "Like what women wear on their faces to look pale."

"Noblewomen, you mean," said Zachariah, since the commoners and servants were always out in the sun and their skin was tanned and they had no need to want to look pale.

"Do you think that Robin Hood imposter was really a woman?" asked Isaac.

"I'm not sure," Vivienne said in thought. "He...or she...was about my height, but they were also very strong."

"What did you find out about that hefty woman?" asked Zachariah.

"Her name is Gunora and she is the laundress. She said she did have an alewife costume, but it disappeared."

"Hmph. Convenient," mumbled Zachariah, wiping off his hand.

"She could be lying," said Isaac, continuing to inspect the corpse.

"She did seem to be hiding something," agreed Vivienne. "Zachariah, who would want to hide the fact that this was a murder and not just an accident?"

"The murderer," said Isaac.

"I know that." Vivienne scowled at him. "What I mean is, who would do such a thing? And why?"

"So they won't be caught." Isaac smiled.

"Isaac, don't make me regret I made you my deputy," Zachariah told him. "Stop stating the obvious. We are trying to find answers here."

"You won't regret making me your deputy as soon as you see what I just found." Isaac's back was toward them when he spoke. He bent down and picked up something from the floor.

"What it is?" asked Vivienne.

"Let me check something." Isaac flipped back the sheet and

pointed to the man's groin. "Uh huh. I thought so. Take a look at that."

"I'd rather not look," said Vivienne, hiding her eyes.

"He's not burned in this area as much as his upper body," said Isaac, reaching out and grabbing something by Lord Lovelle's waist and yanking it off.

"What is that?" asked Zachariah.

"It's a cord." Isaac opened up his hand. "And I'd bet anything that this was attached to it. Mayhap that intruder used his knife to cut this cord that Lord Lovelle wore around his waist."

"He could have come for something and dropped it when I startled him."

Isaac opened up his hand. "It's a stone of some sort. It's in an odd shape." He looked closer at it. "I can't really tell what it is supposed to be."

"Let me see that." Zachariah leaned over and gave a guttural chuckle. "It's in the shape of male genitalia."

"Yuck!" Isaac threw the stone down on the table next to the corpse and wiped his palm on his breeches. "And I touched it?"

"Bag it up, Isaac. It's evidence," instructed Zachariah.

"Why would Lord Lovelle be wearing...that?" Vivienne seemed shocked.

"I can't be sure, but I've heard of things like this before," Zachariah told them. "Sometimes when a man is considered impotent, he'll seek out the services of a witch who will give him an amulet or some herbs or creams to try to help him be able to...do it."

"Ugh," said Vivienne, making a face. "I wonder if Lady Lovelle knew about this."

"I'm sure she'd know if her husband was lacking in that area," said Isaac with a roll of his eyes.

"That's not what I meant. I meant I wonder if she knew he

wore an amulet like that," said Vivienne, still looking disgusted by the idea.

"Usually, from what I've heard, men only use a fertility amulet when they have a little problem," said Zachariah.

"Little problem?" asked Isaac. "I'd say it's a big problem, not being able to make love to a woman. Especially his wife."

"No wonder Lady Lovelle seems to flirt with all the men," said Vivienne. "She is lonely."

"Lord Lovelle was her husband," Isaac reminded her. "Why on earth would any woman marry a man who couldn't do his husbandly duties?"

"Or give them heirs?" added Zachariah.

"Lady Lovelle might not have known about Lord Lovelle's impotency when she married him," suggested Vivienne.

"What a surprise to get on one's wedding night." Isaac kept shaking his head.

"My guess is that Lord Lovelle didn't tell her, but he was trying to fix his little problem on his own."

"Hello? Is someone down there?" came a male voice and then the sound of footsteps coming down the stairs.

"Isaac, put this in your pouch." Zachariah picked up the stone amulet and tossed it to Isaac. Isaac caught it, looked like he was going to retch, and then quickly hid it in the pouch at his side. "Don't breathe a word of this to anyone yet," he whispered to the others.

"Good idea," Vivienne whispered back.

"Yes, we're here," Zachariah called out. "It's Sheriff Fitch, Isaac, and Lady Vivienne." Zachariah looked over to see Jerome, the steward, making his way down the stairs.

"Oh, I wondered who would be down here with the corpse." Jerome walked into the firelight of the candle and Zachariah was speechless.

"That's quite a costume you're wearing, Jerome."

"Yes, it looks similar to mine," said Isaac, eying him up and down.

Vivienne gasped and held her hand to her mouth. "You...you're the Grim Reaper."

"Yes, do you like it?" asked Jerome with a smile. "I'm dressed as Death."

Chapter Seven

Vivienne was totally exhausted by the time she returned to her room that night. Maleine helped her undress, while Grunt lay upon the bed with his legs in the air, waiting for someone to scratch his stomach.

"So that must be why Grunt gave me so much trouble when I tried to take him back to the room," said Maleine, having heard Vivienne's report of what had happened in the undercroft. "The dog must have known that wasn't Zachariah you were following, and he was trying to protect you."

"I think from now on, I want Grunt by my side all the time."

"My lady, if I must say, you've been in many harrowing situations before, but never have they seemed to rile you and upset you as much as now."

"You're right, Maleine." She held up her arms and Maleine helped her to put on her night rail. "I guess I'm just jittery because I'm going to be wed soon."

"And that makes you nervous? I mean...you already have a child, so you're not a stranger to the ways of lovemaking."

"That's not it. I'm just starting to wonder if I should have been so adamant about not giving up investigating murders."

"Is it starting to be too much?" Maleine folded up Vivienne's costume and shoved it into the bag of clothes.

"Not too much. Not really. I mean, I'd do anything to help others find justice for their murdered loved ones."

"I know. You always put everyone else first. But mayhap it is time to start thinking of putting yourself first."

"I can't."

"Why not?" Maleine pulled the covers up around Vivienne.

"Because, I just can't do that."

"Don't you feel you deserve it?"

"I suppose so. But there are so many others who need my help. I don't want to let them down."

"Well, mayhap you just need to get a good night's sleep. I'll blow out the candle and you can shut your eyes."

"You sound as if you're going somewhere, Maleine."

"I am. I'm meeting Isaac in the great hall."

"Isaac?" Vivienne thought this was a little odd. "You have a boyfriend, Maleine. And Isaac is too old for you."

Maleine giggled. "Oh Lady Vivienne, it's not like that at all. I am in love with Wymond and would never choose Isaac over him. Isaac is not my type at all."

Vivienne giggled now too. "I am not sure that Isaac is anyone's type."

"Whether that is true or not, I can't say. But I asked Isaac to join me as Morgana gives me a card reading."

"What? Nay, don't do it, Maleine." Vivienne sat up straight in bed. "I am starting to think that witchery and magic should be left alone."

"Oh, my lady, I cannot lie to you. Isaac didn't want me to tell you or Zachariah, but the truth is that I'm not the one getting the reading. Isaac wanted another one and asked me to go with him."

"Why does he want you there with him?"

"I'm not sure. Mayhap he's afraid of choosing the Death card?"

"Well, why didn't he want me or Zachariah to know? I don't understand. Is it because he knows we would both disapprove?"

"Mayhap." Maleine got a gleam in her eye. "But if you ask me, he doesn't really want a reading. He just wants to flirt with your half-sister, and he thinks Morgana doesn't like him."

"Oh, so he thought he'd have a better chance if you're there too?"

"Yes. I guess in his head it would be less threatening to Morgana, or perhaps make him more intriguing to her, if she thought I had eyes for him."

"Oh, please! Isaac is acting like a dolt again. Morgana has vision. She'll be able to see right through that."

"Then, I suppose Isaac will have a rude awakening. Either way, I was hoping to find out if they had any more of those blackberry tarts left from the party. I want to talk to the cook and learn what that secret ingredient is in them that makes them taste so good."

"You are interested in baking? I didn't know that Maleine."

"Nay, not really. I just want to be able to tell Cook and Maria when we get back to Mablethorpe Castle so they can make them for everyone else."

"Go on. Have fun," said Vivienne with a yawn. "I think some sleep will do me good."

When Maleine opened the door, Grunt ran over to her.

"Oh, I think Grunt may need to go outside to relieve himself. I'll take him and bring him back with me later."

"Thank you," said Vivienne, her eyes already closing.

She had just drifted off to sleep when she heard a knock on the door.

"It's open," she called out, thinking it was Maleine, half-asleep and not even wondering why Maleine would be knocking.

The door squeaked open and Zachariah's head popped inside the room. "Lady Vivienne? Are you already in bed? I'm sorry, I'll come back tomorrow."

"Nay," she called out, sitting up in bed. "What did you want?"

"Well, Isaac didn't come back to the room, and I was hoping to talk things over about the clues we've found."

"Please. Come in."

He hesitated. "I'm not sure that would be proper, my lady."

"Zachariah, we're about to be married. No one will question things if they see you leaving my chamber. After all, it's common knowledge I'm not a virgin and that we've both been married before."

"I suppose you're right." Still, Zachariah looked up and down the corridor before entering. Then he nervously stepped inside quickly and closed the door. "It's quite dark in here. Mayhap I should light a fire on the hearth."

"Oh, don't bother. I'm hot," she said, flipping off the covers. The only light came from the nighttime candle burning next to the bed. "Come, sit down and we'll talk." She patted the bed next to her, inviting him to join her.

He slowly approached the bed and gingerly sat on the edge. He had changed out of his costume and now wore a simple tunic and breeches.

"What did you want to talk about?" she asked.

"I...are you all right? I mean, you were attacked tonight. You were in danger and I feel like I should have been there to protect you." He looked around the room. "Where is Maleine? And what about Grunt? They should both be here for your protection."

"Just relax, Zachariah. Everything is fine. Maleine is helping Isaac flirt with the girls, and Grunt had to piss." She giggled.

"Vivienne, your door was unlocked. Anyone could come in. What if your attacker was watching and knew you'd be alone? He could have sneaked in while you were sleeping and...and done something horrible to you."

"Quit trying to scare me, Zachariah."

"I'm not. I'm only stating the facts."

"As you always do."

"Aren't you worried about that?"

"You're the one who said Morgana told you that Death card didn't mean I was going to die, so why are you so concerned?"

"We're all going to die someday, Vivienne."

"Then I think we need to live for the day. Since tomorrow is not promised." Vivienne boldly reached out and kissed him, having wanted to do this for days but never having had any time away from prying eyes to do so. Zachariah's hand went to the back of her head and his other arm went around her waist as he pulled her closer and returned the kiss.

"I think I'd better stay with you until Maleine and Grunt return."

"I think that would be a grand idea." She leaned against him liking the feel against her of the heat of his body.

"Vivienne, sometimes a man cannot control his urges as well as a woman."

"And sometimes a woman has those same urges, my love." She looked up into his eyes and saw the desire in them strong and clear. In the light of the lone candle, he looked ever so handsome that she couldn't stop herself from wanting him too. In every way.

"You know I can't stay here much longer. Because if I do...I might do something I'll regret in the morning."

"Really?" she asked, rubbing circles on his back with her hand. "You'd regret it?"

"Nay. I just meant, mayhap we should wait. Until we're married."

"Zachariah, we are both adults, have been married before, and have children of our own. We are not under anyone's expectations to wait to make love until we're married."

"You...really mean that, Vivienne?"

"I think we've both waited long enough. We've known each other for a long, long time now. We've been best friends our entire lives. To be honest, I am tired of waiting."

"Me too."

"So we agree?"

He pulled her closer and kissed her again. "We are getting married in a few weeks."

"That's right." She kissed him back, feeling herself coming to life in his embrace.

"Vivienne. What do you want me to do?"

"Well, Zachariah, for starters, you can blow out that candle."

"Gladly." With the flame doused, it only seemed to feed the desire burning in each of them. And in each other's arms, they found comfort, security, excitement, and love. This was the night Vivienne had been hoping for, and one that she truly would never forget as long as she lived.

Zachariah felt something wet on his face and opened his eyes to see Grunt atop him, licking him. "Grunt, stop that," he said softly, so as not to awaken Vivienne.

"Sheriff, is that you?" Maleine lit a candle and Zachariah

sprang up in bed, remembering now where he was, whom he was with, and what he had done.

"Maleine! It's not what you think."

"Zachariah, what on earth are you doing in Lady Vivienne's bed?" Isaac peeked into the room, obviously having walked Maleine back to her bedchamber.

"I'm here guarding Vivienne. Until Maleine and Grunt return."

"Uh huh." Isaac crossed his arms over his chest. "Half-dressed?"

Zachariah reached down to the floor and quickly donned his tunic. He couldn't remember anything after that exciting love-making with Vivienne.

"Where is Lady Vivienne?" asked Maleine.

"She's right...here." Zachariah turned to look, but Vivienne wasn't lying next to him like she was when he'd held her in his arms and they'd both fallen asleep. He jumped up, frantic, wondering where she'd gone.

"Brother, put on your breeches, please. There is a girl in the room," Isaac told him.

"Ooops." Zachariah reached down and quickly pulled on his breeches and then slipped into his shoes.

"It's all right. I didn't see anything." Maleine faced the other way and busied herself playing with the dog.

"Like there was anything to see?" asked Isaac with a chuckle.

"Isaac, stop it. Vivienne is gone and I don't know where she went." Zachariah felt like the worst protector in the world right now. How could she have left the room and he'd slept right through her departure?

"Good thing you were here *protecting* her," said Isaac, stressing the word protecting.

"I've got to find her. I'll never forgive myself if anything happens to her." Zachariah ran out of the room with Grunt following right behind him. "Grunt, find Vivienne. Where is she?"

As if the dog understood, he ran down the stairs and Zachariah followed. He followed Grunt through the dark corridors and to a back passageway that led to the kitchen. Entering the room, he saw Vivienne sitting by the cook fire, eating something. Grunt ran up to her and she broke off a piece and gave it to the dog.

"Vivienne? What are you doing?" he asked, confused, but at the same time happy to have found her.

"I became hungry after our lovemaking," she told him, licking her fingers. "Maleine was talking about blackberry tarts and I remembered seeing a tray of them tucked away in the back of the kitchen. Thankfully I found a few left." She picked one up off the tray and held it out to him. "Would you like one?"

"What in heaven's name is the matter with you?"

"I told you. I was hungry." She took a big bite and gave the rest to Grunt. Then she proceeded to brush the crumbs off her hands.

"You are sitting here in your night rail and all alone."

"I have my cloak on over it. See?" She held out the sides to prove her point. "And I am alone right now, but up until a few minutes ago, there were several cooks here with me."

"I think you're losing your mind. Please don't wander out alone again."

"Zachariah, I've decided that I don't want to live in fear." She got up to join them while Grunt sniffed around the floor for crumbs. "But if you'd like, you can escort me back to my room now." She held on to his arm, smiling so sweetly that he couldn't find it in his heart to reprimand her anymore.

"That was wonderful, what we had together," he said in a low voice as they walked.

"Yes. I agree. That's why I worked up an appetite, I guess."

They both laughed. "Yes, I guess so," he answered.

"You don't regret it, do you?" she asked him. Vivienne peeked up at him and he could see the blush on her face.

"Not at all. Do you?"

"It was my idea," she said. "Of course, I don't regret it. Not in the least. It only makes me want to marry you quicker than we've planned."

"Nay. We'll wait the three weeks. Your aunt and uncle are planning a grand wedding celebration for us and we don't want to let them down."

"I suppose you're right. Three weeks will go by quickly."

Grunt growled lowly, taking their attention.

"What is it, boy?" asked Zachariah, looking around.

"Something's bothering Grunt," said Vivienne, her smile disappearing as she looked around as well. "Do you hear voices coming from Lady Lovelle's room?"

"I don't know. I wasn't paying attention," said Zachariah, seeing light under the door as they approached, and then hearing the voices that Vivienne mentioned. "Yes, you're right. I wonder who she is talking with at this time of night?"

"I hope she's all right."

"Mayhap we should check." Zachariah was about to knock on the door when it opened and the physician walked out.

"Oh!" The physician looked up in surprise. "I didn't expect anyone to be here this time of night."

"Sigbald? What are you doing here? This is Lady Lovelle's chamber," said Zachariah.

"Yes, I know," the man answered, clearing his throat.

"I thought I heard voices out here." Lady Lovelle pulled open the door. She was in her nightshift but had a robe around her and pulled it closed when she saw them.

"Is everything all right, my lady?" asked Vivienne. "Where is your handmaid?"

"I sent Ester to fetch me some hot water," answered the lady of the castle.

"So you and Sigbald were in here alone?" asked Zachariah.

"Yes. I summoned the physician because I had a bad headache. Sigbald came to check on me and to make sure everything was all right."

"And...is it?" asked Zachariah, wondering what the man was really doing in her room. "Are you well then?"

"Yes," Sigbald answered for her. "She is quite fine. I gave her some infused herbs in hot water to drink. They should cure the headache, and also make her sleepy."

"I thought Ester went to get the hot water," said Vivienne.

"She did." Lady Lovelle's face reddened. "She was here but just left. To get more." It all seemed strange to Zachariah, and he was sure at least one of them or perhaps both of them were lying. "What are you doing out in your night rail, Lady Vivienne?" asked Lady Lovelle, causing Vivienne to pull her cloak closer around her.

"I couldn't sleep and went down to the kitchen for a blackberry hand pie. The sheriff escorted me."

"So I guess none of us can sleep tonight," said Lady Lovelle. "However, I feel better now and think I can." She yawned, covering her mouth. "Yes, I feel suddenly very tired. If you'll excuse me, I've had some hectic days. Plus, I'm still distraught from losing my husband. I'd like to get some sleep."

"Of course," said Zachariah. "But just remember, there is a killer on the loose yet, so be sure to lock the door."

"I will," she said, closing the door and turning the key in the lock.

"But what about Ester?" asked Vivienne, with her finger

raised in the air. No one seemed to hear her except for Zachariah.

"Good night," said Sigbald with a nod of his head, not able to look them in the eye. As he left, Grunt growled lowly once again.

They continued to walk back to Vivienne's chamber in silence. Then Vivienne asked the same thing that was on Zachariah's mind.

"Do you think that Sigbald and Lady Lovelle are lovers?"

"Who knows. But it kind of looks that way. I mean, I didn't believe her story of having a headache at all."

"Me neither," said Vivienne. "And that yawn looked fake to me. And where was her handmaid and why did she lock the door if Ester was about to return with hot water?"

"Something is going on here, and we can't leave until we find out what it is."

"I agree." Vivienne stopped at her door. "But you know we can't stop the funeral from happening tomorrow. We have no reason not to let it happen."

"Then we won't try to stop it," he told her.

"We won't?"

"Nay. I don't think we need the body for anything else."

"Not even to prove that someone was trying to cover up the strangulation marks?"

"We know they were there. So does Isaac and Maleine. Ludwig and Sigbald also saw them, even if they don't want to admit it."

"Then we're going to stay? In Grimsthorpe?"

"I don't want to leave before we find the killer. Do you?"

"Nay, I don't. But what excuse are we going to give Lady Lovelle?" she asked him.

"We'll tell her we want to stay for the funeral."

"And afterward? She will wonder why we're still here. Plus, we'll need permission from her to even stay."

"I'm not sure about any of it. But we have all night to sleep on it. I'm sure we'll come up with a good excuse by morning." He leaned over and kissed her on the mouth. "Sweet dreams, Vivienne. Now, take Grunt into the room with you and lock the door behind you for protection."

"I will," she told him. "But I'll never feel as safe as I do when I have you by my side."

Zachariah stood there at her door until he heard her turn the lock from the other side. Yes, this marriage to Vivienne was going to be challenging unless he could convince her to give up the idea of always having to help investigate murders with him. But he knew Vivienne. She'd never stop wanting to help others, no matter how much danger she put herself in to do so. And she'd never want to stop working with him until she found justice for those who had loved ones murdered.

Seeing her parents murdered had to have been the hardest thing she'd ever had to endure. He was only glad they'd found the murderer and that tragedy was now solved and behind them. But he'd never stop worrying about her because she was the woman he loved. She was about to become his wife, and also a mother to his daughter. His desire was for her to do whatever she chose. He never wanted to tell her how to live her life because that would take away from the wonderful woman that she was.

So why did it still feel wrong to allow her to investigate murders with him? And would he ever regret not stopping his wife and possibly his children from being put right into the path of danger in the future? Hell, he already regretted that part! But still, he could never ask Vivienne to stop being the woman she wanted to be. If so, it would be the biggest mistake of his life.

Chapter Eight

The funeral for Lord Daniel Lovelle took place the next morning right there at Grimsthorpe Manor. There was a chapel inside the keep, and a small graveyard in the farthermost reaches of the estate, a good distance behind the manor house and near a stretch of quiet, deep-looking woods. A crowd of people stood around the hole in the ground as the priest, Father Willard from town, said a prayer and several servants lowered the coffin into the grave.

Vivienne looked over to see the servants, as well as Gunora, the washerwoman, standing farther back on one end. Gunora constantly looked around and whispered behind her hand to some of the other female servants.

Across from them and closer up was Sheriff Ludwig, his deputy Rodger, and Sigbald the physician. They just looked bored, and Rodger even yawned. No one seemed distraught by the death of the lord of the manor at all.

Vivienne stood up in front near the coffin with Zachariah, Maleine, Isaac, and, of course, Lady Amelia Lovelle, who continued to whimper and dab at her eyes with a small square of cloth. Her handmaid, Ester, was clinging to her arm. Jerome, the steward, stood at her other side. For some reason, Vivienne thought Lady Lovelle's reactions were faked. Nothing about this woman seemed sincere to her at all.

"We invite Lord Lovelle's loved ones now to please step forward and proceed to drop a shovelful of dirt over the deceased in a final goodbye," said the priest. It was custom for the mourners to pay honor and respect by dropping dirt on the dead person to symbolize not only closure and their farewells, but also that the deceased would turn back to dust and become part of the earth now.

One of the servants scooped up some dirt and handed the shovel to Lady Lovelle. She reached for it, but then stopped and shook her head and wailed. Her hand went to her stomach. Jerome stepped forward to take the shovel and do it for her.

"Let's go do our part and say our farewells," said Zachariah, taking Vivienne by the hand.

"You all go on and drop the dirt into the grave. There is something I need to do first," she told him. Grunt lay on the ground with his nose between his paws, but once Vivienne started to walk in the direction of Lady Lovelle, the dog quickly followed.

There was quiet talking amongst the onlookers and Vivienne tried to be discreet, walking up behind Lady Lovelle trying to eavesdrop on what she and the steward were saying.

"My lady, you should go back to the manor and lie down," Jerome told her.

"I agree," said Ester. "I'll take her."

"Nay. I'm not going to do that with all these people here," she told them.

"Do you think it's wise to stay? You need to rest," said Ester.

"I'll be fine, now leave me be. Both of you. Go now. I want to be alone." She talked from the side of her mouth and barely looked at either of them.

Jerome walked away from her, and Ester stepped back, seeing Vivienne, and stopped.

"I'll comfort her," said Vivienne, dismissing the handmaid, who didn't look happy about it at all. Vivienne approached Lady Lovelle and laid her hand on the woman's shoulder. "Lady Lovelle, I am so sorry for your loss," said Vivienne, but Lady Lovelle didn't even turn to look at her. She just kept staring at her husband's grave.

"Yes. Thank you." She sniffled and wiped her nose on a cloth.

"I'm sure this must be so hard for you, since you recently wed. How long had you two been married?"

"We'd only been married for two months," she told Vivienne.

"Really." Vivienne knew it hadn't been long, but the short time surprised her for some reason.

"Did you know Lord Lovelle long before you two were betrothed?"

"Nay. We met for the first time on our wedding day." She looked down, folding up the square of cloth.

"Oh, I see. I'm betrothed now, so I realize how hard it is to wait for three weeks for the banns to be posted."

"There was no posting of the banns."

"Nay? Why not? After all, it is custom."

"We didn't see any need to wait. My father made an alliance with Lord Lovelle, and they agreed we should marry immediately without waiting."

"That's uncommon. Why the rush?"

"Lord Lovelle was old and my father was ill. I suppose it was because he wanted me to be married before he died. And Daniel wanted a wife before he died as well."

"So Lord Lovelle had never been married before he married you?"

"Nay."

"Why not?"

Her head snapped up. "Why are you asking me all these questions? My husband is dead and I am in mourning and would rather not speak of these things, since they make me feel lightheaded and weak."

"Of course not. I understand. I'm sorry. But tell me, how is your father?"

"He passed away the day after we wed."

"I'm sorry, once again."

They were both silent for a moment, watching the others drop dirt into the grave. Then Vivienne took a chance and spoke up once more. "What will happen to you now that your husband is gone? I suspect his manor and holdings will revert back to the Crown. Will you take another husband in order to keep the manor and not lose Lord Lovelle's holdings? Or will you take up the veil and join the convent instead?" Vivienne wasn't trying to upset the woman, but she wanted to learn more about her since she didn't trust her at all.

"Take up the veil?" Lady Lovelle's eyes opened wide. "That will never happen!" She seemed to shudder. Vivienne figured it was because this woman liked men too much to ever want to give up coupling to be dedicated to God.

"Then you'll need to find another husband."

"Yes. I need one. I want one. Quickly. Lady Vivienne, your father is the King. Perhaps you can talk to him about finding me a rich baron. One who is handsome and closer to my age?"

"I don't ever see King Edward to talk to him, so I'm afraid not. Besides, it would be up to the King to choose a husband for you. I am afraid I couldn't convince him of anything."

This seemed to really upset the woman. Her body swayed and her hand went to her stomach once again.

"If you'll excuse me Lady Vivienne, I'd like to go back to my chamber and lie down. Daniel's death has overwhelmed me and I am filled with grief."

"Yes, of course. I'd be happy to walk with you."

"Nay, I'll be fine."

Before Vivienne could summon Lady Lovelle's handmaid, the steward walked up to Lady Lovelle and put out his arm to escort her back to the manor. The handmaid silently followed behind them.

Grunt whined and looked up at her with wide eyes.

"Yes, Grunt, I think it is odd too."

"What's odd, my lady?" asked Maleine, joining her, brushing dirt from her hands.

"I just find it curious that the steward is taking so much interest in the lady of the castle when it is the handmaid's job to see to her needs."

Zachariah, Isaac, Sheriff Ludwig, and his deputy Rodger walked over to join her.

"Well, since the masquerade as well as the funeral is over, I expect you'll be leaving for Mablethorpe now," said Ludwig. "I see Lady Lovelle is leaving. I'd better go to her and make sure she is all right. She told me this morning that a pouch of her husband's money is missing. She thinks someone may have stolen it."

"So now there is a thief afoot, as well as a possible murderer?" asked Zachariah.

"Don't worry about it, Sheriff Fitch. I'll handle matters. It is my job to see to Lady Lovelle's protection."

Now the sheriff was acting like it was his job to see to the lady of the castle's needs, and not just for her protection. Vivienne had never seen anything like this.

"Nay, we're not leaving," Vivienne spoke up before Zachariah could answer. She didn't want to go yet, because something didn't feel right and she wanted to investigate further to figure out what it was.

"Nay?" asked the deputy. "Why would you want to stay?"

"Lord Lovelle was a good friend of my uncle," she told the men. "I feel I owe it to him to comfort Lady Lovelle for at least a few days. She seems so...distraught."

"I'm sure she'll be fine," said Ludwig. "She has many people around her to fulfill her needs. I will personally vouch for her safety."

"Just the same, we'd like to stay for a few more days," said Zachariah.

"Whatever for?" This didn't seem to please the Sheriff of Grimsthorpe in the least.

"I still have some clues to follow up on," said Zachariah.

"You still think it was a murder?" asked Ludwig.

"Yes, we do," Isaac answered for him. "We won't leave without first overturning every stone trying to find the truth."

"Stay if you want, then," said Ludwig with a shrug of his shoulders. "But I think you are all wrong. There has been no foul play here and I don't want your accusations upsetting Lady Lovelle."

"Sheriff," said Zachariah. "We have a few questions about things, and would really appreciate if you could help us out since you know these people better than we do."

"Well, yes I do." Ludwig seemed to like that, and stood taller, pushing back his shoulders. "I have been sheriff here for a long time and have seen many people come and go."

"Then you'll help us?" asked Zachariah.

He looked back at Lady Lovelle, seeming as if he would rather be with her. Finally, he answered. "I'd be glad to help however I can. But I still believe that you are wrong about thinking it was a murder."

"There are clues we can't ignore," said Isaac.

"Clues? What kind of clues?" asked Rodger.

"Well, for one, someone tried to cover up the strangulation marks on Lord Lovelle's neck using chalk," Zachariah told them.

"Really." Ludwig's face became solemn. "Why didn't you mention this before now?"

"We tried to," said Vivienne. "But you didn't seem to want to listen."

"That's not true. I always listen," the man answered, seeming highly insulted now.

"Lady Vivienne was also attacked in the undercroft by a man wearing the costume of Robin Hood," Maleine spoke up.

"What? Why didn't anyone tell me this?" growled Ludwig. "Was he armed?"

"He had a knife, and was looking over the corpse when I surprised him," said Vivienne. "He turned around and I bit him on the forearm."

"Who was it?" asked Ludwig. "Did you get a look at his face?"

"No, Lady Vivienne wasn't able to see the man's face," Zachariah spoke up. "He was wearing a mask at the time."

"Everything happened so fast, and it was dark in the undercroft," explained Vivienne. "He ran out of there before I could see who he, or she, might have been."

"If someone assaulted you, Lady Vivienne, you shouldn't have kept it from me." Ludwig frowned. "I am the sheriff of this town and I need to know everything that happens."

"I...I guess I didn't bother to tell you since I didn't think you'd believe me."

"Why wouldn't I? And is the reason you didn't mention it because your precious betrothed knew about it and wanted to take the credit for catching an attacker?"

"What?" This confused Vivienne. The man was clearly accusing them of something that wasn't true.

"Or is it because you don't trust me, and think I might have had something to do with this supposed murder?" Ludwig seemed to go crazy now.

"Nay, of course not," Zachariah answered as Vivienne's jaw dropped. "No one thinks that. We just seemed to get off on the wrong foot. However, if we work together, I think we can be a strong team and solve this case once and for all."

"Then meet me in the great hall in two hours," said Ludwig. "I want to know everything you've found and any suspicions you might have about who did it. Do I need to keep everyone here any longer?" he asked.

"I don't think that's necessary," said Zachariah. "We've already questioned most of them and they are free to leave. However, I still want to talk to the staff again. And I have some more questions for the card-reader too."

"Morgana. Her name is Morgana," said Vivienne.

"God's teeth, is she still here?" whined Ludwig. "I don't want her anywhere around Lady Lovelle."

"I'm not sure," said Vivienne, but I'll look for her."

Isaac cleared his throat.

"Did you have something to add, Isaac?" asked Zachariah.

"I think you'll be able to find Morgana in the stable."

"In the stable?" asked Maleine. "What would she be doing there? I would have thought she'd have left by now."

"I'm...meeting her there after the funeral. Which is now."

"What on earth for?" gasped Vivienne.

"I mentioned to her about the amulet we found on Lord Lovelle's body, and she told me she gave it to him. I wanted to ask her more about it."

"What amulet?" asked Ludwig. "Is this another secret you have kept from me? I don't like this at all."

"Isaac, show it to him," said Zachariah. "We're working together now and need to share our findings."

"I don't have it on me. It's in the room," said Isaac. "I didn't feel like I wanted to carry that thing around with me." He shuddered and made a silly face.

"Sheriff Fitch, if you've been keeping evidence from me, I can have you arrested," threatened Ludwig.

"Yes, I'm sure you can. But what would that solve? If you did that, we'd only be tied up here in Grimsthorpe even longer, and still be no closer to learning the truth about Lord Lovelle's death. We said we'd work together instead of fighting each other like we've been doing, so I say we start doing that right now."

"Fine," said Ludwig. "Like I already said, meet me and my deputy in the great hall in two hours." Ludwig and Rodger walked away, talking amongst themselves.

As soon as they left, Isaac reached into his pouch and used his kerchief to pull something out. Opening his palm, he gazed at the amulet and groaned. "Ugh. I can't believe I'm even touching this thing again."

"You had the amulet all along?" asked Vivienne in surprise.

"Why didn't you tell Ludwig?" asked Maleine.

"Because we want to talk to Morgana about it first," Zachariah told her.

"You knew?" This surprised Vivienne as well.

"Vivienne, there is something about Ludwig that I still don't trust." Zachariah took the cloth with the stone amulet in it and put it in his pouch.

Grunt barked as if saying he agreed.

"But you said you were going to work together with Ludwig and his deputy to figure this out," said Vivienne. "Didn't you mean it?"

"I did say that. And yes, we are." Zachariah squinted his eyes as he watched Ludwig and Rodger walk away. "I figure the closer I am to him, the easier it will be for him to slip up with information if he really is guilty."

"And if he's innocent?" asked Vivienne. "What then?"

"Then I'll apologize and it'll be the end of it," said Zachariah with a shrug.

"I see." Vivienne looked back at the keep, thinking how she'd like to find out more about Lady Lovelle too. "I think I'll play that game as well," she told him.

"What game?" asked Isaac. "Are we playing a game?"

"My lady, you're going to try to get close to Lady Lovelle, aren't you?" asked Maleine.

"I am," said Vivienne. "You can always read me like a book, Maleine. You are sharp and that is what I like the most about you."

"You don't trust Lady Lovelle?" asked Zachariah.

"Nay. Then again, there is not a lot of people around this place that I do trust," she told him.

"Excuse me," said Gunora, walking up with a basket of dirty laundry. "Is there anything you need washed? I'm washing everyone's costumes today, now that the masquerade is over."

"Nay, but thank you for asking," said Zachariah. "But why are you out here in the graveyard? Shouldn't you be inside?"

"I was at the funeral like everyone else," said the woman. "But I'm going back to work now."

Vivienne looked down and saw something of interest in the basket. "Is that an alewife's costume?" She reached in and pulled it out.

"Ah, so that's where it is." Gunora snatched it away from her. "I have to return this to the alewife who leant it to me in the first place. She was upset when she heard it had been stolen."

"So that is your costume," said Vivienne.

"Yes. It's the costume that disappeared. I told you about it. I wonder how it got in this basket since I didn't put it there."

"Whose laundry did you pick up today?" she asked the woman.

"I went to Lady Lovelle's chamber, then down to the great hall to collect the costumes of the servants before coming out to the graveyard for the funeral."

"Did you leave the basket out of your sight at any time?" asked Zachariah.

"Well, yes. But not for too long. Just long enough for me to go the kitchen for a little snack. And to participate in dropping dirt on Lord Lovelle."

"Someone might have put the costume in there when she wasn't looking," suggested Maleine.

"Why would they want to do that?" asked Gunora. "If I don't know who put it there, I couldn't give it back once it was clean. Not that I'd want to, mind you. I mean, they stole it from me to begin with."

"They wanted to dump it before they were caught." Isaac nodded.

Gunora put the basket on the ground while she shoved the alewife's costume back into the pile. Grunt ran over to sniff it, causing the woman to scream and hold up her hands. When she did so, Vivienne saw something of interest.

"Grunt, get down." Isaac pulled the dog away.

"Might I see your forearm?" asked Vivienne. Gunora covered her forearm with her other hand.

"What for?"

"It looked like you had bite marks on your arm," said Vivienne.

"Awk, it's nothing. I got bit by one of the castle dogs last night. The mutt tried to get the lamb chop I was eating. When I pushed him away, he bit me."

Grunt made a guttural noise in his throat.

"Hold out your arm," said Zachariah.

"Yes, Sheriff." She did as asked, and Zachariah pushed up

her sleeve and took a look at the bite marks. "It's hard to tell but it could be from a dog."

"Or mayhap a person?" asked Vivienne.

"A person?" Gunora seemed confused. "Bid the devil, who would be biting me? I'm sure I don't taste that good."

"Lady Vivienne was attacked in the undercroft yesterday and she bit the arm of the intruder before they ran off," explained Zachariah.

"You don't think that was me, do you? If so, you're daft, Sheriff. I am too fat to barely fit through the door of the undercroft, if I must point that out to you. Plus, I don't go down there for nothing because I hate rats. It wasn't me in the undercroft, my lady, I swear it's true."

"Nay, I suppose it wasn't," said Vivienne. "I'm sorry if we've offended you."

"Thank you, Gunora. You may leave," the sheriff told her. Gunora picked up her basket of laundry and hurried away, mumbling to herself.

"That was interesting," said Isaac.

"Vivienne, do you trust the washwoman?" Zachariah asked, once Gunora had walked away.

"I don't know," said Vivienne. "She did have the costume as well as the bite marks on her arm. But I don't think my attacker was as short or as fat as her. It all happened so fast, that I don't really remember more, but I wish that I did."

"I'd like to find the physician and question him once more before we meet with the sheriff," announced Zachariah.

"Go on," said Vivienne. "I'll take Grunt and Maleine and meet up with Morgana in the stables."

"Nay, I don't think that's a good idea," said Isaac.

"Why not?" she asked him.

"Because, she is expecting me and doesn't really like you."

"Of course she does! She's my half-sister, Isaac. What an absurd thing to say."

"Isaac, I'd like you to stay by Vivienne," said the sheriff. "You go with her. Maleine can come with me."

"What about Grunt?" asked Maleine. "Should I put him back in the room?"

"Nay," said 'Vivienne. "Grunt will go where he likes, and might be beneficial in helping us find more clues."

"I am also curious to know about that stolen pouch of Lord Lovelle's money," said Zachariah.

"Do you think it is somehow connected to the murder?" asked Vivienne.

"I don't know. But I do know that I saw a pouch with the letter L on it in Morgana's bag."

"Oh, Zachariah, you don't really think my sister would steal, do you?" asked Vivienne.

"Well, she is an entertainer, and they don't have a reputation for being that honest."

"Stop saying that," pouted Vivienne. "I am sure Morgana had nothing to do with it."

"I'll find out," Isaac told him. "But it could just be a simple misunderstanding or a coincidence of some sort."

"Let's hope so," said the sheriff. "But whatever we're going to do to prove this was a murder and catch the killer, we need to move fast. I'm anxious to get home to Starah. Besides, I get the feeling we're not wanted here, and I'm not sure how long we can stay before we wear out our welcome."

Chapter Nine

Vivienne entered the stables with Grunt, sure she heard a woman's voice and she sounded as if she were talking to someone.

"Get away. Leave me alone. Do you hear me? Leave me be," said the woman.

"Morgana? Is that you?" Vivienne walked over to a stall to see her newfound sister sitting inside. She stood up abruptly, looking startled. Isaac was right behind Vivienne. The horses didn't like the dog being there, and whinnied and jostled their heads.

"Lady Vivienne? What are you doing here?" Morgana looked back inside the stall and shook her head, and then opened the gate and slipped out. "Isaac, you didn't tell me she was coming with you."

Vivienne's heart ached to hear Morgana say this, since it almost really did sound as if she didn't like her and that hurt.

"What difference does it make if I'm here?" Vivienne sat down on a wooden bench outside the stall and pulled Grunt over to her. "After all, we are half-sisters. Whom were you talking to when we entered?"

"I wasn't talking to anyone." Morgana hugged her arms around her body.

"But I heard you. You were telling someone to leave you alone and to go away." Vivienne stood up and peered over the gate and into the stall. There wasn't a person in sight. Only a horse.

"It was the horse. I was talking to the horse. He was nibbling my hair, that's all." Morgana seemed visibly upset. Vivienne knew that what her half-sister just said wasn't true, since Morgana had been sitting and the horse had been munching on hay.

"Morgana, what can you tell us about this?" Isaac took the stone amulet out of his pouch. He opened up the cloth it was in to show it to her. The stone in the shape of male genitalia had a hole at the top that a cord had been strung through, and that cord had held the amulet around Lord Lovelle's waist.

Morgana stretched her neck and looked at it from the side of her eye. "It's a witch's amulet, made for a man. To cure his impotency."

"Did you give that to Lord Lovelle?" asked Vivienne.

"I'm not a witch, if that is what you really mean to ask me."

"Nay, Morgana, no one thinks that. We just want to know more about Lord Lovelle. Did he ask you for it?" said Isaac.

"Not exactly."

"What does that mean?" Vivienne sat back down and scratched behind Grunt's ears.

"Someone told me to get it and to bring it to him, since I had been asked by the King to come here to do readings at the masquerade."

"The King really asked you to come?" Vivienne was surprised to hear this.

"Yes. Father thought you'd like that, Lady Vivienne." It was odd to hear Morgana call the King 'Father' while she was talking about both of them. Then again, in a way it felt good too. It was a common bond she now had with Morgana.

"He thought that I'd like that? Why? I've never even had a card reading before, and neither do I know anything about fortunes."

"He said you saw a ghost in a graveyard."

"Yes, that's true. I did." Vivienne wondered how the King knew that, since she didn't remember saying anything about it to him.

"So you believe in ghosts?" Morgana asked her.

"Of course I do," said Vivienne. "I've seen not one but two of them with my own eyes. My son and some others saw them too, including Sheriff Fitch."

"Did either of the two ghosts you saw ever talk to you?" she asked, with urgency in her voice. "Tell me. What did they say? What did they want?"

"Nay, they didn't say anything." Vivienne shook her head. "Why? Have ghosts spoken to you?"

"Nay. Of course not." Morgana looked to the ground.

"Who asked you to bring that amulet to Lord Lovelle?" Vivienne asked her.

"No one." Morgana leaned her arms on the top of the gate and looked in the opposite direction. Vivienne could see that the young woman was keeping something from them and needed to find out what it was.

"Did Lord Lovelle tell you he was impotent?" asked Isaac. "We need to know."

"He wanted to ask about it in a card reading, but it didn't matter that it never took place because I already knew all about it. That's why I gave him the amulet. He was happy to get it."

"How did you know about his sad state?" asked Isaac. "Did his wife tell you?"

"Nay! Lady Lovelle is stuffy and didn't want me here in the

first place, and even tried to convince her husband to make me leave. I am sure she'd never admit to anyone that her husband was impotent."

"Tell us more about the amulet," said Vivienne. "Does it really help cure impotency if one wears it?"

"I don't know." She shrugged. "But I suppose if one truly believes in the stone's power, well, then, yes, it could help."

"Who told you to bring it to him?" Vivienne asked once again.

"I'd rather not say."

"Well, whom did you get it from?"

"It doesn't matter," answered the girl, suddenly becoming close-lipped.

"You need to tell us, Morgana," said Isaac. "We're in the midst of a murder investigation, and keeping information from us could make you an accessory to a crime."

"What crime? Killing a man? I had nothing to do with that. I was reading the cards for Lady Vivienne when it happened."

"Yes, and you told me someone was going to die that night and they did. How did you know?" Vivienne pushed Morgana with her questions, needing to know more.

"I am a fortune-teller. We just know things."

"I don't believe if I truly believe that," said Vivienne. She let go of Grunt and he wandered off, sniffing around the stables.

"It's true. Sometimes we just...know things. Even before they happen."

"Morgana," said Isaac, stepping around Vivienne to get closer. "You have to realize that it sounds very suspicious that you just know things, including that a man was going to die that night and then he did."

"I didn't know it was going to be a man. Just the death of someone at the party."

Grunt started pawing at the hay and barking from the far side of the stable.

"Isaac, would you be kind enough to see what has my hound so worked up?" said Vivienne, really wanting to talk to Morgana alone. When he left, she spoke in hushed tones.

"Morgana, we are of the same blood, and I will do anything I can to help you, but you need to be honest with me and tell me all you know."

"I did," she replied.

"Nay, you didn't. Who asked you to go find the witch and bring the fertility amulet to Lord Lovelle? Please, tell me."

Morgana was quiet for a moment, her eyes roaming over to Isaac who was chasing Grunt around in the hay, trying to catch him. Vivienne figured the dog was after a rat. "Oh, all right, I'll tell you. It was Lord Lovelle's mother."

"His mother? She must be very old if she's still alive. Where did you see her? I don't remember meeting her at the masquerade."

"She wasn't at the masquerade, and it doesn't matter. I was told to bring the amulet and I did. I tried to give a card reading to Lord Lovelle, but Lady Lovelle entered the solar and stopped me, so I got up and left. That's everything that I know."

"I see. Well, thank you for telling me that," she said, not wanting to push harder or she might just shove Morgana away. Vivienne liked having a half-sister, and wanted to get to know her and possibly spend time with her too, someday. Even if she was a mysterious fortune-teller, Vivienne didn't care. She was friends with people from all walks of life, not just the nobles. Although, if Morgana was King Edward's bastard, then she was a half-noble. Hopefully, someday there would be time to learn about Morgana's mother or perhaps any siblings, but she didn't want to ask about that right now.

"Grunt, get back here!" shouted Isaac, chasing Grunt as the dog headed right toward Vivienne with something in his mouth.

"Grunt are you causing trouble?" Vivienne caught the hound. "What have you got in your mouth? Are you killing rats again?"

"It's not a rat." Morgana dropped her bag and got to her knees in front of Grunt, gently taking the animal from the dog's mouth. "It is a cat! A scrawny, very dirty cat." She held up the cat by the scruff of its neck and the animal purred. It looked at them with big green eyes as if begging them to save it. It was very dirty, but looked to be black, and seemed to be somewhat young yet. The cat was a female.

"Here, I'll take it and throw it outside." Isaac reached for the poor cat, but Morgana slapped his hand away.

"Ow! Why do you always slap me?" he complained.

"I wonder if this is someone's cat?" said Morgana, running her hand over the cat's head.

"I see you found that pesky cat that's been scaring the horses." One of the stablehands walked in to the stable with Jerome.

"Lady Lovelle hates that blasted thing. Give it to me, I'll drown it in the horse trough," said the stablehand.

"Nay!" shouted Morgana, hugging the young cat to her chest. "No one is going to hurt this poor thing. She is scared and needs a home. She is going to be mine from now on." Morgana ran out of the stables with the cat in her arms and Grunt at her heels.

"Morgana forgot her bag," said Isaac, picking it up and going after her.

"What's going on out here?" asked Jerome, looking at them suspiciously. "This is no place for a lady."

"We were just leaving." Vivienne got up and shook out her skirts. "Jerome, can you tell me where I'd find Lord Lovelle's mother?"

Jerome looked at her oddly. "Aye."

"Is she nearby?"

"Aye," he said again. "Right here at the castle, actually."

"Really? Oh, good! Would you please take me to her?"

"I...suppose I could. But why would you want to do that?"

"To talk to her, of course. About her son."

"I don't think so."

"The lady made a request, now carry it out and don't give her trouble," said Isaac, returning. "And just in case you do, I'm coming with her."

"All right. Follow me." Jerome made his way to the keep, but instead of going inside, he turned and headed for the little graveyard down by the woods outside the manor house, and right where Lord Lovelle had been buried.

"Oh, is she visiting the grave of her son?" asked Vivienne, surprised he was taking them there. "I don't think I saw her here earlier during the funeral."

"She was here, where she always is," said Jerome, opening the gate and letting Vivienne enter first. Vivienne looked around, but there was no one there.

"I don't see anyone," she told him.

"If you're playing silly games, you'll be sorry." Isaac rested his hand on the hilt of his sword.

"You asked me to bring you to Lord Lovelle's mother, and I did. May I go now?" asked Jerome.

"Not until you bring us to her," said Isaac. "Now tell us, where is she?"

"Look down," said the man with no emotion at all on his face.

Vivienne looked down and there at her feet was a grave. The marker stone read Mabel Lovelle.

"There must be some mistake," said Vivienne. Is this the grave of Lord Lovelle's first wife?"

"Nay. He was never married before marrying Amelia."

"Oh, that's right. Then is it his sister or perhaps an aunt?" she asked.

"Lady Vivienne, I don't know what you want me to say," said Jerome. "You asked me to bring you to Lord Lovelle's mother and I did. Now, if you'll excuse me, Lady Lovelle is in need of my services."

"Of course," she said in shock, watching him go.

"She's dead," said Isaac, staring down at the grave.

"I can see that, Isaac."

"Why would Morgana tell us she spoke to the woman when, by the looks of that grave, she's been dead for a very long time?"

"I'm not sure."

"She must be a horrendous liar as well as a thief." Isaac shook his head and held out a velvet pouch with the letter L stitched on it.

"What is that, Isaac?"

"I found it in Morgana's bag when I went to give it to her."

"Why did you take it? It's not yours."

"It's not hers either. You heard what Zachariah said, as well as Ludwig saying a pouch of Lord Lovelle's money had been stolen. Look." He spilled a lot of coins out into his palm. "And the L on it proves it belongs to the Lovelles."

"Isaac, you don't know that."

"The proof is in my hand."

"Oh, there's my money pouch," said Morgana, walking up with her bag over her shoulder and the cat tucked under one arm. Grunt trotted along behind her with his tail wagging, probably wanting to play with the cat. "Where did you find it?"

"I found it right where you hid it, in your damned bag," spat Isaac.

"So you stole it from me?" Morgana reached for it, but Isaac slapped her hand away.

"No, you don't," he told her. "This is evidence."

"Evidence? What are you talking about? Now give it back to me." Morgana reached for it once more, getting angry when Isaac slapped her hand again and pulled it away from her.

"Sister," said Morgana, talking to Vivienne. "Will you please tell this addlepated fool to give me my money and to stop stealing from me. He's a deputy but he really belongs behind bars."

"Me? You're the one who stole this money pouch from the Lovelles," said Isaac. "The L on the bag proves it."

"Is this true?" asked Vivienne. "Did you steal that, Morgana?" She really hoped it wasn't so because she didn't want to think her half-sister was a thief.

"It's true that the L on the pouch stands for Lovelle."

"It is?" This was the last thing that Vivienne wanted to hear right now.

"Lord Lovelle gave it to me in payment for the stone amulet I gave him. I told him there was no need to pay me since he didn't ask for the amulet, but he insisted. He also was very adamant that I did not tell his wife about it."

"Really?" Isaac closed his fingers over the coins looking like he felt foolish now. "But Zachariah told me you stole it."

"I didn't."

"Well, why is there so much money in here?" asked Isaac. "Lord Lovelle certainly wouldn't have paid this much for a stupid stone." He jostled the coins up and down in his hand.

"I added the payment that Lady Lovelle gave me for doing the card readings at the masquerade. She can vouch for that. However, like I told you, she didn't know about the money that her husband gave me in payment of the amulet."

"And with Lord Lovelle dead, there is no way we can verify that," said Vivienne.

"Nay, I suppose not. You'll just have to take my word for it. Sister," she added, causing Vivienne to feel a pain in her heart. "That is all I have to live on, and now I have another mouth to feed." Morgana held up the pathetic-looking cat to prove her point. The cat mewed softly, and Grunt actually barked at Isaac as if he were scolding him and saying she was telling the truth.

"Give it back to her," Vivienne told Isaac, since her heart was telling her that Morgana was telling the truth.

"But it's evidence, my lady. I need to show it to Zachariah," Isaac protested. "You can't really believe her. God's eyes, she's not to be trusted!"

"I do believe her Isaac, now give it back to her," Vivienne ordered. "I'll be responsible for any consequences."

"Fine." Isaac shoved the coins back into the pouch and dangled the bag from the drawstrings, holding it in front of Morgana's face by two fingers.

"You really are a fool, just like the cards said." Morgana snatched it away from him and shoved it into her bag. "Now, if you'll stop pestering me, Deputy, I'll be on my way." She turned and stormed off in a huff. Grunt whined as if he didn't want her to leave.

"How can you believe that woman?" asked Isaac.

"I just feel that she was telling us the truth."

"So, you're making decisions from your heart and not your head again? Zachariah is not going to be happy to hear this."

Vivienne smiled and shook her head. She had used her heart instead of her head, but that was what felt right and she couldn't deny it. "And you thought I was the one that Morgana didn't like? If you truly believe that, Isaac Fitch, then mayhap you are just like that Fool on the card like Morgana said." The words spoken, her mind set, she turned and walked away, with Isaac standing there with his jaw dropped.

Chapter Ten

Zachariah looked up to see Vivienne and Isaac enter the great hall. A little ways behind them came Ludwig and Rodger.

"Oh good, you two are finally here." Zachariah jumped up and escorted Vivienne to the table, where Maleine was busy pouring cups of ale for all of them. "Did you find out anything of interest?"

"Nothing worth talking about." Isaac plopped down on the bench, grabbing a cup and cradling it in his hands. "Other than the card-reader is a liar, and I still believe she's a thief."

"What are you talking about?" asked Zachariah.

"Isaac accused her of stealing from the Lovelles," said Vivienne.

"Yes. I saw the money pouch with the L stitched on it in her bag," answered Zachariah.

"It was indeed an L for Lovelle, but it was given to her by Lord Lovelle as payment for the amulet."

"Then Lady Lovelle would know that."

"Nay, she wouldn't," said Vivienne. "Lord Lovelle wanted to keep it a secret and told Morgana not to tell his wife."

"Of course he did," said Zachariah with a deep sigh.

"I believe Morgana is telling the truth, Zachariah.

"Of course, you do." He released another sigh.

"And don't bother saying I am thinking with my heart instead of my head, because I just know Morgana is a good person." Vivienne was not about to change her belief.

"Because she's your half-sister?" asked Zachariah.

"She's a damned witch," grumbled Isaac.

"Isaac, you're just upset since Morgana has no attraction to you, even after all your flirting," Vivienne told him.

"We'll discuss this later," said Zachariah. "Here come the sheriff and his deputy. Mayhap don't mention any of it to them right now."

"But it could be evidence," said Isaac.

"That is the least of our worries, Isaac. By the way, where is Grunt?" asked Zachariah.

"He's in the kitchen begging for food," Vivienne told him. "He'll find me when he either gives up or the cooks chase him out of the kitchen."

"I'm glad you and Isaac are both here, because I want to question Ludwig again. I think something doesn't add up, but I can't put my finger on what it is."

"Sheriff Fitch." Ludwig approached the table and sat on the bench. Rodger sat down next to him. "We're here. Now, tell us your suspicions." Ludwig picked up a cup and slurped some ale.

"Let's review the evidence first," said Zachariah. "A man was strangled and then someone tried to burn his body, probably hoping it would look like an accident."

"That doesn't make sense," said Ludwig. "I can't think of anyone who would want to kill Lord Lovelle."

"Me neither," said Rodger. "Everyone liked him."

"Well, that is what we're trying to figure out," said Isaac, still scowling.

"Certainly you must have some suspicions." Ludwig stared down into his cup when he spoke.

"Yes. Tell us who you think killed Lord Lovelle," said the normally quiet deputy.

Zachariah continued. "Lady Lovelle mentioned that when she left her husband in the solar the day of the murder, she bumped into a large woman dressed in an alewife's attire."

"So, an alewife is the suspect?" asked Ludwig, repositioning himself on the bench.

"Nay. But someone wearing an alewife's attire is," Zachariah answered.

"It must be that fat washerwoman. Laundress, if you will. What's her name?" Ludwig looked over to his deputy.

"I believe her name is Gunora, Sheriff," said Rodger.

"Yes, that's it. I never did like her. I'll have her arrested right away." Ludwig slurped some more ale.

"Hold on," said Zachariah, shocked that the sheriff would come to that conclusion so quickly. "Gunora told us that someone stole her costume and she never got to wear it that night. That's why, the next day, she was dressed as a fairy. She no longer had the alewife's costume."

"People lie," said Ludwig. "She's a big woman who is very strong, like a man, you could say. She sounds just like the person Lady Lovelle bumped into."

"Besides her size, there is no real evidence pointing to her," Vivienne spoke up.

"What other clues do you have, then?" asked Rodger.

"Well, Lady Lovelle also saw someone dressed like the Grim Reaper that night," Isaac answered.

"That was the steward, Jerome. I saw him in that costume. I never liked him either, since he is always lurking around Lady Lovelle." Ludwig eagerly shared his opinion. "I'll apprehend him for questioning."

"Nay," said Zachariah. "Right now, we're just talking and discussing things. Nothing more. Lady Lovelle also mentioned seeing someone in a Robin Hood costume."

"That was your costume, wasn't it?" asked Rodger.

"Yes, it was, but someone else had the same costume that night, because she saw him before I even arrived."

"And that person was also down in the undercroft doing something with the dead body when Lady Vivienne walked in and surprised him," added Isaac.

"He came at me with a knife," said Vivienne. "That's when I bit his arm."

"The washerwoman had a bite on her arm but said it was from a dog." Isaac downed some ale.

"Gunora seems to be the one who did it," said Ludwig. "It all adds up now."

"Not so fast. There are still more suspects," said Vivienne. "Lady Lovelle, herself, seems more distracted and upset with something else that doesn't even seem to have anything to do with her husband's death."

"It's true," blurted out Maleine. "We think her tears are fake."

"Nay, Lady Lovelle is sincere," argued Ludwig. "I've known her for a long time, and she'd never do a thing to hurt anyone. She's a true angel."

"She's only been at the manor for two months," Vivienne spoke up. "How could you have known her for a long time?"

"I knew her when I was sheriff back in her home town," said Ludwig. "I was happy to hear that she was coming to Grimsthorpe. I just don't know why she had to bring that lurking steward with her."

"Jerome once worked for Lady Lovelle in her home town?" asked Zachariah in surprise. "No one has mentioned that to us."

"Aye," said Rodger. "And her handmaid was from there too. Isn't that right, Sheriff Ludwig."

"It is," he said, sounding disgusted.

"You're talking about Ester?" asked Vivienne. "She seems old to be a handmaid."

"Jerome probably talked Lady Lovelle into bringing her along since the woman is his mother." Ludwig held out his cup and Maleine refilled it.

"Well, that is some interesting information indeed," said Zachariah, not knowing what to think now. But one thing was for sure. Not many were willing to share information willingly.

"Sigbald is also a suspect since he was seen coming from Lady Lovelle's room late last night," Vivienne added the information to their list.

"He was?" The sheriff's head shot up and he frowned. "Are you sure about that?"

"Yes, we talked to him when we saw him leaving her bedchamber," said Vivienne. "He told us he was called to Lady Lovelle's chamber to cure her headache."

"He lies," growled Ludwig.

"Well, Lady Lovelle opened the door and confirmed it," Zachariah added.

"What about her handmaid, Ester?" asked Rodger. "Was she there too?"

"Nay, she wasn't," said Zachariah. "It was just the physician and Lady Lovelle."

"He shouldn't have been in her chamber without Lady Lovelle having someone else there. I don't like this," snapped Ludwig. "It's not right for a man to be in a noblewoman's room without her having a chaperone."

"He is her physician," Vivienne pointed out. "I'm sure that is acceptable to anyone."

"Excuse me, but I've got work to do." Ludwig stood up and so did his deputy.

"Are you leaving? Already?" asked Zachariah. "I thought we were going to work together to solve this case."

"I'm not even sure there really is a case," said Ludwig. "I think you're trying to stir up trouble in my town, Sheriff Fitch, and I don't like it. Mayhap it is time for you and your friends to leave."

"No, we're not leaving," said Isaac. "We're trying to find a murderer and won't go anywhere until we solve the case."

"That's right," said Vivienne. "We need to make sure that justice is served."

Ludwig glared at them. "There is no need for you to stay here anymore, Sheriff Fitch. I have things under control. Rodger and I will take things from here. You and your entourage should leave here first thing in the morning."

"Not unless Lady Lovelle asks us to go," said Vivienne, standing up. "You are just the town sheriff and have no say over what goes on at the manor house of a noble."

"Let's go, Rodger," mumbled Ludwig, as the men hurriedly walked away.

"What do you make of all that?" asked Isaac, pouring himself another drink.

"I'm no longer sure what to think," said Zachariah, sitting down on the bench and putting his head in his hands. "But there are still a few more people we need to question to possibly learn some answers. And Lady Lovelle is the first one."

Isaac looked around and made a face. "Mayhap that can wait until after the meal? After all, I work better on a full stomach."

"Here comes Morgana with Grunt," Maleine pointed across the great hall toward the kitchen.

"Oh good," said Vivienne seeming pleased. "I thought she'd left, but I am glad that she didn't. I want to talk to her."

Vivienne turned around to see Morgana in her traveling cloak and with her bag over her shoulder coming from the kitchen with Grunt following right behind. She held the wet cat in her hands.

"Morgana, your cat looks so different," Vivienne told her.

"Yes, I washed her in the scullery and discovered that she isn't totally black, but has a small white patch on her chest. Isn't she pretty?" Morgana held up the cat. Grunt sat at Morgana's feet looking up and wagging his tail. Vivienne knew that look. Grunt wanted to play, or perhaps chase the cat the way he always did with Midnight, the sheriff's daughter's pet.

"Did you name her?" asked Maleine, walking over to pet the cat.

"I think since that spot looks almost heart-shaped, I am going to name her Locket." Morgana snuggled her nose into the cat's fur and the cat mewed.

"Locket? What a stupid name," complained Isaac.

Morgana's brows dipped and her mouth clenched. "Well, what do you think I should name her? Fool? After you?"

"Are you going somewhere, Morgana?" asked Vivienne before a fight broke out between Morgana and Isaac.

"Yes, I'm leaving now and taking *Locket* with me." She stressed the name of the cat and looked directly as Isaac when she said it.

"Where are you going?" asked Maleine. "Home?"

"Where is your home?" asked Isaac with interest. "With a bunch of others of your kind?"

"I am a fortune-teller, Isaac, that's true," she told him.

"However, I live by myself now. I have for a long time. I travel and live in many places. I don't really have a home."

"You don't?" Isaac stood up and came to her side, no longer seeming angry but more concerned than anything. "Well, mayhap we'll run into each other again someday." He almost seemed sad that the woman was leaving.

"I doubt it." Morgana looked the other way.

"What if I want another card reading?" asked Vivienne. "How can I find you?"

"There's no need. I'll find you," said Morgana, as she turned and started to leave.

"Morgana, wait." Vivienne rushed over to her. "I have to ask you something."

"I'm not sure I'll be able to answer," said Morgana, sounding as if she already knew what Vivienne was about to say.

"You said Lord Lovelle's mother told you to get that amulet for her son, isn't that right?"

"That's right. She did."

"But his mother is dead! Jerome took us to her grave right here at the manor."

"I must be going now, Lady Vivienne." She turned to go and Vivienne reached out and grabbed her arm, forcing her to turn back around.

"You were talking to a ghost, weren't you? Just admit it. That is also whom I heard you speaking to in the stables. Isn't that true?"

"I don't know what you mean." Morgana was back to showing no emotion. "I don't know anything about ghosts." Once again, she started to walk away and Vivienne ran after her.

"It's all right, you can tell me. I believe it really happened. Remember, I told you that I've seen ghosts before too. Please tell me about it, Morgana. I want to know more."

She stopped and turned to face her. "Mayhap someday I will, since we are half-sisters. But for now, I cannot explain things that I don't understand or even fully believe. Now, once again, goodbye, Lady Vivienne. And if it is meant for us to meet again, then it will happen, but not before." The cat mewed and Morgana gave her new pet a kiss, and then turned and left.

"You're just going to let her walk out of here?" Isaac was at Vivienne's side.

"Did you want me to stop her for some reason?"

"Me?" Isaac's palm hit his chest. "Nay. Why on earth would I want that? Let her go. Who cares? She's crazy!" He waved his hand through the air and turned back and started talking with Maleine and petting Grunt.

"Vivienne, is everything all right?" Zachariah's hand was on her arm and she felt the warmth of his body. His touch calmed her immediately.

"Yes, everything is fine, Zachariah."

"Mayhap I shouldn't let the witch leave yet. Isaac is convinced she lied, and we don't know yet if she is guilty or not where the murder is concerned."

"She's not a killer—anyone can see that. And stop calling her a witch." Vivienne's gaze focused on Morgana as she left the great hall. "I feel as if she's a very special person. And I'd like to meet with her to talk to her again sometime."

"Well, did you find out where you can find her?"

"Nay. But it doesn't matter. Our paths are destined to cross again, I know it. So I'll just wait for our next meeting to happen."

"You sound as if you really like the girl," said Zachariah.

"I do," Vivienne admitted. "She's not only my half-sister, but reminds me a lot of myself in more ways than I can count."

"Well, you're the only *you* I want, Vivienne." Zachariah turned her around and stared into her eyes. "I'd kiss you right now, here, in front of everyone, if I didn't think tongues would wag because of it."

Vivienne no longer cared and neither would she live in fear of what others would say about her any longer. She would be married soon, and none of it even mattered. She boldly reached up and gave him a quick peck on the mouth. "Since when did I ever care about gossip?" she asked him with a wide grin.

"Never. That's what I like about you, Vivienne. You're not afraid of anything." Zachariah quickly looked around and gave her a swift peck on the mouth as well.

If only he knew all the fears creeping up inside of her lately, Vivienne thought. And most of them had to do with the future that they were about to have together.

Chapter Eleven

"Grunt, what is the matter with you?" asked Maleine that night as they were about to prepare for bed. The dog whined and pawed at the base of the door.

"He probably needs to go out," said Vivienne.

"Oh. All right, I'll take him." Maleine looked tired and as if she really didn't want to take the dog down the stairs and out to the back of the castle.

"I'll do it, Maleine. I'm still dressed." Vivienne walked over to the door.

"Sheriff Fitch won't like that, my lady. Perhaps you should get him to escort you."

"Don't be silly. Grunt will scare away any predators or people lurking in the shadows. I'll be fine. Come on, Grunt, let's go." She opened the door and the dog shot out into the corridor and ran from her, stopping in front of Lady Lovelle's door, pawing at the floor and sniffing under the crack. "Come away from there, Grunt. We don't want to wake the lady of the castle."

When Vivienne reached for her dog, she heard voices inside the room, right through the door. She swore she heard not only

Lady Lovelle's voice, but the voice of a male again as well. When she heard footsteps coming toward the door, she ran and hid behind a pillar, bringing Grunt with her. Peeking out, she saw Sigbald the physician once again, as he left the room. Lady Lovelle was in the doorway and it looked as if she'd been crying.

"I wonder what that is all about," Vivienne spoke to herself. She made her way outside with the dog, and on her way back in, she decided she was going to knock on Lady Lovelle's door to see if she was all right. She raised her hand to knock and heard weeping coming from within. "Lady Lovelle? Are you all right?" she called out, but the woman didn't hear her. Vivienne put her hand on the door latch and to her surprise, the door was open. "Lady Lovelle?"

Lady Lovelle was naked and looking at herself in a standing mirror. She spun around and gasped when she saw Vivienne. Grabbing her robe from the bed, she quickly put it on. When she had turned around, Vivienne noticed that the woman had a small bump at her waist. It was obvious she was pregnant!

"I'm sorry. I knocked because I heard you crying, but I guess you didn't hear me. I just wanted to make sure you were all right."

"Yes. I'm fine," she said wiping her eyes on her sleeve and flashing a smile. "Won't you come in?"

"Nay, it's late and I should be getting back to my room." Grunt darted inside the room and Vivienne had no choice but to go in after him. "Grunt, get back here." She entered the room, chasing after Grunt. The dog jumped up on the woman's bed and lay down, making himself comfortable. "Well, I guess Grunt has other ideas. I'm sorry. Come on, Grunt, we need to go." She tried to pull him off the bed but he wouldn't budge.

"It's all right. Stay for a while." Lady Lovelle reached out and her cold fingers wrapped around Vivienne's wrist. "It would be nice to have another woman to talk to right now."

"Well, all right," she said, gently sliding onto the edge of the bed next to the dog. "Did you want to tell me why you were you crying?"

"I'm just missing my husband a lot right now, that's all."

"I can imagine that's true." She could see Lady Lovelle wasn't going to offer information freely, so she had no choice other than to come right out and say it. "Did Daniel know you were pregnant?"

"What?" Her eyes opened wide and she tightened the belt around her robe. "Why would you say that I'm pregnant? Where would you even get such a silly idea like that?"

"I saw your thickening waist, my lady," she told her. "I was pregnant at one time too, and I know how it looks and feels. The pregnancy is also making you emotional."

"Oh, you do know." She sank down atop the bed.

"Is that why the physician was in your room? To examine you?" Now it was all starting to make sense to Vivienne.

"Yes. Sigbald told me yesterday that I was pregnant, but I couldn't believe it and called him back today to confirm it."

"I see."

There was an awkward silence, and then Vivienne just had to say what was on her mind. "How did you get pregnant if your husband was impotent?"

Once again, the woman's eyes widened. "You know about that too?"

"Yes, I do. And I'm not the only one either."

"It's a miracle," she said, forcing a smile and sounding awfully nervous. "It must be that amulet that Daniel had. I didn't believe it, but he said it was magical and that it was going to help us have children."

"The amulet?" This didn't make any sense to Vivienne since Morgana had just brought the stone to him a few days ago.

"Are you talking about the stone that looks like male genitalia that he wore around his waist, hanging from a cord?"

"Yes. I gave it to my husband right after the wedding night when I discovered he couldn't perform his husbandly duties."

"Two months ago," said Vivienne.

"Yes, that's right."

"Excuse me for saying so, but your belly looks more like a woman who is at least in her fourth month of pregnancy, not just two."

"I know I'm bigger than most women at this stage, but the physician said I'm probably carrying twins and that's why."

"Well, I'm sure your husband would have been thrilled to know that he was about to have an heir or two, after all."

"Yes. I was going to tell him right after the masquerade, but then he died."

"So you knew about being pregnant during the masquerade? Lady Lovelle, I saw the doctor leaving your chamber twice now, and both times it was already after your husband was murdered so how could this be?"

"No, you misunderstood. What I meant was that I *thought* I was pregnant and was going to tell him. It wasn't actually confirmed until after his death, that's true." She whimpered and wiped away some more fake tears.

"Well, congratulations. You must be very excited by this news."

"Thank you. And yes, I am."

"So, are you going to tell everyone about it?"

"That's my dilemma, Lady Vivienne." Her smile disappeared. "I want to make it known, but now that Daniel is gone, I'll be required to marry another man. No man will want me once he discovers I am pregnant. Oh, Lady Vivienne, can you talk to the King for me and ask him to help me find a nobleman to marry quickly? Mayhap my new husband will think the child is his then."

"You want me to be deceitful?"

"I am only thinking about the baby...or babies, if I do have twins." She put her hand on her belly and pouted. "Besides, I am sure I'll have many more children with whomever I marry, so he will have true heirs. I don't feel that it makes a difference if he really knows about it."

"I'm sorry, Lady Lovelle, but I can't do that."

"Can't? Or won't?" Lady Lovelle's nose stuck up in the air. "Don't think you are better than me, because everyone knows that you are only marrying a commoner."

"Whom I marry has nothing to do with it," spat Vivienne. "I will not help you with your deceitful plan, because I will not compromise my integrity that way. It is not right."

"Please, understand how desperate I am." She reached across the bed and grabbed Vivienne's wrist. "You are woman. Surely you can understand how I feel. Please, Lady Vivienne, talk to the King for me."

"Nay!" Vivienne pulled out of the woman's grip and got to her feet. "I can't ask that of my father. I don't agree with it, and neither would I ever purposely deceive the King. It wouldn't be right and I won't lie for you. I could never live with myself if I did what you are asking." She turned and hurried to the door and Grunt jumped off the bed and followed. "Besides," said Vivienne with her hand on the door. She looked back over her shoulder. "I have a feeling you need to tell the true father about this, and that you should marry him instead."

"What! How can you insult me like that?" Lady Lovelle was up on her knees atop the bed. "This baby, or these babies, belong to Daniel. He was my husband, unless you've forgotten." She put her hand on her belly. "I was never disloyal to him."

"I wouldn't want to be in your position, my lady," Vivienne

told her. "But then again, I have a feeling that you will find a way to get exactly what you want, and always do."

"What does that mean?"

"It means, I believe the quick wedding with Daniel was because your father knew you were already pregnant before you ever arrived in Grimsthorpe. The two of you were trying to pull something off by betrothing you to Lord Lovelle and having a quick wedding without even waiting for the banns to be posted."

"How can you say that?"

Vivienne continued. "Neither of you knew at the time that Lord Lovelle was impotent. Isn't that right? It's probably why Lord Lovelle agreed to the fast wedding, because no other woman would marry him. And now that he's dead, you are scrambling to find another fool to deceive and marry so you can have power and riches and make the poor man think this is his progeny."

"How dare you say such things! Leave here at once!" She pointed at the door.

"Gladly. I'm going."

"If you don't believe me you can speak to the physician because he will confirm that I am just two months pregnant and that my baby is Daniel's. He'll also tell you that he believes I am carrying twins. Just ask him about it."

"Oh, I will talk to him, I assure you," said Vivienne, opening the door. Grunt ran out. "And I think you'd better come up with a really good excuse, because all your deception is about to be exposed."

Vivienne left, closing the door behind her, hearing something shatter against the other side of the door. She hurried to her room with Grunt, closing the door behind her and locking it.

"My lady? Is something wrong?" asked Maleine. "You seem shaken. Did something happen?"

"Yes, Maleine, and it made me very upset."

"Please, tell me what's troubling you, and mayhap I can be of help." Maleine took Vivienne's cloak and hung it on a hook.

"Maleine, it is awful. I just found out some things about Lady Lovelle that I don't like in the least. I should probably tell Sheriff Fitch about my discovery right away."

"Oh no. All right. Did you want me to go with you to the sheriff's room?"

Vivienne didn't know what to do. In a way, part of her felt sorry for Lady Lovelle and she wanted to help her. After all, no one knew better than Vivienne how hard it was to be pregnant and not have a husband to be there. She had gone through that with her son, when her husband died before Martin was born. It was a hard time and left her to fend for herself.

Then again, Lady Lovelle was being deceitful. Zachariah always said Vivienne shouldn't make decisions with her heart but rather with her head. Perhaps that was what she was doing. Still, it was all so confusing. Vivienne just knew somehow that the baby was not sired by Lord Lovelle and that she was not really carrying twins. It was clear to her that Lady Lovelle had a secret lover. Someone that she probably really cared for and who was not a much older man like Daniel. This lover was also able to give her children, something that Daniel was never able to do with any woman. The whole situation was really sad. Vivienne now regretted getting into the middle of it and wished she had never walked into Lady Lovelle's room in the first place.

Vivienne sighed and sat down on the bed. Grunt jumped up and she put her arm around the dog. "It's late," said Vivienne. "I'm sure the sheriff is sleeping. I'll tell him about it first thing in the morning."

"All right, if you think that is best. But tell me, my lady. What is it you learned about Lady Lovelle?" Maleine was curious just like Vivienne, and always wanted to assist if she could. "Is it something that could help with the murder investigation?"

"Yes. Well...mayhap. Oh, I'm not really sure." Vivienne flopped back on the bed and grabbed a pillow and hugged it.

"My lady, I've never seen you so emotional over aspects of an investigation. Doesn't the sheriff always say to think with your head and not your heart, or it will only confuse you and cause you to make bad decisions?"

"He does," she agreed. "However, now that I'm about to be married and my whole life is about to change, I've been wondering if thinking with my heart is better than making decisions with my head, after all."

"What?" Maleine sat down on the edge of the bed as well. "I'm sorry, Lady Vivienne, but I don't understand exactly what it is that you are trying to say. Somehow, I get the feeling we are not talking about Lady Lovelle anymore."

"I'm not sure myself." Vivienne turned on her side and closed her eyes and continued to hug the pillow. "I think a good night's sleep will make everything more clear in the morning."

"Don't you want me to help you change into your night clothes, my lady?"

"Nay. Don't bother." Vivienne sighed again, and pulled up a blanket from the bed to cover her against the cold. Right now, all she wanted was to leave all her doubts and worries behind, and go to a dream world where hopefully she could escape all her problems once and for all.

Vivienne started to have her recurring nightmare again about the night that she saw her parents murdered. But this time, something was different. In this dream, she wasn't crying as her parents lay on the ground bleeding and dead, while the horses took off with the wagon, her son and brother still inside it. This time, the unfolding scene was peaceful. Vivienne saw herself leaving the main road, then seeing a light shining on something in the woods. As she walked toward it, she noticed standing stones that were placed in a circle. Inside the circle, were little blobs of light whizzing about. Curious, she moved closer. A woman's voice then whispered to her, calling her name on the breeze. *Vivienne*, she heard, wondering who it was. Why did someone summon her, and what could they possibly want? She had the strong desire to move even closer, as if she were being pulled toward the stone circle. Vivienne didn't fight the sensation and needed to find out more. She held no fear, only a peaceful, warm feeling. One of comfort, happiness...and possibly love.

Vivienne. She heard the voice again, calling her name, and saw a ghostly form inside the circle, but she couldn't tell who it was. Once more, the mysterious apparition summoned her, but this time, the voice wasn't high like a woman's but sounded much lower, like a man.

"Vivienne? Vivienne? Wake up," came a deep voice causing Vivienne to jolt right out of her dream. She suddenly realized it was morning and she was lying in bed.

"My lady, are you all right?" This time it was Maleine speaking from across the room as the girl opened the shutters on the window and the morning sunlight streamed in. "Sheriff Fitch is here to see you."

"Zachariah?" She sat up, seeing him sitting on the edge of the bed. Grunt was wedged between them, wanting attention as usual.

"Vivienne, is something wrong? When you didn't meet me in the great hall this morning as planned, I came to get you." Zachariah's face showed concern.

"Nay, nothing is wrong." She blinked several times in succession. "I was just...dreaming."

"Egads, I hope you weren't having that awful nightmare again. I thought since we caught your parents' murderer, those dreams would finally stop."

"Nay, and you are right. They did stop. This was different."

"How so?"

"Well, this time the dream was actually a very pleasant one, but mysterious. And it took place inside a stone circle."

"It's good to know that you aren't still being haunted by those awful nightmares," said the sheriff, not seeming to care to hear about her dream. She supposed it didn't matter since she couldn't really explain it, and had no idea who the disembodied voice belonged to. Perhaps it was just a silly dream and meant nothing at all.

"Yes, I am happy that my nightmares have subsided as well," she admitted.

"Good, then." Zachariah reached to smooth his knuckles down her cheek. "I am glad to hear that. After we break our fast, I will send a missive with a messenger to Mablethorpe Castle for Richard to bring the wagon for us. It is time we go home."

"Oh, Zachariah, do you really believe we should? I mean, we haven't solved the case yet."

"I don't feel as if we're wanted here anymore, Vivienne. Besides, without proper evidence and not having been able to catch the killer, I am not sure there is anything else we can do to prove that Lord Lovelle was truly murdered. Perhaps it is time we leave the matter to local authorities."

"I didn't think you believed in quitting," she said, shocked to hear that he was going to leave before things were finalized regarding the murder.

"I suppose I don't. However, I am missing Starah and I am also anxious, thinking about our wedding. Ludwig is the Sheriff of Grimsthorpe, and honestly, I have no authority to stay so long and try to prove him wrong."

"But he is wrong and you know it. I do too."

"Even so, Vivienne, since the only evidence we had was a mark of strangulation and now the body is buried, we have nothing to back up our claims. Sadly, I believe it is time for us to go home."

"Mayhap not," said Maleine from the window. "Lady Vivienne visited with Lady Lovelle last night and found out some information that might help. Tell him, my lady. She was going to go to your chamber last night with the news, but decided to wait until this morning instead. Isn't that right, Lady Vivienne?"

"Well, yes." Vivienne nodded. "I did learn something."

"You did? What did you discover?" asked Zachariah.

Before Vivienne could answer, Maleine gasped and called out to them while still looking out the window. Her eyes grew wide with surprise. "Excuse me, Lady Vivienne and Sheriff Fitch, but I think you need to see this for yourselves."

"What is it?" asked Vivienne with a yawn, stretching her arms over her head.

"There is a visitor approaching the manor right now."

"That's nice," said Vivienne, swinging her feet to the side of the bed. "I'm sure Lady Lovelle will greet them."

"*You* might want to greet this visitor," said Maleine. "After all, he is your father."

"My father? The King is here?" Vivienne jumped out of bed and ran to the window with Zachariah right behind her.

"God's eyes, what is King Edward doing here?" asked Zachariah, stretching his neck to see out the window. "And why does he have such a small traveling party with him instead of his entire household in his entourage? Did any of you know he was coming?"

"Nay, and I have a funny feeling that Lady Lovelle doesn't

know about it either." Vivienne strained her eyes to see who was leading the procession up the road to the manor. "That looks like my half-brother, Rowen, in front of the line."

"Rowen the Restless?" asked Zachariah, taking another look. "The Legendary Bastard of the Crown?"

Vivienne scowled at him. "Yes, my bastard half-brother," she confirmed. "But do you really need to refer to him as such?" She ran to find her shoes, not bothering to sit down put them on, but instead standing and leaning against the bedpost. Maleine grabbed a boar's bristle brush and followed her around the room, running it through Vivienne's hair. Grunt barked anxiously, already waiting at the door.

"I wonder if something is wrong." Zachariah grabbed Vivienne's cloak from the hook on the wall and helped her don it. "King Edward doesn't just show up for casual visits. And never unannounced. This is odd indeed." With his hand on the small of her back they headed to the door.

"Mayhap he heard about the murder of Lord Lovelle and that's why he's here," said Maleine, running ahead of them and pulling open the door. Grunt ran out into the corridor, leading the way.

"I doubt it," Zachariah answered. "The murder just happened. As far as I know, Lord Lovelle's death is not common knowledge yet, except for those who attended the masquerade."

"Well, let's go find out and stop all the guessing, shall we?" Vivienne raced down the corridor, curious, excited, and actually anxious to see her birth father once again.

Chapter Twelve

By the time they got out to the courtyard to greet the King, there was already a big crowd gathered around him. Vivienne pushed her way through them all, finally reaching the front edge of the throng, only to see Lady Lovelle and her steward, Jerome, standing there, ready to greet Edward. Her handmaid was not with her.

"Lady Lovelle, did you know King Edward was going to be here?" asked Vivienne.

"Nay." The woman turned toward her, grabbed Vivienne's arm and leaned in to speak without anyone overhearing. "About last night, Lady Vivienne, please don't mention my state to anyone just yet."

"You're asking me to keep your secret from the King?"

"I am asking you as a woman to please help me. I am frightened and confused. I don't want to end up in a worse position than I am in right now. Since the King is here, this might be a perfect opportunity for you to ask him about finding me a husband, and quickly."

"I don't know." Vivienne just stared at Lady Lovelle, not liking to be in this position.

Slowly, the woman's fingers released Vivienne's arm and despair filled her eyes. "Please, Lady Vivienne," she whispered with her bottom lip trembling. "You are the only one who can help me."

"Vivienne? What's going on?" Zachariah was on the other side of her and saw her speaking to Lady Lovelle.

"Nothing." Vivienne turned to face him and smiled. "Let's go greet my father, shall we?"

"Shouldn't Lady Lovelle be the first one to do that?" asked Zachariah, seeming more than confused.

"Yes, I suppose so." She looked back at Lady Lovelle and nodded. "Please join me," she said, causing the lady of the manor to step closer to Vivienne.

"I'm frightened," Lady Lovelle whispered to her. Vivienne could see the woman's body shaking.

"We need to greet him as is proper." Vivienne held on to Lady Lovelle's arm, and together they walked up to greet the royal party.

"Lady Vivienne. So good to see you again." Rowen the Restless slid off his horse and walked over, reaching out to give her a half-hug. "How have you been, Sister?" he whispered into her ear. When he pulled back, she noticed his huge smile. He didn't seem to know that anything was wrong, so she guessed that they had not yet heard about the murder. "And this must be the lady of the manor?" Rowen looked over at Lady Lovelle next.

"Yes, this is Lady Lovelle," said Vivienne. Rowen kissed the woman's hand and when he finished, Vivienne moved closer to her brother. "Why are you here, Rowen? And why on earth is our father with you?"

"Not now," said Rowen with a scowl. "It is proper that the lord and lady of the manor greet the King before we start a conversation. Where is Lord Lovelle?" Rowen looked around, scanning the crowd as the curious pressed closer, many of them speaking softly to each other.

"Oh, no," cried Lady Lovelle, wringing her hands together. "Could this get any worse?"

"Come on," said Vivienne, dragging Lady Lovelle along with her as she approached the King's horse. One of his men was helping him to dismount.

Vivienne's heart sped up. This was her father! Her birth father. The man who'd sired her, even if he wasn't the man who had raised her. King Edward looked elegant as always, in his ermine fur-lined cloak and with his gold crown on his head. His many jeweled rings on his fingers glittered in the sun. Her hand automatically went to the ring she wore on a chain around her neck. It was her father's—the King's gemstone ring. Her mother had given it to her right before she died, explaining that King Edward was Vivienne's true father.

Vivienne had always worn the ring hidden, since her mother had told her to tell no one about it. But the truth had presented itself at the joust at Mablethorpe Castle not long ago. Now, everyone knew that Vivienne was the King's bastard daughter. There was no reason to hide the ring anymore, but Vivienne had continued to wear it under her clothing. She supposed it was because she still didn't feel comfortable saying she was the daughter of King Edward. Plus, she didn't want to flaunt the ring or her status in front of anyone.

Today was different, however. Today, she wanted the King to remember her and that she was his daughter. She quickly slipped the ring out from under her clothes, wearing it in full sight atop her bodice.

"Hello, King Edward," she said, curtsying to the man who had spawned her. He was a big man with reddish hair that, these days, was mostly graying. He had wide shoulders and a round belly. Still, he was aging with an air of flawless preeminence, so managing to keep a royal composure about him at all times.

"Ah, Lady Vivienne, so nice to see you again." King Edward smiled and looked genuinely happy. Still, he hadn't called her *daughter,* and for some reason that bothered her a little. Still, she realized he couldn't go around addressing all his bastards as *daughter* or *son.* Not when he hadn't properly claimed them, anyway.

"My King," said Rowen, coming to Edward's side, drawing a woman along with him. "This is Lady Lovelle, lady of Grimsthorpe Manor."

"It is an honor to meet you, my King," said Lady Lovelle with a nervous curtsey. Before he had a chance to ask about the woman's husband and why he wasn't there to greet him as well, Vivienne spoke up, trying to change the subject.

"What brings you here, Your Majesty? I didn't know you were coming," said Vivienne.

"Nay?" Edward looked confused. "I told Daniel myself that I'd be here for the masquerade, since I didn't want to miss it. I only wish I could have made it here sooner."

"I'm afraid to say the masquerade ball was over with, days ago," Vivienne explained.

"By the rood, I knew losing the wheel on the wagon was going to cause problems and slow us down. Plus, we ran into a bit of bad weather coming from Whitehaven."

"I'd like to visit Whitehaven someday," said Vivienne, knowing that is where Rowen's castle was, and that the King was probably there visiting Rowen or going over a battle plan of some kind, she really wasn't sure.

Edward looked around. "Why isn't my good friend Daniel here to greet me? I'll have his head for being so rude."

Instead of answering, Vivienne once again turned around the conversation. "So, you were truly coming to the masquerade for the celebration of my betrothal to Sheriff Fitch?" asked Vivienne, as Zachariah walked up and stopped at her side. "I am honored that you would even consider such a thing."

"My good King," said Zachariah, approaching and bowing deeply.

"Hello, Sheriff Fitch." King Edward nodded. "It is always good to see the man who protected me and kept me from being assassinated."

"Just doing my duty," Zachariah answered, speaking about the assassination attempt on the King at Mablethorpe Castle, a shocking and unfortunate incident that happened in the not-so-distant past.

"And to answer your question, Vivienne, yes, I wanted to be here because I love masquerade balls. I also wanted to help celebrate your betrothal, since I feel grateful to both you and Sheriff Fitch for helping me. I was just in Whitehaven with Rowen and he said he'd escort me and my traveling party here, and I thought it a nice distraction before I needed to get back home and tend to my duties. I'm surprised Daniel didn't tell you all this. I guess he wanted to keep it a surprise that I was coming."

"So you were traveling for days," said Vivienne, still steering the conversation away from the murder.

"Yes, we were. And I am famished," said the King. "Lord Lovelle promised a huge feast when I arrived, and I only hope there is some food left since we were detained. Why isn't he here to greet me?" Edward asked again, now seeming very confused. And it was evident that no one in his entourage knew about the man's death. As much as Vivienne didn't want to share the bad news, she realized it couldn't be avoided any longer. So when Zachariah stepped in to tell him, she didn't stop him.

"My King, did you not hear the news?" asked Zachariah.

"News? What news?" asked Edward, making Vivienne

cringe. She wasn't looking forward to having Edward hear what happened. Especially since he'd been calling the late Daniel Lovelle his good friend. "And why does the air smell like smoke?"

"My husband died several days ago," Lady Lovelle spoke up, her voice wavering when she said it.

"Died?" Edward's brow furrowed. "Good Lord, nay. I had no idea. Was he ill?"

"He died in a fire," said Lady Lovelle."

"It was more than that. He was murdered," said Isaac walking up with Maleine and stopping next to Zachariah. "You really haven't heard, Sire?"

"What on earth are you talking about?" asked Edward, squinting his eyes.

Zachariah scowled at Isaac.

"My King?" Isaac quickly added, and bowed deeply, looking over at Zachariah for some kind of approval.

"Will someone please get me an ale and take me to the great hall and kindly explain to me what the hell is going on here?" King Edward's voice boomed out, and everyone heard him.

"Of course, Your Majesty. Right this way, My King," said Rowen, leading the way to the keep. Hearing Rowen talk this way to the King made Vivienne wonder if he ever actually called Edward *Father* to his face. Most likely not, she supposed. Bastards had no right to speak to the King in that manner.

Vivienne walked side-by-side with Zachariah, following right behind Rowen and the King, while Isaac escorted Lady Lovelle to the keep.

"I didn't know he was good friends with Lord Lovelle," Zachariah whispered to her. "Did your uncle ever tell you that?"

"Nay. Unfortunately not," she answered. "And I can guarantee that we won't be leaving any time soon. Now, having seen his affection for Lord Lovelle, I am sure Edward will not let this murder rest until we find the man's killer."

"Then it is a damned good thing you found out something from Lady Lovelle last night, because mayhap whatever it is will shed some light on the situation. You never did tell me what it was."

"Later, Zachariah," she whispered back. "Right now, we need to do everything we can to help make the King comfortable. After all, he traveled here to help us celebrate our betrothal. That must mean that he cares for us, so we need to show our gratitude."

"It also means that unless we quickly find his good friend's murderer, King Edward might change his mind about how he feels about us, after all."

Vivienne's stomach clenched as she reached up to clutch the royal ring she wore. She was only a bastard of the King, but still, he was her father. She wanted Edward to like her. She also wanted to get to know him better. If her mother was his mistress, she must have seen a good side of him, and Vivienne wanted to see what her mother saw about this man too. But most of all, she didn't want to disappoint King Edward because he was family now, and family meant everything to Vivienne. She hoped she wouldn't do anything to anger him, because she wasn't about to lose another family member in any way.

The King had insisted that Zachariah sit at the dais along with him, Rowen, Lady Lovelle, and Vivienne, even though Zachariah didn't feel as if he belonged here. He would have felt much more comfortable on a stool below the salt. But because the King insisted, Zachariah had no choice but to obey. And so he sat up on the dais, there at the high table with the King and his nobles, doing his best to appear at ease, also trying hard not to look out at the crowd. He was sure seeing Isaac below the salt while he sat up here would only make him feel more uncomfortable.

Once ale had been served to all and the musicians started to play a quiet tune, King Edward looked over and asked about Lord Lovelle once again.

"Sheriff Fitch, tell me everything. Why would anyone want to kill Daniel?"

"I'm not sure," Zachariah answered.

"Well, have you taken measures to apprehended Daniel's murderer yet?" Edward raised the goblet to his mouth and took a drink.

"Nay, not yet, Your Majesty." Zachariah felt his throat going dry. The last thing he wanted to tell his ruler was that he'd failed at his job. "However, we are still investigating some clues so the case is not yet closed."

"Clues? What clues? And how was Daniel killed exactly?" asked the King. "He was such an amiable man. It is hard to believe someone would want to ever hurt him."

"My husband died in a fire, Your Majesty," Lady Lovelle spoke up.

"Yes, I can still smell the lingering smoke. Still, I'm confused," said the King. "I thought you said he was murdered, Sheriff." Edward's attention snapped back to Zachariah and he didn't look happy.

"Yes, that is true too." Zachariah cleared his throat. "Evidence shows that he was strangled before being set on fire."

"Then there is still a murderer on the loose? Why haven't you apprehended him by now?" asked Edward.

"It's complicated, but we are working on it, Sire."

"You did say Daniel died several days ago?"

"That's right," Zachariah answered.

"Then I want to see the body."

"Sheriff Ludwig Shireman doesn't believe it was a murder," Vivienne quickly explained. "He insisted that it was an accident, and so Lord Lovelle's body has already been buried."

"Mmph," grunted the King. "Ludwig Shireman is a fool and I never liked him. I always told Daniel he needed someone better in the position of Sheriff of Grimsthorpe, but Daniel didn't like to disappoint others. What this town needs is someone more like you, Zachariah, as their sheriff."

"Thank you, Your Majesty," said Zachariah with a nod. "But in Sheriff Ludwig's defense, there has not been enough evidence to actually call it a murder and arrest anyone. Yet."

"Yet?" Edward raised a brow. "So, are you saying you have more evidence? If so, what is it? Do tell me."

"Vivienne, would you like to explain?" asked Zachariah, waiting for her to tell what she'd learned concerning Lady Lovelle. But instead of revealing the information, she seemed to purposely change the conversation once again.

"Oh, here comes the food. It does smell delicious," said Vivienne. "I hope it is to your liking, my good King. If not, I am sure the cooks in the kitchen could quickly prepare another dish or two for you."

"Oh, nay, this will be fine. I don't want to wait to eat since I am starving," said the King, his eyes already devouring the food and his attention focused on his stomach now, since he liked to eat.

Vivienne's consistent distractions since the King arrived worked once more. The only thing Zachariah couldn't figure out was why she was doing it instead of telling King Edward what he wanted to know. Since the King momentarily forgot all about his question and instead started eating, Zachariah figured he'd do the same for now. As if he knew, Grunt put his chin on Zachariah's leg from under the table and, Zachariah reached down to pet him on the head.

"Vivienne, what is it you're keeping from me?" Zachariah asked in a low voice, looking down when he spoke, so the King wouldn't hear him.

"Lady Lovelle is pregnant," she whispered back.

"What?" Zachariah looked up in surprise. "So that fertility amulet Lord Lovelle was wearing actually worked? I cannot believe it. So fast, too."

"I don't know about that," she said softly, holding her cup up to her mouth so no one could read her lips. "But I will tell you that I don't think her baby is Daniel's."

"You don't? Why not?"

"Zachariah, she only got married two months ago and didn't even know Daniel before then. Not to mention, he was impotent! I saw her waistline. She's at least a good four-months pregnant, if not more."

"Oh, nay. No wonder she seems so nervous. Mayhap she had something to do with Daniel's death after all."

"I doubt it." Vivienne turned her back slightly to the King, who was sitting next to her. "I think she was pregnant before she married Daniel. She wanted a fast wedding, hoping to pretend the baby was his but not knowing he was impotent. I don't believe her father knew either, or he never would have betrothed her to the man."

Zachariah chuckled at that. "Well, I guess she got what she deserved."

"It's not funny, Zachariah." Vivienne held a stern look in her eyes.

Zachariah cleared his throat and quickly took a drink. "Nay, it's not. You're right."

"And I don't think Lady Lovelle could ever purposely kill anyone."

"If not, then mayhap her lover is the murderer. Do you have any idea who he is?"

"Nay, I don't. I can't even get Lady Lovelle to admit that the baby is not her late husband's. However, I saw the physician coming from her room two days in a row now. I had planned on speaking with him this morning and finding out the truth of how pregnant she really is, but now that the King is here, I haven't had a chance."

"Don't worry. I'll send Isaac to town to talk to the physician and tell him to report back to us right away with the answer. We should know the truth about how far along she is before we even finish this meal." Zachariah started to get up.

"Send Maleine with him," suggested Vivienne. "Mayhap she'll be able to help draw out information."

Grunt nudged Zachariah from under the table. "I will. And I'll tell them to take this pesky hound with them as well."

They ate course after course of delicious food, everything from sliced, roasted goose, hens, and duck, all well-seasoned with herbs and served with special sauces, to savory wild-boar pie. Then they turned their attention to platters piled high with filets of deer, beef, and lamb, while the choices grew when new servants arrived from the kitchens, these bringing small, individual-sized kettles of steaming rabbit stew. There were even extra baskets of fresh-baked bread, plus a fine assortment of cheese. Spiced ginger cakes, sugared almonds, and honeyed wafers tempted those desiring something sweet between the heartier fare.

Ever circling and decorous, still more servants and a squire or two poured endless streams of wine, ale, and mead.

A handful of young pages went from table to table with small bowls of newly-churned butter, yellow and creamy, 'fresh and delicious' as the pages duly announced on approaching each waiting guest.

A good number of lads, these being older than the squires and pages, but likewise in the estate's employ, stood watch in shadowed alcoves, making certain not a single torch or oil lantern spat too frequently or too far. The guests paid these still-beardless young men no heed, their attention on the well-laid and groaning tables.

Indeed, the feast that should have been the highlight of the masquerade did not go to waste, and there was thankfully enough left over to serve this supple array of food worthy of a King.

And thankfully, King Edward, who was a big man with a famously voracious appetite, seemed ever so happy as well as distracted by the generous and festive meal.

Zachariah kept watching the door, hoping Isaac would hurry back with word from Sigbald about Lady Lovelle's state of pregnancy.

"Vivienne," he whispered, leaning over to talk to her again. "If the King starts asking more questions about the murder before Isaac returns, I think we need to tell him what we learned about Lady Lovelle."

"Nay," she whispered back in a firm tone. "I don't want to do that. Not yet."

"Why the hell not? And why are you attempting to shield that deceitful woman? I almost believe you wish to protect her from the law." Zachariah angled his head, his eyes narrowing. "From me. Is that so, Vivienne?"

"I guess I kind of feel sorry for her," Vivienne admitted, feeling uncomfortable but not wanting to lie. "Her husband just died, and I know what it's like to have to birth a baby without the father present. It's not easy."

"But Daniel is not even the child's father, so stop letting your womanly emotions control your judgment.'"

By the look on her face he could tell she didn't like that comment in the least.

"Zachariah, I know what you always tell me, but I've been

thinking lately that I do better in life when I listen to my heart and not my head. Therefore, that is what I'll do."

"Vivienne," he groaned, wondering why she was acting so stubborn. "Don't be that way." He'd worked so hard with her to get her to push aside her emotions and use her mind to face facts while investigating with him. She seemed for some reason to have taken a step or two backward. This was only going to make matters even more difficult for him. Vivienne seemed to like Lady Lovelle, or at least feel sorry for her. And if they ended up discovering that she was the one to have murdered her husband or had anything at all to do with his death, well, he wasn't sure how Vivienne would react.

"I heed my heart not my head, Sheriff, and I'm sorry if you don't agree with that." Vivienne wasn't going to let up about this.

Finally, to his relief, Zachariah saw Isaac flagging him down from the other side of the great hall. Maleine and Grunt were with him, as well as a woman he'd never seen before.

"Oh good, they've returned." Zachariah pushed up from the table. "I'll go see what they've found out from Sigbald."

"I'm coming with you." Vivienne put down her cup and was on her feet and leading the way off the dais before Zachariah could stop her.

"Zachariah, over here," called out Isaac, still waving at him as if Zachariah couldn't see him. It made Zachariah want to hit his brother over the head since all he was doing was attracting a lot of attention from everyone there. Hopefully King Edward would be too busy eating to notice.

"Did you talk to Sigbald?" asked Vivienne, as they walked up to greet them. "What did he say?"

"My lady," said Maleine, stepping forward with a peasant woman at her side. "This is Sigbald's wife, Ida."

· · ·

Vivienne couldn't understand why Isaac and Maleine had brought the physician's wife back from town with them. And where was Sigbald? None of this made any sense.

"Nice to meet you, Ida," said Vivienne, able to tell the woman was very worried, although Ida lowered her head and curtsied in respect.

"What did Sigbald say?" Zachariah asked Isaac. "And why didn't you bring the physician back with you as well?"

"Ida's husband is missing," Isaac provided the information. "We searched the entire town for him, but no one has seen him since yesterday."

"He's missing?" Vivienne didn't like the sound of this at all. Without the physician's testimony how pregnant Lady Lovelle truly was, they would have no proof of anything. Once again, it seemed as if they had wasted precious time.

"He never came home from the manor last night," said Ida, her brow wrinkled as she twisted a piece of clothing in her hands. "I don't even know if he was really here."

"He was," said Vivienne. "I saw him late last night."

"Where?" asked Ida, but Vivienne didn't tell her. She didn't know if Ida even knew Lady Lovelle was pregnant, and wanted to keep it hushed for now. Then again, she wasn't even sure if Sigbald wasn't perhaps Lady Lovelle's secret lover. If so, Sigbald's wife was going to be devastated to learn her husband's eye had wandered.

"It doesn't matter," said Vivienne. "Right now we need to focus on finding him."

"I suppose I could start questioning people to see if anyone has seen him." Zachariah looked around the great hall. "But I haven't seen him here at all either."

"Neither have I," said Vivienne. "And with the King here, it is going to make everything more difficult. This could take some time."

"Why don't we have Grunt help us?" suggested Maleine. "I had Ida bring one of her husband's tunics for Grunt to sniff. If Sigbald is here at the manor, I am sure Grunt will be able to find him."

As if Grunt knew he was being talked about, he whined and looked up at Vivienne with big eyes, furiously wagging his tail.

"I think that is a wonderful idea, Maleine. Grunt is a bloodhound and could easily sniff out his presence. Ida, would that be all right with you?" asked Vivienne.

"I'll do anything at all to find my husband," Ida answered. "We have three children at home and we can't survive without him." Ida had dark circles under her eyes, and looked as if she hadn't slept a wink last night.

"Allow me." Vivienne reached out and Ida placed her husband's tunic in her hands. Then Vivienne hunkered down and with one hand on Grunt, she used the other to hold the tunic to the hound's nose. "Take a good sniff, Grunt. I need you to find Sigbald."

Grunt, being the bloodhound that he was, used his big nose to smell the garment thoroughly. Then Vivienne stood up and gave the tunic back to Ida. "All right, Grunt. Find him," she gave the command, sending Grunt running around the great hall and under the tables sniffing everyone and searching everywhere. Some of the women cried out and the children squealed in delight, chasing the dog around the room creating a good amount of chaos.

"What's going on here?" growled King Edward from the dais.

"I'm sorry, Your Majesty," Zachariah called out. "I'll get the dog out of here right away."

"Wait." King Edward stood up and so did everyone else when they saw his action. "Lady Vivienne, is that your bloodhound sniffing out a trail by any chance?"

"Yes. That is Grunt and he is doing just what you said," she answered, rushing over to the dais.

"Then let Grunt do his work." King Edward nodded. "Mayhap since two sheriffs couldn't find the murderer, Grunt can."

Vivienne noticed the disgruntled look on Zachariah's face when her father said what he did.

"Grunt is not searching for a killer, he is trying to help us find the physician, Sigbald Leach," Vivienne informed him. "He seems to have gone missing."

"What's all this?" Sheriff Ludwig asked, as he entered the great hall and quickly made his way over to Vivienne and Zachariah. "Your Majesty?" Ludwig's eyes opened wide when he saw the King sitting at the dais. He bowed lowly. "I just came from town and had no idea you were here, Sire. I'm not sure why I wasn't notified that you would be visiting."

"Sheriff Ludwig," King Edward said, in a deep monotonous tone. It was obvious by his voice that he didn't care for the Sheriff of Grimsthorpe much at all. "No one knew. It was a surprise."

"I see." Ludwig looked around, seeming very uncomfortable.

"Sheriff Fitch tells me my good friend, Lord Daniel Lovelle, has been murdered," Edward continued.

Ludwig's eyes went from the King to Zachariah and then back to the King again. "Well, yes, Lord Lovelle has died, but there is no real proof that he was murdered, Your Majesty."

"If Sheriff Fitch says it was a murder, then I believe him. His word is as good as gold." The King made his thoughts and feelings known.

"With all due respect, Sire, Sheriff Fitch might have the last word back in Mablethorpe, but I am the Sheriff of Grimsthorpe and I tell you that Lord Lovelle's death was naught but an accident and nothing more." Ludwig was being very bold to speak to the King in such a manner.

"Grunt has picked up the physician's scent," Isaac called out from the far side of the great hall." Grunt, with his nose to the ground left the great hall and ran up the stairs to the second floor.

"Fast, follow him!" shouted Zachariah, sprinting after the dog and Isaac. Vivienne picked up her skirts and followed with Maleine keeping pace. The dog went past the bedchambers, making his way toward the garderobe at the end of the corridor.

Vivienne heard a woman scream, and when she caught up, she saw Gunora, the washerwoman on the floor with a basket of dirty clothes on her lap. Grunt was atop her, sniffing the basket she held.

"Someone get this hound off of me!" screamed Gunora."

"Grunt, come here." Isaac made it to the dog first, pulling Grunt off the woman.

"Let me help you up," said Zachariah, meaning to aid Gunora to her feet.

"I'll help her." Rodger seemed to appear from nowhere, helping the washerwoman to her feet.

Grunt pulled at his collar and Isaac tried to hold him back as the dog continued to bark.

"I think Grunt picked up a scent from your clothes basket," said Vivienne, looking down at the dirty laundry. "Isaac, let Grunt go."

Isaac did as told. Grunt ran over to the basket, sticking his head under the pile of laundry and pulling out a green velvet piece of clothing that looked more than familiar to Vivienne.

"It's the Robin Hood costume." She held it up for the others to see. It was the coat.

"Sheriff Fitch's costume?" asked Maleine.

"Nay, Maleine," answered Vivienne. "It must be the

costume of the other Robin Hood from the party. From the man who abducted me in the undercroft."

"So, it must have been Sigbald, then, who abducted you," said Rodger.

"Nay," said Ida, peeking out from behind the group of people. "My husband didn't have a costume because he wasn't at the masquerade ball. He was out of town, assisting a midwife who was having trouble with her patient who was giving birth at the time."

"Yes, that's true," said Vivienne. "Because when we found Lord Lovelle's body, the physician wasn't there to examine him and we were told he was out of town."

"Can that patient vouch for your husband?" Zachariah asked Ida.

"Yes, I'm sure she could." Ida nodded. "And so can the midwife who was there at the time."

"Where did you get this costume?" Vivienne asked Gunora.

"I didn't even know it was in the basket," answered the large woman. "I just collect all the dirty clothes that are lying around in the garderobe and wash them and return them."

Grunt barked and pawed at the door leading into the garderobe.

"Excuse me, Lady Vivienne, but I think Grunt is trying to tell us something," said Maleine.

"Yes, it seems so," Vivienne agreed.

"Well, let's find out for sure." Isaac opened the door to the garderobe and Grunt rushed in. The hound sniffed the floor and then ran over to one of the holes that was a seat for those to use while emptying their bowels. The excrement fell down a long shaft and into a gongpit far below, outside the back of the castle. Grunt continued to bark and actually put his paws up on the seat.

"Grunt, get away from there," scolded Vivienne, holding her

hand over her nose since it smelled so foul in there. There were clothes hanging off to the side, since the garderobe was a place where garments were sometimes stored because moths would not come here.

"I'll get him." Zachariah went to fetch the dog, stopping and peering down into the hole. He bent over and looked harder. "Vivienne, take the women back to the great hall," he said in a low voice. "Isaac, I'm going to need your help out back of the castle, immediately."

"Really? Why?" Isaac walked over and looked into the hole and made a face. "Oh, I see."

"What is it?" Vivienne rushed forward and gazed down into the hole, immediately wishing that she hadn't. Her stomach had been churning, but now it only got worse. She could see the gongpit and daylight down below the chute that led from the hole. And she could also see Sigbald lying on his back, atop a pile of feces. From where she stood, she noticed blood on his tunic and what looked like a knife sticking right into the man's heart.

"What's going on?" Ida tried to get into the garderobe, but Vivienne stepped back and held her away to keep her from looking. "Is it my husband? Did you find him? God's teeth, please don't tell me he's down there. Please don't say he is dead."

Vivienne didn't know how to comfort the woman, and there was nothing else to do but to tell her the truth. By the bad feeling in her belly, there was no doubt in her mind that the man was truly dead.

"What's happening?" Ludwig stood outside the door, looking into the garderobe. Lady Lovelle's handmaid, Ester, towered over him, standing right behind. Vivienne hadn't even seen either of them arrive.

Grunt continued to sniff around and rushed over, sticking his nose up against Rodger's groin next.

"Get this mangy mutt away from me," shouted the deputy-in-training, swatting at the dog.

"Come on, Grunt." Maleine ran over and pulled the hound away.

"Get the womenfolk back to the great hall. Now," shouted Zachariah.

"Why?" asked the sheriff.

"We've found the physician," said Isaac, looking down into the hole again. "And by the looks of things...he's most likely been murdered too."

Chapter Thirteen

Vivienne took Grunt and the women back to the great hall while Zachariah, Isaac, Ludwig, and Rodger made their way out to the gongpit to collect Sigbald's body. She tried her best to comfort the physician's wife, but the woman was bawling hysterically and nothing she could say or do seemed to calm her down.

"What is it? Has something happened?" Jerome, Lady Lovelle's steward, met them at the entrance to the great hall.

"Yes, something has happened," said Vivienne. "But we can't talk about it just yet. Can you take Ida to the kitchen to get her a cup of soup please, Jerome?"

"Of course," said Jerome.

"I'll help," said Ester, and they both led the woman away.

"Well, I've got to get back to work," said Gunora, still holding her basket of laundry under one arm. "There are lots of clothes to wash and work to do."

"Did you see anyone leave the garderobe before you picked up the laundry?" Vivienne asked her.

"I don't look at those with bare arses as they're going about

177

their business," said the woman in a huff. "And I don't know nothing about anyone dying in the garderobe either. I just do my work and mind my own business."

"Did I hear you say someone died?" King Edward walked over with Rowen escorting him. Lady Lovelle was with them.

Vivienne sighed. "I suppose there is no use in trying to keep this quiet since everyone will find out as soon as the sheriffs return from the gongpit."

"The...gongpit, did you say?" Rowen wrinkled his nose.

"Yes," said Vivienne. "Sigbald Leach, the physician, went missing last night."

"He went missing?" asked Lady Lovelle. "So...have you found him then?" She looked very worried, if Vivienne wasn't mistaken.

"Yes. Grunt found him, actually."

"Where is he? Is he all right?" asked Lady Lovelle.

"Nay, my lady, he is not," Vivienne answered. "Going by what I just saw up in the garderobe, I believe Sigbald is no longer alive."

"Egads," said King Edward. "A man dies while relieving himself in the garderobe? Not a good way to pass on at all."

"King Edward, he isn't in the garderobe anymore. It seems his body...fell down the hole," she explained.

"How could that possibly happen?" asked the King.

"I don't know for sure yet, but I don't believe the man fell into the hole on his own," Vivienne said, without going into detail.

"What are you saying, Lady Vivienne?" asked the King. "Was this an intentional act?"

"Of course, nothing is confirmed yet, but we'll know more as soon as Sheriff Fitch returns." She put her hand on her churning stomach feeling like she was about to retch, just at the thought of what most likely happened. "But I believe there was a second death at Grimsthorpe Manor, and that Sigbald, the physician...might have been murdered as well."

Zachariah stood behind the manor house as servants picked Sigbald's body out of the gongpit and laid him atop an elevated board being used as a make-shift stretcher. Because of the smell of the corpse from being in feces and urine, and the fact that the King was visiting, they decided not to bring Sigbald's body into the keep, but to leave it outside for now.

After the servants finished dumping water over the body, Zachariah and the others walked closer to inspect it.

"He's been stabbed through the heart," commented Rodger.

"By the looks of all the blood, he was alive when it happened," said Isaac.

"Yes," said Zachariah, checking for signs of life, even though he more than realized there wouldn't be any. Sigbald's body was cold and stiff and his skin had already turned blue. "My guess would be that he was killed sometime during the night."

"This is awful," said Ludwig, shaking his head. "And now with the King here, it makes things even worse."

"Now do you believe that there is a murderer to be found?" Zachariah asked him.

"Mayhap, but I'm not sure."

"Mayhap? How can you not be sure?" Zachariah thought Ludwig had to be the stubbornest man he'd ever met. Why couldn't he just admit that he was wrong?

"Because, Sigbald could have taken his own life," said Ludwig.

"What?" Zachariah shook his head. "I don't think anyone

would stab themselves in the heart and then throw themselves down the chute of the garderobe. That is preposterous."

"Look at this," said Rodger, pulling up Sigbald's sleeve. "It looks like bite marks of some sort."

"Let me see that." Zachariah rushed over to examine the dead man's arm.

"Didn't Lady Vivienne say she bit the intruder in the undercroft?" asked Ludwig. "This must prove that the intruder in the Robin Hood costume was Sigbald."

"Mayhap, but I'm not sure," Zachariah retuned Ludwig's exact words to him.

"How can't you be sure?" asked Ludwig. "The dog found his Robin Hood costume, and the bite marks prove he was down in the undercroft and most likely was Lord Lovelle's killer as well."

"Yes," agreed Rodger. "Sigbald probably felt so guilty about it that he took his own life afterward."

This had to be the worst excuse Zachariah had ever heard. These two fools didn't deserve to be sheriff and deputy-in-training because they were both too dumb to find their noses on their own faces. Hell, even Isaac was much better at what he did than these two put together.

"Ida said her husband wasn't here the night Lord Lovelle was murdered," Zachariah pointed out. "So until I can find the patient he visited out of town and ask them, we won't be able to draw any conclusions."

"What about that washerwoman?" asked Isaac. "Mayhap she had something to do with it. She was right there by the garderobe when Grunt sniffed out the trail."

"I agree," said Ludwig. "Didn't Lady Lovelle say she knocked into the woman right outside the solar just before her husband died?"

"She did," agreed Zachariah. "But that doesn't mean it was

Gunora. She said someone stole her alewife costume that night."

"You really believe that?" asked Ludwig. "You're going to take the word of a servant? Sheriff Fitch, I think you are a damned fool if you believe her story."

"Well, I think you're a damned fool if you truly believe a man killed himself and then purposely fell down a garderobe shaft. Isaac, stay here and make sure Sigbald's body is brought back to his office in town. I am sure his wife and children will want to pay their last respects before he's buried."

"Aye," said Isaac with a nod.

"Where are you going?" Ludwig ran after Zachariah as he headed inside the keep through the kitchen.

"Stop following me," growled Zachariah. "And stop contradicting everything I say, because it only makes me suspicious that you might have been involved in these murders instead."

"Me?" Ludwig didn't like that accusation at all. "How can you say that? I am sheriff of this town and I find justice when it is due."

"Really." Zachariah stopped just inside the kitchen and turned to face the man. "Well, it's due right now and you don't seem to be doing anything to help the cause. Two innocent people have died, and their families need to find closure. Did you want to go tell Ida that her husband has been murdered but you're not going to lift a finger to look for the killer? That she's going to have to raise her children on her own and you're not going to do a damned thing to help her?"

"Now, wait a minute, Sheriff Fitch. I never said that."

"Nay, and neither did you say you would do anything to help find answers either. Now let's go tell Ida about her husband. Together." Zachariah held out his arm, pointing the way to where Jerome and Ester had the woman sitting at a kitchen table with a cup of soup clasped in her hands.

"Fine," said Ludwig as they made their way over to the widow.

"Sheriff, tell me it isn't true that Sigbald is dead," cried Ida, looking at Ludwig when she spoke, and not Zachariah.

"I'm sorry, it's true," mumbled Ludwig, looking at the ground.

"How did he die?" asked Jerome.

"Was it another murder?" asked Ester.

"Sigbald was stabbed through the heart," Zachariah told them when the Ludwig stayed quiet and didn't answer.

"Nay!" Ida dropped the cup and soup spilled all over the table. A kitchen maid rushed over with a towel to clean it up.

"Was it murder then?" asked Jerome.

Ludwig once again stayed quiet.

"Some of us believe so," said Zachariah. "But Sheriff Ludwig seems to feel as if Sigbald took his own life."

"Nay!" shouted Ida, crying even harder. "My husband would never do that. Why would he? He had a family that he loved."

Finally, Ludwig spoke, but Zachariah didn't like what he was telling the poor widow. "Ida, we have evidence that leads us to believe that your husband murdered Lord Lovelle and then attacked Lady Vivienne in the undercroft. He must have felt so guilty about it, that he took his own life in the end."

"That's a lie!" shouted Ida. "My husband admired Lord Lovelle and would never have hurt him. And he would never attack a noblewoman, I can promise you that."

"Hush up, woman, you are causing a scene," snapped Ludwig, his gaze flashing back and forth at all the servants in the kitchen who were watching and listening.

"Zachariah?" Vivienne rushed into the kitchen with Maleine and Grunt right behind her. He could see King Edward and Lady Lovelle leaving the dais and heading for the kitchen. Grunt went over by the fire to beg for meat from the cook. "What did you find out?"

"I'd like to talk to you in private," he told her. "But first, we need to calm down Sigbald's widow."

"Maleine, take Ida up to our chamber and give her some wine," instructed Vivienne.

"Yes, my lady." Maleine put her arm around the woman's shoulders, and Ester helped her to stand as well.

"Take Grunt too," ordered Zachariah. "He'll protect both of you."

"Aye, Sheriff," said Maleine, calling the dog over.

"What happened?" asked King Edward, walking into the kitchen. Rowen saw him from the other room and ran to his side.

"Was Sigbald really dead?" asked Lady Lovelle.

"I think I'll let Sheriff Ludwig answer all your questions. But I will say that I'm convinced it was a murder, no matter what he tells you happened." Zachariah took Vivienne by the arm and pulled her out of the kitchen.

"Zachariah, what on earth is going on?" Vivienne looked up at him with confusion in her eyes.

"We'll talk outside where hopefully we can get some privacy." He took her toward the stables, and when he was sure no one was listening, he explained everything to her.

"So, Sigbald was the one who attacked me in the undercroft? Why would he do that? And why was he even down there that night? It doesn't make sense."

"I agree," said Zachariah. "However, the Sheriff of Grimsthorpe has his mind made up that Sigbald is Lord Lovelle's murderer, and that he attacked you and then felt so guilty that he took his own life in the end."

"It's hard to believe that a man with a wife and three children would do such a thing."

"He wouldn't."

"What?" Vivienne's head snapped up and she frowned. They stopped just outside the stables. "Zachariah, what are you saying?"

"I'm saying that someone is lying and that is what they want us to think so the suspicion is off of them."

"Lying," she repeated, looking at the ground.

"Vivienne, I know you too well to not believe that you are keeping something from me. Now tell me, what is it?"

"Oh, Zachariah, I don't want to believe it could be true, but Lady Lovelle lied to me, I just know she did."

"About her pregnancy."

"Yes. And last night I might have gotten a little angry with her and...threatened her."

"Threatened her? How? Why?"

"Well, she told me to ask Sigbald and he'd tell me that she was only two months pregnant and that her waist was already getting large because she's pregnant with twins."

"And?"

"And I told her that I was going to talk to him."

"So?"

"I might have also said she knew she was pregnant before ever marrying Daniel, and that she was being deceitful and wanted him to think it was his baby."

"And because Daniel was impotent, it couldn't possibly be."

"Right. I accused her of having a lover. I told her she was being deceitful and better come up with a good excuse because I was going to expose all her lies."

"That does make sense, Vivienne. And if Lady Lovelle thought for a moment that Sigbald would tell you that she wasn't carrying Daniel's child, or that she was really four months along in the pregnancy, then she'd have good motive for killing him before he had a chance to confess."

"Oh, I know that makes sense but I don't want it to make sense. It can't possibly be true."

"You're letting your heart rule your decisions again instead of facing the facts and using your head."

"Mayhap so."

"Vivienne, no one else has a double motive like Lady Lovelle does. Not only could she have killed Sigbald to keep him from telling anyone the truth about her pregnancy, but she could have very well killed, or possibly hired someone to kill Daniel, if she thought at all that he might have found out that she was carrying someone else's baby."

"Oh, Zachariah, I can't believe that."

"Well, can you think of anyone else who would have a motive for killing these two?"

"Nay," she said, sadly shaking her head. "I cannot.

"There were bite marks on Sigbald's arm."

"Oh, no," said Vivienne, shaking her head.

"And Grunt sniffed out the Robin Hood costume, as well as Sigbald's scent," said Zachariah.

"That does seem to prove that Sigbald was the one in the undercroft who attacked me," Vivienne agreed. "But honestly, I can't think of a single reason why he would do that."

"Lady Vivienne?" Rowen walked up to join them. "King Edward wants to say goodbye to you."

"Goodbye?" Vivienne's head twisted around to look at the King, who was mounting his horse. "But my father can't leave yet. I haven't even had a chance to talk to him."

"I'm sorry, but since there seems to have been a double murder here, I need to protect the King and get him away from here as fast as possible."

"I understand." Vivienne sounded so sad that it tugged at Zachariah's heart. "I'll come say farewell."

The three of them walked over to the small entourage that was preparing to leave.

"Vivienne, I'm sorry that once again, another of your plans has been ruined by a murder," said the King, shaking his head from atop his horse. "It just doesn't seem as if you can get away from it."

"Nay. Nay, it doesn't," she told him. "I had hoped to have some time to talk with you and to visit. To get to know you," she said, her bottom lip sticking out in a small pout.

"Don't fret, Daughter," said the King, causing Vivienne's frown to turn into a smile because he'd acknowledged her as his daughter. "I've been informed that your wedding banns will be posted as soon as you return to Mablethorpe. Your wedding will be very soon."

"Yes, that's right," she answered. "Will you perhaps be attending our wedding? Zachariah and I would be honored if you attended the ceremony."

"I'll do better than that," he told her. "I'll let you use my castle grounds for your wedding. I'll make sure you have a huge ceremony, lots of people, lots of food, and everything you want."

"You'd...do that for me? Even though I'm just your bastard child?"

"Why not? Like I've told you in the past, your mother was one of my favorite mistresses."

When the King said the word *mistress*, it only brought Vivienne back to her senses. While her father was offering her the chance of a lifetime, in her heart she didn't feel as if she wanted it. Not when her mother was a mistress to the man, no matter how much he claimed to have liked her. The fact remained that Vivienne was naught but a product of infidelity on the King's part.

"What will your mistress, Alice, say about that?" she boldly asked her sovereign.

"Alice won't like it in the least, I'm sure. But that is not your worry, it is mine." Edward chuckled lowly.

Suddenly, Vivienne had thoughts flashing through her mind that were downright disturbing. Did she really want to be displayed in front of wagging tongues as naught but his bastard daughter? Even if he was King? Vivienne didn't need or want a lot of attention. Neither did she need a lot of money spent for her wedding to a commoner. It would most likely only bring about problems from the nobles and to her aunt and uncle as well.

She, a bastard, and Zachariah, a commoner, would only end up being the laughing stock of the King's court if she took Edward up on his offer. Zachariah deserved so much better than that. He'd been through enough hardships of his own and she didn't want him to feel uncomfortable on their wedding day since it was supposed to be the most important day of their lives.

Vivienne truly didn't want a show. She didn't need a lot of people around them either. All she wanted was a small wedding with her immediate friends and family. And although King Edward was her birth father, she didn't know him or even feel any connection to him at all. Nay, this did not feel right. Her head said to be grateful and not turn down the King. Her heart said it wasn't right and she should be true to what she really wanted...not just because it was handed to her on a silver platter. She struggled with what to do.

"Thank you, My King," she said with a slight curtsy.

The King smiled proudly.

"However, I am afraid I will have to decline your offer."

"What?" both Rowen and Zachariah gasped at the same time.

"Vivienne, what are you saying?" whispered Zachariah. "Didn't you hear the King?"

"Of course I did."

"Then why would you turn him down instead of just saying thank you?"

"King Edward, as much as I would like to know you better, I don't think my wedding is the time or place to make that happen," she told him. "I appreciate your offer, but I think I'd rather have a small wedding with just a handful of people around me who are good friends or family."

"I see," said the King, seeming disturbed at first. But then he started laughing instead of getting angry and shouting at her. "You are a lot like Flanie," he told her, speaking of her mother. "But I think you might have made the right choice."

"You do?" she asked, curious as to why he would say this.

"Yes. It might be for the better since Alice has a mean temper that I'd rather avoid at all costs. Well, goodbye, my dear. Sheriff, I hope you catch the killer." The King nodded.

"Thank you, Sire." Zachariah bowed. "I'll be sure to send word to you on what I discover."

"You do that," said Edward, turning his horse to go. Then he leaned over atop his horse and spoke in a low voice. "I never liked Ludwig. Don't tell him but I might be replacing him soon as Sheriff of Grimsthorpe."

"Oh, that reminds me," said Vivienne. "Will you be finding a new husband for Lady Lovelle now that she is a widow?"

"I don't know," said Edward with a shrug. "Why do you ask?"

"I was just wondering if perhaps you'd allow her to choose her own husband." Vivienne knew that Lady Lovelle wanted her to ask King Edward if he'd send her a baron to marry quickly. However, Vivienne couldn't do that since she didn't want any future husband of Lady Lovelle to be deceived. There was enough deception lately and that wasn't going to solve any problems. Still, she wanted to try to help the woman if she could, because that is what Vivienne did. She helped those in need. It felt like the right thing to do.

"That's an odd request."

"I believe that every woman should be able to marry a man of her choice, if she so loves him."

"Like you and Sheriff Fitch." He smiled widely.

"Yes. Like me and Zachariah."

"Well, I'll have to think on that one, I suppose. I never liked the idea that Daniel married her, because I had someone else chosen for him, but I gave in at the last moment."

"You did? May I ask who?" Vivienne was surprised to hear this.

"It was a widow more his age, and who already had five children from her previous husband."

"You were trying to make sure Daniel had children before he died, weren't you?"

"Lady Vivienne, I suppose there is no need to keep it a secret any longer since poor Daniel is gone, but he was impotent. I knew he'd never have an heir, but he just never gave up and didn't want to stop trying."

"That was kind of you, My King," she said, rather than to admit that she knew Lord Lovelle could never sire a child. Now more than ever, it was crucial that he didn't find out Lady Lovelle was pregnant, because he'd know she had another lover. A noblewoman in such a position had a doomed fate ahead of her.

"If Lady Lovelle wanted to move away from Grimsthorpe Manor to live somewhere else, would you allow it?" asked Vivienne.

"Why would she want to do that? She has everything she could possibly want here. This manor house is nicer than some of my barons' castles. And almost as big, too."

"Of course, and I am sure she is grateful. I don't pretend to know what she'll want, but being a woman, I know what is important to me, Your Majesty."

"You, my dear, are much bolder than most noblewomen. If Lady Lovelle has you on her side to speak for her, she should consider herself lucky."

"Will you grant her my request then to choose her own husband? I mean...if it should be what she really wants?"

"Let's wait and see what happens with this murder investigation before I start making too many decisions," said the King. "We'll discuss this again later when things settle down."

"Thank you," said Vivienne with a curtsy.

"Rowen, we need to go," Edward called out.

"Yes, My King," said Rowen, holding out his hand to shake Zachariah's hand. "Sheriff Fitch, it was good to see you again, and I wish you the best with your marriage to my sister." He looked at Vivienne and smiled. She smiled back, liking how he hadn't called her his *half*-sister. "And Vivienne, I hope to see you again soon so we can get to know each other better. Someday, I'd like to introduce you to the rest of my family. Especially, Reed, the last of your triplet brothers that you've yet to meet. He lives in Scotland, but if you ever want to visit him, Lord Rook and I would gladly give you an escort."

"Thank you," she said, feeling happy. "I would like that. And I want you and your brothers to come to my wedding," she blurted out as he gave her a hug goodbye.

"You do?" Rowen pulled back, his hands on her shoulders. "But I just heard you tell our father that you wanted a small wedding with just a handful of your good friends and family there."

"And you are my family. Are you not?"

He let go of her and gave a sharp nod. "Yes, I suppose I am. And I'll tell Rook and Reed your wish too. However, I cannot promise any of us will actually make it back in time for the ceremony."

"I hope with all my heart that you can. It will take place in three weeks from now."

"And...where will that be?" Rowen raised a brow.

Vivienne exchanged glances with Zachariah. This is one thing they'd yet to decide.

"We're not sure yet, but we'll make sure to send a missive to let you know," said Zachariah.

"Good. And I'll be waiting to receive it. Goodbye to both of you, and good luck." Rowen hopped atop his horse and led the way, with King Edward raising his hand to wave to Vivienne as they headed out the gate.

"Are you sure you did the right thing by rejecting an enormous offer like that from the King?" asked Zachariah, watching them go.

"I acted with my heart and not my head, I know. But yes, I am sure I did the right thing."

"If you say so. I don't think anyone has ever turned him down before, but if it was going to be someone, my money was on you."

Vivienne giggled and reached up and kissed him on the cheek. "We can talk about our wedding plans later, when we're back at Mablethorpe. Right now, we have a murder to solve."

"Vivienne, I can't wait to get home," said Zachariah with want in his eyes as he kissed her back. "So let's put our heads together and solve this mystery quickly, because I'm tired of it and want to move on to the next phase of our lives."

"What would that be?" she asked him.

"Being husband and wife, of course." He used his fingertip to tap her on the nose. "To be a family. Or start a family. Or mayhap both."

"Zachariah."

"Yes?"

"I'd love to feel all romantic right now with you, but honestly you rather smell like the gongpit and it's a little hard to even want to stand close to you at the moment."

That made them both laugh, and it broke the tension they were feeling having to do with murders and weddings and anything else. Now they were both in a hurry to solve this murder mystery, because home was looking quite inviting at the moment.

Chapter Fourteen

It was decided that the body of Sigbald would be brought back to town instead of keeping it at the manor house. Even though Zachariah was familiar with Grimsthorpe, having been there several times, Vivienne was not. As she rode with him atop a borrowed horse later that day, they followed the wagon driven by the sheriff and his deputy as they headed to the town of Grimsthorpe. Isaac and Maleine rode together on yet another horse following behind Zachariah and Vivienne.

"Is this town similar to Mablethorpe?" she asked Zachariah as they got closer.

"I haven't been here in quite a while, and it was when I was a child and my father came here on business, so I don't remember all that much. But yes, I believe it is similar, just smaller."

"Was Sheriff Ludwig here when you visited as a child?" she asked.

"Nay. At the time there was no sheriff at all."

"No sheriff? Didn't that bring about a lot of problems?" she asked.

"Not really since Grimsthorpe had the Town Watch."

"Town Watch? What is that?"

"The residents of the town helped to patrol and watch for trouble. They all worked together."

"That's nice. I like the idea."

"The lord of the manor, who happened to be Lord Lovelle back then, oversaw everything and he had his bailiff collect the rents for the King."

"The bailiff? I don't remember even meeting one at the manor." Vivienne hadn't even realized until now that a bailiff was never mentioned.

"I don't remember much about the bailiff, just that he was a kind man. I wonder what happened to him? Surely, I would have seen him by now if he was still here."

"Zachariah," said Isaac, riding up next to them. Maleine sat behind him, holding on to Isaac since she wasn't sitting in the saddle. "Do you think we'll be going back to Mablethorpe soon?"

"As soon as we solve the murder."

"What if it's never solved?" asked Maleine.

"I have a feeling it'll all be over soon," Vivienne told them.

"Is there something you know that I don't?" asked Zachariah.

"Nay." She shrugged. "But it could be possible that Sheriff Ludwig is correct, and that Sigbald killed Lord Lovelle and then killed himself in grief for what he did."

"Vivienne, be serious." Zachariah's voice was low and vibrated against her back since she sat in front of him and leaned back against his chest. "I know you too well to even think you believe that addlepated story."

"Well...we don't have any other clues."

"Are you just saying this because you want to go home too? Or is it because for some god-forsaken reason you are still trying to protect Lady Lovelle?"

"Zachariah, I feel it in my heart that Lady Lovelle is innocent." Vivienne looked back at him from the corner of her eye.

"She's the only one who had a motive to kill both men," Isaac pointed out. "I'm leaning toward the idea that she did it. I say we arrest her and head on home."

"Stop it, all of you," growled Zachariah. "If you want to leave so badly, then go, and I will figure this out by myself. But I am not leaving Grimsthorpe until I feel confident that we've caught the true killer."

"Sheriff Fitch is right," said Vivienne with a sigh. "Even though we're all a little homesick, we need to focus on our work. It is important to find justice for the families of the men who were murdered. We have to push our own wants and needs aside."

"Fine, but let's hurry it up," said Isaac. "I don't really like this town."

"I, too, wouldn't mind getting home to Wymond and the ferrets," said Maleine, speaking of her boyfriend and his pet ferrets that used to be used to help the local rat catcher.

"Grimsthorpe isn't a bad town," Zachariah told his brother. "You haven't even given it a chance, so don't judge it without first knowing all about it."

They stopped in front of the sheriff's office, which was a two-story house in the center of town. Like Mablethorpe, the streets were dirt and filled with ruts and there was garbage and excrement dumped in the street, causing a foul stench. At least in Mablethorpe, the stench and most of the garbage was down on Rotten Row. Here, it was like the entire town was one big Rotten Row, and it turned Vivienne's stomach. She could see why Isaac said he didn't like it.

"We'll take the body into my office," said Ludwig, stopping the wagon and walking around the back with Rodger. Isaac helped Maleine dismount and Zachariah aided Vivienne.

"Do you get the feeling we're being watched?" Zachariah whispered to Vivienne.

"Yes. By rats," she answered with a shiver, noticing rats roaming the streets.

"Not just rats." He nodded and Vivienne turned around to look down the street. Residents were either standing in the shadows, sweeping in front of their stores, or silently watching them from every window. It sent a chill up her spine.

"It's almost like one big Rotten Row, isn't it?" she asked him.

"I will say that I remember this town in a much better light from when I was a child," Zachariah told her. "My feeling is that once Sheriff Ludwig took over, he must have let things go to the dogs."

Just as he said that, they heard a dog barking, and Vivienne turned to look down the street. "Oh no, Grunt followed us here."

"Isaac, I thought you locked the dog in the bedchamber," said Zachariah.

"Me? I thought you did it," said Isaac with a yawn.

"It's fine. Grunt come here, boy." Vivienne clapped her hands, and the dog ran up to her with something in its mouth. "What on earth do you have there?" She reached down and realized it was the scrawny cat they'd found in the stables. "I thought Morgana took this cat with her." Vivienne held the cat to her chest, gingerly petting it as it mewed, and the poor thing's body shook in fright from having been in Grunt's mouth.

"Locket, there you are," came a woman's voice, causing Vivienne to turn around. She spied Morgana coming out of a building that looked to be deserted and abandoned. The door hung on one hinge, and the sign above the door swung back and forth in the breeze making an eerie squeaking sound. The paint was nearly worn off of it, but Vivienne could see that at one time there had been a unicorn's head painted on it. She'd never seen this depicted before, but had been told that it was a sign sometimes put in front of an apothecary, since the mythical unicorn's horn was said to be magical and hold medicinal properties.

"Hello, Morgana," Vivienne called out.

"I've been looking everywhere for that cat." Morgana walked up and reached out and took the cat from Vivienne.

"Morgana. Hello." Isaac cleared his throat, suddenly seeming to have regained his energy. He hurried over to greet Vivienne's half-sister.

"Morgana, I didn't expect to see you here." Vivienne rather liked the surprise.

"Do you live in Grimsthorpe?" asked Isaac, but Vivienne knew it wasn't true since Morgana had told them she always traveled.

"Nay, she doesn't live in my town and neither is she allowed here." Ludwig rushed over, anger turning his face a bright red. "We don't want your kind here. Now leave my town before I throw you out."

"Her kind?" Vivienne was taken aback. "And what kind might that be, Sheriff Ludwig?" For some reason she thought he meant a bastard like she was, but that wasn't what he was complaining about at all, it seemed.

"She's a witch!" Grimsthorpe's sheriff ground out. "She'll only bring this town bad luck and a whole lot of trouble."

Vivienne heard the slamming of doors and window shutters, and looked back down the street to see everyone rushing inside and trying to get away from Morgana. They'd all been eaves-dropping and just heard Ludwig call Morgana a witch, and it obviously scared them.

"Don't worry, I'm leaving." With the cat under one arm, Morgana hurried back to the apothecary to pick up her large carpet bag that she had left there.

"Nay, don't leave. Not yet." Isaac started to go after her, but Zachariah's hand on his arm stopped him.

"In case you've forgotten, we're working," Zachariah sullenly reminded him.

"Let's get the body inside before everyone wanders over to see it." Ludwig didn't seem to want the town to know what was happening.

"We'll give you a hand," offered Zachariah, taking a few steps toward the wagon, but stopping when he saw Isaac just standing there, staring down the street, watching Morgana walk away. "Isaac? If you're not too busy?" He raised a brow. "We could use your help."

"I'm here." Isaac jerked and shook his head, and then hurried over to the wagon with the men to move the corpse.

"I wonder where Morgana really lives?" Maleine reached down to pet Grunt.

"I'm not sure, but I wish we had time to talk to her," Vivienne answered. "After all, she is my sibling, and I would really like to get to know more about her."

"Mayhap we should follow her then," said Maleine.

"We can't. I promised the sheriff I'd help solve this murder. Plus, he won't like us going off on our own. And honestly, by the looks of this town, I want us to stay as close to Zachariah as we can."

"I agree," said Maleine. "This town is a little spooky."

Vivienne looked down the street, but Morgana had disappeared. "She seems to just show up when its least expected."

"Then hopefully she'll show up again at a later date so you two can get to know each other," Maleine told her with a smile.

"Yes. That would be nice," said Vivienne, wishing she had at least had the thought before now of inviting Morgana to her wedding.

ONCE THE BODY was laid out on the table in the sheriff's office, Zachariah started to inspect it. "Where's the knife that was stabbed into his heart?"

"Here it is," said Rodger, handing it to him.

"Is this the physician's knife?" Zachariah turned it over and over in his hand.

"I don't remember seeing him carrying a knife at all." Vivienne walked up behind him and peered over his shoulder. "Oh, I know that blade. It's the one my attacker used on me in the undercroft. I remember that cracked handle."

"Like I said, this is our killer." Ludwig sounded so arrogant, like he was sure of it.

"I want to see the bite marks on his arm," said Vivienne, pushing up Sigbald's left sleeve. "I don't see any bite marks. I thought you said they were here, but there aren't any."

"Nay, they are there. You're just looking at the wrong arm. Let me show you." Zachariah put down the knife and walked over and rolled up Sigbald's right sleeve to show her. "See? Just like I said."

"Zachariah, those bite marks are not from me," Vivienne told him, sounding very sure of herself.

"Of course they are," Ludwig spoke up. "You told us you bit him and there are your teeth marks to prove it. That's all the proof we need to wrap up this case."

"Nay. I tell you, that is not from me."

"Vivienne, what are you saying?" asked Zachariah.

"I bit the man on his left arm, not his right," stated Vivienne. "My attacker was left-handed."

There was a moment of silence, and Vivienne didn't know what was going on.

"Are you sure, my lady?" asked Maleine from behind her.

"You were distraught so mayhap you're mistaken?" Zachariah almost didn't seem to believe her, and that made her angry.

"Are you all saying I'm lying?"

"Of course not." Ludwig walked around the table. "Just mistaken, that's all. After all, I'm sure it happened so fast that your mind is muddled."

"Zachariah, I'd like to go back to the manor house now," said Vivienne, not wanting to stay there a minute longer.

"But we're not finished yet," he told her.

"I'm not feeling well and need to lie down." It wasn't really a lie, because her stomach was aching, but that was because of the murder, she supposed. She could have pushed through like she had in the past, but it was the only thing she could think of to be able to leave there right now.

Grunt started sniffing Rodger's crotch again, and Rodger pushed the dog away. "Take this bloody mutt with you. He is very irritating."

"I'll stay here for now with Maleine if you want to take Lady Vivienne back to the manor," Isaac offered. Vivienne was sure it was because Isaac was hoping to see Morgana again, but it didn't matter. She wanted to speak to Zachariah in private and this would be the perfect way to do it.

"All right. We'll check on Lady Lovelle and her story in the meantime," said Zachariah heading for the door.

"Come on, Grunt," Vivienne called to her dog. "Isaac, please watch over Maleine," she added.

"I'll protect her, don't worry," Isaac called back.

They mounted the horse and rode back to the manor with Grunt leading the way.

"Why did you really want to return to the manor?" asked Zachariah.

"How do you know I'm not really feeling ill?"

"On past murder investigations, I couldn't drag you away from a corpse or anyplace where we might find clues. Now what is going on?"

"I wanted to talk to you in private," she told him.

"Go on."

Part of her wanted to admit to him that she was starting to feel as if once they were married that she might not want to be so involved in the cases anymore. But her mind was confused and she would rather have time to think it through before she made such a rash decision.

"I bit my attacker on the left arm, not the right," she told him. "I told you, however you don't seem to believe me."

"I do believe you, Vivienne. I just wanted to play the devil's advocate to see what Ludwig would do and say."

"Oh. I see."

"Plus, in case you didn't notice, that bite mark was from a much wider mouth than yours. The closer I studied it, I could also see that it almost looked to me as if whoever bit Sigbald had one of his side teeth chipped."

"Not to mention, it looked fresher than it should have. If it really was done by me, by now, they would all be scabbed over since it would have started to heal."

"And they weren't," Zachariah agreed. "I'm starting to get the feeling that Ludwig knows something about the murders, or mayhap is even our killer."

"I thought the same thing," said Vivienne. "But if so, what would his motive be for killing the men?"

"I'm not sure on that yet, but mayhap if we speak to Lady Lovelle or her staff some more, we can find out some things about Ludwig."

"And Rodger," added Vivienne.

"You suspect him?" Zachariah's brows raised. "He certainly doesn't seem to have the evil mind of a killer."

"Nay, and he doesn't seem smart enough to pull it off and blame it on someone else, either," said Vivienne. "It's just a feeling, that's all."

"Don't come to conclusions by using your heart instead of your head."

"You're right." They stopped in the courtyard, and when they dismounted, Vivienne spied the washerwoman in the shadows talking to someone. It looked to be a tall man and his back was toward her so she couldn't see his face. "Isn't that Gunora over there?" she asked.

"Where?" Zachariah turned around but the woman must have known she'd been seen and was now gone.

"She was right there behind the well." Vivienne pointed. "She was talking behind her hand to a tall man wearing a dark cloak."

"I'll try to find her. You find Lady Lovelle and question her again. Convince her to tell you who her lover might be."

"I will," said Vivienne, heading for the keep with Grunt trotting along right beside her. She had just entered the keep when Lady Lovelle's handmaid came running toward her, crying. She noticed Ester was wearing a dark cloak and now wondered if she had been the one talking to Gunora.

"What is it, Ester?" Vivienne asked.

"Lady Lovelle is bleeding," cried the woman. "I don't know what's wrong with her."

"I think I do," said Vivienne. "Does the castle have a midwife?"

"Nay," she answered. "And there isn't one in town either."

"Of course not," she said with a sigh. "And the physician is dead. I'll go to Lady Lovelle, but I need you to do something for me."

"What is it, my lady?"

"Take the horse and ride to town. At the sheriff's office

you'll find Mablethorpe's deputy, Isaac, and my handmaid, Maleine. Please tell them Lady Lovelle's condition and have them return immediately."

"I will, my lady," said Ester, running off to get them.

Grunt whined from her side.

"It'll be all right, Grunt," said Vivienne. "But I need you to go and find Zachariah and bring him to me. Go on. Find Sheriff Fitch."

Grunt barked twice and turned around and ran down the stairs. Vivienne didn't have time to look for Zachariah herself and her hound knew the sheriff's name so she was sure Grunt would bring him to her.

Vivienne ran up the stairs to Lady Lovelle's room to find the door partially open. Gunora and Jerome were both inside.

"Lady Lovelle, I am here to help." Vivienne rushed into the room and up to the bed. Lady Lovelle looked to be in pain and was crying. Her sheets were covered in blood.

"We don't know what's wrong with her," said Gunora.

"Can you help her?" asked Jerome.

"First of all, calm down everyone. She isn't dying. But I do think I know what is happening here. I've sent Ester to town to get my handmaid since I'll need all the assistance I can get."

"What is it?" asked Gunora. "Why is she bleeding so much? She says it is not her flux."

"Lady Lovelle is having a miscarriage," she told them.

"What?" Gunora looked surprised and Jerome just stood there with his mouth opened. "Now Gunora, I need more towels and a basin of water," Vivienne instructed. "And Jerome, you will have to step out to give Lady Lovelle some privacy."

"I'm going," said Gunora, waddling off at a near run, but Jerome just stood next to the bed and wasn't leaving.

"Certainly there must be something I can do," he mumbled. "Please, let me help. I don't want to leave."

Lady Lovelle looked up at the steward and held out her hand. "I want him to stay, Lady Vivienne."

Things became immediately clear to Vivienne now. "Jerome, you are a man and need to leave the room immediately, because it isn't proper. Even if you are the father of Lady Lovelle's baby."

Chapter Fifteen

"Grunt? What is it?" Zachariah had been talking to some of the occupants of the manor as well as searching for Gunora, when Grunt ran up to him in the courtyard, barking like crazy. "Stop all that fuss. Why aren't you with Lady Vivienne?"

When he mentioned Vivienne's name, the dog took a few steps toward the manor, then turned around and barked some more.

"Oh, you want me to follow you? All right." Zachariah was starting to wonder if there was a problem and just hoped that Vivienne was safe. He followed Grunt at high speed, chasing the dog up the stairs where he stopped just outside of Lady Lovelle's room. Zachariah could hear crying from within.

"Vivienne? Are you in there?" He knocked on the door, anxious to enter but knowing it wouldn't be proper to do so. "Vivienne? Is everything all right?" He continued to knock while Grunt barked and even started to howl.

The door swung open and Vivienne stood there looking bedraggled. "Zachariah. Good, you're here."

He could see Lady Lovelle lying on the bed with blood on

the sheets. Gunora was trying to sit her up and had a wet rag in her hand that she was pushing against Lady Lovelle's forehead.

"What's happening?" He looked over Vivienne's shoulder again to see Lady Lovelle crying now.

"Is she going to be all right?" Jerome appeared from somewhere nearby, obviously having been watching and listening.

"I don't know yet," said Vivienne. "Without a midwife, I can't even say if I'll be able to save her baby because I honestly don't know what to do. I have never been thrown into such a situation before."

"Please, don't let our baby die," said Jerome softly.

"*Your* baby?" Zachariah looked at him in question. "So you're Lady Lovelle's secret lover?"

"Zachariah, please. Not now," said Vivienne. "I've sent the handmaid to get Isaac and Maleine from town. I am hoping Maleine can assist me."

"Maleine is young and knows nothing about healing or pregnant women as far as I know," said Zachariah. "You are going to need more help than just her."

"I'm sure my mother will do all she can to help as well, once she returns with your handmaid, Lady Vivienne," said Jerome.

"The more hands the better," she answered.

"Vivienne, you shouldn't have to do this," said Zachariah, knowing she had a good heart and never walked away from those in need. It was an admirable trait about her, but in his opinion, it was also her weakness. She always put others before herself. He'd never seen a noble act the way that she did. "You are a noblewoman. Leave this situation to the servants. This is not your responsibility."

Vivienne let out a deep sigh. "I know that, Zachariah. But there is no one else who can help Lady Lovelle, since this godforsaken town doesn't have a midwife and now their physician is dead. I cannot just turn my back on the poor woman and walk away. She is suffering and is very frightened. I am needed here right now."

"Mayhap I can help," came a small voice from behind them. Zachariah stepped aside and there stood Morgana.

"Morgana? What are you doing here?" gasped Vivienne, surprised to see her newly discovered half-sister.

"Let me in, Vivienne. I know about all about herbs and healing potions. It is part of my training. I think I might be able to help her." Morgana looked up at them with no emotion at all on her face. She was just the opposite of Vivienne, who had too much emotion most of the time. Morgana's big green eyes that reminded Zachariah of a cat seemed to stare right through him.

"Nay, I don't want that witch anywhere near Lady Lovelle." Jerome voiced his opinion, showing his concern and being very cautious of Morgana.

"She is not a witch!" snapped Vivienne. "Morgana is a talented entertainer who happens to tell fortunes."

"Same thing," mumbled Zachariah, getting a stern but silent glare of reprimand from his betrothed.

"She knows how to heal and is Lady Lovelle's best chance right now," Vivienne told them.

"I don't care. I still don't want her here," said Jerome. "Amelia doesn't like her."

"Look," said Vivienne. "We either let Morgana help, or you can say goodbye to your future child for certain. If we don't stop the flow of blood quickly, Lady Lovelle might die as well."

"Jerome, I don't want to die," cried Lady Lovelle from the bed, looking very ashen since she'd lost so much blood.

"Nay, I don't want that either, my love," Jerome called back to her, as they all stood in the doorway without entering, since men were not allowed in a noblewoman's room. Especially with something like this happening. "Please. Go to her," said Jerome, talking to Morgana. "Do whatever you can to save her and save our baby too."

"All right then. I'll need some white wine brought to the room immediately," commanded Morgana stepping around the men and heading into the room. "And have the servants start heating up water because I'll need a tub brought up here soon for a bath."

"Really? She's worried about having a drink and hot bath at a time like this?" asked Zachariah, not understanding the woman. First she showed no emotion at all, and now she was thinking of herself and her own needs, putting them before a noble? Unbelievable.

"Zachariah, please. Just do as Morgana says." Vivienne scowled at him and then her head turned and her gaze followed Morgana across the room.

"I'll get what she needs," said Jerome, taking off at a run. All of a sudden, the door slammed shut in Zachariah's face, leaving him standing there alone with Grunt in the corridor.

"Well, I guess it's just me and you now, Grunt. Mayhap you can tell me what the hell just happened, because I am honestly shocked and confused." Grunt whined and wagged his tail as he sat at Zachariah's feet. "On second thought, let's go down to the great hall and get something to drink, because I'm feeling like I really need some whisky."

Zachariah entered the great hall, snitching a goblet of wine off the platter of a kitchen servant walking past, disappointed that it wasn't whisky. He had just taken a swallow when he saw Isaac and Maleine enter the keep with Ester. He put down the cup and hurried over to them with Grunt at his side.

"Zachariah? What's going on?" asked Isaac. "Lady Lovelle's handmaid came to town to get us and said something is wrong with the lady of the castle?"

Zachariah saw Ludwig and Rodger enter the keep right

behind them. He didn't think it would be wise to talk about Lady Lovelle being pregnant in front of them, since he wasn't sure that anyone really knew about the woman's condition or that it should be common knowledge at this point. He also didn't want to expose Jerome's secret of being the baby's father.

"Fitch, what's going on here?" ground out Ludwig, stomping across the great hall heading toward him. "We were pulled away from our investigation by this handmaid. I can't be distracted if I'm expected to do my job as sheriff."

Zachariah found Ludwig's comment almost amusing, since he was he laziest sheriff Zachariah had ever met, and never seemed concerned with actually doing what he was supposed to.

"Excuse me," said Ester, wringing her hands together. "I need to get back to Lady Lovelle." She turned and ran up the stairs.

"Lady Lovelle is...not well," Zachariah told them. "Lady Vivienne is with her and so is Morgana." That was all he said.

"Morgana is here?" Isaac perked up when he heard that.

"That witch is with Lady Lovelle?" snapped Ludwig. "I need to get the devil-woman away from that angel." Zachariah found it an odd thing for the man to say. Ludwig started to walk toward the stairs, but Zachariah reached out and grabbed his arm to stop him.

"Maleine, will you please go see if you can help Lady Vivienne?" asked Zachariah.

"Of course, Sheriff." Maleine left in a hurry.

"I'm going to help as well," said the Sheriff of Grimsthorpe.

"Nay," said Zachariah, still holding on to the man's arm. "Ludwig, no men are allowed up there and you know that." Zachariah didn't like Ludwig or anything about him. The last thing he wanted was to let him anywhere near the women. "I suggest the rest of us go have a drink in the great hall and wait until we get word on the lady of the manor's situation."

"Good idea. I could use a drink," said Rodger, leading the way. Ludwig pulled out of Zachariah's grip and followed his deputy-in-training.

Isaac leaned over and whispered. "Zachariah, what is really going on?"

"It has to do with Lady Lovelle's pregnancy, but don't say anything in front of the others," he answered his brother.

"All right," said Isaac, following the others into the great hall. They all sat down at a table, and Ludwig raised his hand, calling over a server with a tray containing a bottle of wine and cups with wine already poured into them.

Zachariah watched as each of the men took a cup from the tray. He noticed they all used their right hand, but Rodger used his left. The server put the bottle with the rest of the wine in the middle of the table and walked away.

"Did you find any more clues on the corpse?" Zachariah asked, taking a drink of wine, still searching for information.

"Nay. There is nothing more to find," said Ludwig. His attention was not on the conversation but rather on the stairs, as he kept looking over in that direction. "Sigbald was our murderer and he killed himself. His body will be buried tomorrow."

"What about the attacker in the undercroft?" Zachariah watched the reactions of the men as he took another drink. Neither Ludwig or Rodger could even look at him.

"It was Sigbald. We saw the bite marks on his arm," said Rodger, staring down into his cup.

"Rodger, would you mind passing me that wine bottle?" asked Zachariah.

"I'll get it." Isaac started to reach for it, but Zachariah grabbed his arm to stop him. "Rodger?"

"Sure, Sheriff Fitch." Rodger reached for it with his left hand and gave it to Zachariah. When he did, Zachariah grabbed the man's arm.

"What are you doing?" cried Rodger, trying to pull away.

"Finding out the truth once and for all." Zachariah yanked up the sleeve on Rodger's left arm. Sure enough, just like he thought, there was the scabby skin and the marks from where Vivienne had bitten him. "You attacked Lady Vivienne in the undercroft, and there is the proof." He nodded to his arm. "You are under arrest for attacking a noblewoman, Rodger."

"Nay! Sheriff Ludwig, don't let him do this," cried Rodger.

"It was Rodger?" Isaac asked in surprise.

"I was told to—" Rodger's words were cut off as Ludwig stood up and punched the man in the jaw so hard that there was blood everywhere. Rodger ended up prone on the floor, unconscious.

"What the hell did you do that for?" shouted Zachariah.

"Because he deceived me and made me look like a fool, that's why," screamed Ludwig. "We have our real culprit now. I'll slap him in the dungeon and we'll put an end to this investigation once and for all."

"Nay. Not until Rodger wakes up and we get a full confession out of him first," said Zachariah.

"I'm not going to let you tell me what to do, Fitch! I am Sheriff of Grimsthorpe. I am in charge so you need to stay out of it."

"Not while we're here, you're not." Isaac stood up in front of Ludwig with his arms crossed over his chest.

"There will be hell to pay for your actions," spat Ludwig. "You won't get away with this." He ran off and headed for the stairs.

"Should I go after him?" asked Isaac.

"Nay, not now," said Zachariah, looking down at the floor.

Everyone in the great hall was watching. "Help me get Rodger up and conscious. I think we're about to solve this case, but I need his confession first."

~

"Give me that goblet of wine," said Morgana, taking a small velvet pouch out of her bag.

"What are you going to do and what is in that pouch?" asked Vivienne, handing the goblet to her. Maleine, Ester, and Gunora were next to the bed, trying to help Lady Lovelle in any way that they could, but mainly just by trying to make her comfortable.

"It's dragon's blood." Morgana shook some red powder into the wine. "And cloves." She added some more powder and stirred the wine with the tip of a dagger that she pulled from her waist belt. "It is used to stop internal bleeding."

"Dragon's blood," repeated Vivienne, thinking how mysterious that sounded. She was sure it had to be some kind of plant and not real blood from a dragon. She hoped. Then again, Morgana was a mysterious woman, and Vivienne didn't know anything at all about her kind or even dragons for that matter, so she truly didn't know what to expect.

"Lady Lovelle, you'll need to drink this." Morgana got up with the goblet in her hand.

"Nay!" Gunora blocked her way, crossing her arms over her ample bosom. "You'll not give any of your poison to her."

"Oooooh," cried Lady Lovelle from the bed with her hands on her belly.

"This is medicine that will help her. It's not poison," stated Morgana.

"How do we know what you really put in there?" Gunora was not backing down.

"It's all right, Gunora. You can trust Morgana," said Vivienne. "She is Lady Lovelle's best chance at this point since we don't have a midwife."

"Yes, let her try or we might lose Lady Lovelle as well as the baby," cried Ester, cradling the noblewoman's head in her arms.

"I didn't say a word about what happened when I watched my husband die, but I'll not stand by and watch Lady Lovelle die as well without trying to do something about it," shouted Gunora.

"What do you mean?" asked Vivienne in interest. "Is there something you didn't tell me?"

"Please, move aside or there will be no hope in saving her baby," Morgana instructed. Morgana was cool and calm and didn't seem nearly as upset as Vivienne felt right now. Vivienne had never seen anything like it.

"Please, Gunora, do as she says," begged Lady Lovelle from the bed. "I know you want to protect me, but you can trust Lady Vivienne. If she says the card-reader only has good intentions, then I believe her."

"Well, only because you command it, my lady." Gunora huffed, and stepped aside to let Morgana give the drink to the noblewoman.

"Gunora? Who was your husband?" asked Vivienne curiously, thinking this was a story she needed to hear. Perhaps it could help shed light on the case in some way.

"He's dead, so what does it matter?" Gunora clenched her teeth in aggravation, and Vivienne noticed a tick at the side of her jaw.

"Her husband was once the bailiff here years ago," Ester told her.

"He was the bailiff?" asked Vivienne, finally finding out something about the missing position at the manor. "Well, what happened to him?"

"He was ill, but was left to die," spat Gunora.

"What do you mean?" Vivienne continued, trying to draw out information.

"My husband, Peter, was in town collecting the rents when he had a seizure. I ran to the sheriff's office to ask for help, but that stupid Sheriff Ludwig said there was nothing to be done for him and he wouldn't lift a finger to help us."

"Well, why didn't you call for a physician?" asked Vivienne. "Certainly he'd be more qualified to help than the sheriff."

"I couldn't, my lady. At the time we had no physician because he had just died. The sheriff was in no hurry to get a new one and did nothing about it."

"Oh my, that's awful," said Vivienne. "Didn't Sheriff Ludwig even try to help your husband?"

"Nay, of course not. He never liked Peter, because Peter was good friends with Lord Lovelle and the sheriff was jealous about it. My poor husband died that day in my arms, and everyone just stood and watched, because Sheriff Ludwig told them Peter was contagious and not to touch him. I swear he wasn't contagious, my lady. I believe he just had a bad heart and that's all."

"I'm sorry for your loss, Gunora. That is such a sad story." Vivienne truly felt bad for the woman. It made her wonder how Ludwig could just stand by and watch and do nothing to help a dying man. She couldn't even think of walking away from someone in need.

The door to the room slammed open and hit the wall just then, causing them all to spin around. Vivienne saw Jerome's tall form standing in the doorway. He had an odd expression on his face.

"Jerome, did you get the things that Morgana asked for?" Vivienne took a step toward him and stopped when she realized what was wrong. Right behind Jerome was Ludwig, and he had a knife held to Jerome's back.

"Sheriff Ludwig? What in the world are you doing?" gasped Vivienne.

"I just found out my deputy-in-training was your attacker in the undercroft, Lady Vivienne. And also that Jerome is the murderer and so I am going to take his life just like he took the lives of the others."

"I'm no murderer. I didn't do it, I swear!" Jerome's hands were in the air.

"Nay, he didn't, but you did, Ludwig, you sneaky bastard!" Zachariah walked up behind the two men with Isaac and Rodger. Grunt was with them, growling at Ludwig.

"Zachariah, watch out!" screamed Vivienne, as she noticed Ludwig slip another dagger from his waist belt and lunge for him.

Zachariah stepped to the side and Isaac reached over, slugging Ludwig in the jaw and knocking him to the floor.

"Oh, my!" she heard Lady Lovelle shout from the bed.

"Zachariah, can you explain what's going on here?" asked Vivienne. "We are in the middle of trying to help Lady Lovelle and this is doing nothing to calm her down."

"I can tell you, but mayhap we should do it somewhere other than a noblewoman's chamber."

"Nay, I want to know too," called out Lady Lovelle. "Why was Sheriff Ludwig holding a knife to Jerome? And why is he accusing Jerome of murder?" Lady Lovelle finished off the drink and handed the cup back to Maleine. Her handmaid helped her to sit up straighter.

"You're ill, my lady," said Zachariah. "You should rest and just leave this to me and Isaac."

"She's not ill. She was having a miscarriage," explained Morgana from the bedside.

"Yes, I was, but I am already starting to feel better, thanks to

Morgana," said Lady Lovelle, with a kind smile and nod of thanks.

"It's amazing but I think the bleeding is already starting to slow down," said Maleine checking Lady Lovelle but holding up a blanket for the noblewoman's privacy.

"My angel is pregnant?" Ludwig got to his feet, wiping the blood from his lip with his sleeve. "How can that be? Her husband was impotent."

"Mayhap that amulet Morgana gave him for fertility really worked after all." Isaac smiled at Morgana.

"Nay," said Morgana, collecting up her things, still showing no emotion. Her cat mewed and stuck his head out of her big canvas bag making Grunt whimper.

"Nay, Grunt. Leave the cat alone," Vivienne instructed her dog.

"Lady Lovelle was already pregnant before I ever gave that amulet to Lord Lovelle," Morgana explained.

"Nay, don't say that!" said Ludwig. "It can't be true. Daniel couldn't get her pregnant. You are lying."

"It is true," Lady Lovelle admitted with tears in her eyes. "I was pregnant before I ever came to Grimsthorpe and only married Daniel so my baby would have a father. I didn't tell him, of course. I also didn't know when I married him that he couldn't sire a child."

"None of us did," said Gunora. "Lord Lovelle never told a soul."

"I knew," said Ludwig.

"My mother and I knew too, since Amelia told us, once she found out," said Jerome.

"Lady Lovelle," said Vivienne. "Was I right? Are you four months pregnant?"

"Yes, I believe so," she admitted. "Sigbald told me so, and I made him promise to keep my secret."

"Who got you pregnant?" spat Ludwig.

"Jerome is the father of my baby." Lady Lovelle put her hand on her stomach when she spoke. "He was my steward before I came here to Grimsthorpe. We were in love, but my father wanted me to marry a noble as was expected. He was furious when he discovered I was pregnant, and that is why he married me off as quickly as he could."

"Your baby should be mine, not his," hissed Ludwig from the floor, glaring at Jerome.

"Ludwig, you killed Daniel as well as Sigbald, didn't you? Just admit it," said Zachariah. "And you had Rodger go to the undercroft to find the amulet on Daniel, so we wouldn't know he was impotent. You did everything you could to keep it quiet because you didn't want Lady Lovelle to get pregnant. Isn't that right?"

"I saw that damned witch give the amulet to Lord Lovelle," admitted Ludwig. "I couldn't take the chance that it would work."

"What do you mean?" asked Vivienne. "Why should you even care?"

"I didn't want him to be able to get Amelia pregnant." Ludwig looked over to the bed. "She was mine. I should be the father of her child."

"Oh, this is frightening," said Amelia from the bed, clinging to Ester. "Ludwig was always doting over me and caring for me and always here at the castle instead of in town where he belonged. However, I never knew he wanted me in that manner." Lady Lovelle hid her face against Ester.

"You're damned right I wanted you, Amelia," Ludwig continued. "When you arrived in Grimsthorpe, I knew I'd encountered a true angel. You are so beautiful and didn't belong with that old man! He didn't deserve you. Nay, you belonged with someone much better, like me." Ludwig seemed more than crazy, and hearing his words made Vivienne fear for Amelia now.

"You were in love with Lady Lovelle?" gasped Maleine. "And that's why you killed her husband?"

"If he were gone for good, I knew I'd be able to get closer to her," admitted Ludwig. "She always let me comfort her."

"I wouldn't have if I'd known you had feelings for me," cried Amelia.

"Ludwig, you're a sheriff, not a nobleman," Isaac reminded him. "Or did you forget that part? You could never have had her anyway."

"He's sick in the head, I tell you," shouted Gunora. "He always was. That's why he let my poor husband die when he didn't need to."

"Think what you want, you fat bitch, but I could have had my angel, Lady Lovelle, and I'd almost convinced her of it too," growled Ludwig.

"Oh, nay!" Lady Lovelle continued to hide her face against Ester.

"Ludwig, don't talk that way to Gunora," snapped Zachariah.

"Amelia let a commoner bed her, and that commoner should have been me." Ludwig glared at Jerome in contempt.

"Ludwig, you are a sick, sick man. And it makes no sense why you killed the physician," said Lady Lovelle from the bed.

"I heard he was in your room two nights in a row," said Ludwig. "I should have been with you, not him. I know he was touching you intimately. He deserved to die."

"He was a physician!" spat Lady Lovelle. "Of course he had to touch me, but not in the way you are suggesting."

"Sigbald had a wife and children," ground out Vivienne. "He didn't want Lady Lovelle in the way you thought. And now, because of your jealous actions, a poor widow is going to have to raise her children on her own."

"That is none of my worry," mumbled Ludwig. "And neither do I care."

"What about him?" asked Vivienne, seeing Rodger standing silently behind the men, holding his jaw.

"When Grunt kept sniffing Rodger in the groin, I realized it was because the Robin Hood costume not only smelled like Sigbald, but also like Rodger," explained Zachariah.

"He made me do it," Rodger said, pointing at Ludwig. "He knew that Sheriff Fitch was coming as Robin Hood and that's why he made me dress the same way. I didn't know why at the time, but now I see it was because he wanted Sheriff Fitch to seem like a suspect, once he killed Lord Lovelle. And I swear I wasn't trying to kill you, Lady Vivienne. You just startled me in the undercroft, that's all. I was never going to kill you."

"You were going to blame the murder on me?" asked Zachariah. "Ludwig, you truly are a sick man, the women are right."

"I didn't need another sheriff coming into my town," snapped Ludwig. "You were going to take it away from me. I couldn't allow it to happen."

"Nay, I wasn't," said Zachariah. "I have my own town of Mablethorpe to run."

"You would have taken Grimsthorpe from me," Ludwig continued. "Just like you stepped in and took over the investigation after I told you it was naught but an accident. You wouldn't listen."

"I wouldn't listen because I could see it was clearly a murder. I couldn't just stand by and do nothing. Ludwig, you are not only jealous but seem to be disturbed as well."

"I don't understand," said Vivienne. "Why were there bite marks on Sigbald's arm if he wasn't the one who attacked me?"

"Ludwig put them there. I noticed a chip on his tooth when we were just drinking in the great hall," said Zachariah. "It was him."

"I only did it to keep Rodger from being suspected," said Ludwig.

"Like hell you did." Zachariah's voice beamed. "You were obviously trying to cover your own tracks, and wanted to make it look like Sigbald killed Lord Lovelle and then himself afterward so your name would be cleared."

Isaac jumped in now to add to the explanation. "Ludwig wanted to make it look like Sigbald attacked you, Lady Vivienne, as well as killed Lord Lovelle. If he could convince everyone that was what happened, there would be no further investigation. He might have gotten away with it too if he hadn't put the bite marks on the wrong arm."

"Sheriff Fitch, I think I was mistaken about Rodger trying to kill me," said Vivienne. "He was holding a knife but now that I think about it, he never really tried to stab me. It just must have seemed like it at the time, since I was gripping his arm."

"I was just trying to get away, I tell you," said Rodger. "Please, Sheriff Fitch, let me go."

"I can't," said Zachariah. "You were an accessory to the crime since you helped Ludwig."

"Nay," shouted Rodger. "I didn't know he killed those men. I was just trying to do my job by doing what he told me to do, that's all."

"And you never asked him why you needed to do those things?" asked Isaac.

"He told me not to ask questions or I'd never be his deputy."

"Why should we believe you?" asked Isaac. "It seems stupid on your part."

"Rodger didn't kill anyone, and neither does he have a mean

bone in his body," said Gunora. "I can vouch for him. He's innocent."

"What are you saying?" asked Zachariah. "How would you know?"

Gunora sighed but then answered. "The night that Lord Lovelle was killed, my costume of an alewife was stolen, that part is true."

"My guess is that it was stolen by Ludwig," said Zachariah. "And that's who was wearing it when Lady Lovelle knocked into an alewife while leaving her husband's solar."

"Yes, it was me," admitted the Sheriff of Grimsthorpe from the floor, smiling as if he was proud of his deception. "I found the damned costume just lying on the ground and used it to my advantage."

"It was in the larder where he found it," snapped Gunora. "And it wasn't on me because at the time, I was naked and making love...with Rodger."

"What?" blurted out Isaac before he started laughing. Gunora was a large woman and Rodger was small. Plus, Gunora was quite a bit older than the deputy-in-training.

"It's true," said Rodger, testing his jaw to make sure he could still move it. "We saw Sheriff Ludwig come in and then leave. We discovered that the costume was gone afterward. We stayed quiet because we didn't want him to know we were there."

"Why did the Robin Hood costume smell like Sigbald if you were the one who wore it?" asked Isaac. "Grunt sniffed it out, but my guess is that Sigbald never wore it."

"I don't know," said Rodger with a shrug. "I can't explain it."

"It's because I rubbed the costume all over Sigbald's dead body, and then hid it in the garderobe before I dumped his body down the chute after stabbing him in the heart." Ludwig's confession was shocking, and for a few seconds no one said a word.

"Oh nay!" Lady Lovelle whimpered and held a hand to her mouth. Jerome rushed into the room to be at her side, not caring anymore that men were not allowed in a lady's bedchamber.

"You are a horribly wicked man, Ludwig!" spat Jerome. "How could you do those terrible things?"

"Gunora, when we found you upstairs near the garderobe with the basket of clothes," said Vivienne. "Were you…"

"Yes," Gunora admitted. "Rodger spent the night with me and also the next morning. We find it exciting to couple in odd places."

"In the garderobe? Ugh!" Isaac made a face.

"We didn't know Sigbald was dead at the time and had already been pushed down the garderobe chute," said Rodger.

"Of course you didn't, because I killed him the night before, while most people were sleeping," said Ludwig, laughing now as if the whole thing amused him. His gaze went back to Lady Lovelle. "My lady, I did it all for you. So we could be together. I have always taken such good care of you, and you know I'd never do anything to hurt you. We belong together."

"You were always a pesky pain in the ass," snapped Lady Lovelle, obviously feeling better. "I never wanted anything to do with you, and even tried to convince Daniel to ban you from the manor, but he was too kind-hearted to do so. Everyone loved Daniel. Everyone…but me, I suppose." Lady Lovelle looked down and wrung her hands together. "I didn't really want to be his wife, but I thought it would solve all my problems. Now I feel horrible about how I deceived the man. I didn't want him to die."

"Yes, I'll bet that was a shocking surprise to find out he was impotent and you had no way to explain your pregnancy," said Isaac.

"All I've ever wanted was to be with Jerome," she said, looking up to her lover with stars in her eyes. "But I knew we could never be together since he was a commoner and I was noble."

"Amelia, I'm so sorry you had to go through all this," said Jerome, bending over and kissing her on the mouth right in front of everyone.

"Get away from her, you fool! She doesn't want you, she wants me. She's mine!" Ludwig yanked a hidden dagger from his boot and sprang up and rushed across the room with the blade over his head and pointed right at Jerome.

"Nay you don't!" Isaac dove through the air and brought the man down, ripping the weapon away from him while sitting on top of him so he couldn't move.

"Ludwig, you're under arrest for the murder of Lord Daniel Lovelle and also the murder of Sigbald Leach," announced Zachariah. "Isaac, get him up and we'll lock him in the dungeon for now."

"What about me?" asked Rodger.

"Please, Sheriff Fitch, don't arrest Rodger. He's innocent," cried Gunora.

"I'm sorry, Rodger, but you're arrested for now too, because of your part in this and also for attacking a noblewoman," Zachariah told him.

"Zachariah, you heard him. He wasn't really trying to hurt me," said Vivienne. "Can't you let him go?"

"Vivienne, you're thinking with your heart and not your head again," said Zachariah, taking ahold of Rodger. "However, since Ludwig confessed to the killings and Gunora can verify that Rodger was with her at the times of the murders, Rodger will go to trial, but only for attacking a noblewoman."

"Thank you, Sheriff Fitch," said Rodger, lowering his head.

"Don't thank me, because your fate will now be determined by the people of this town," said Zachariah. "And I am personally going to tell the King everything and advise that you not be allowed to return to Grimsthorpe, if you do go free."

"I understand," said Rodger. "Fair enough, I guess."

"I'll leave Grimsthorpe with you, Rodger," Gunora promised. "And I'll convince the jury to let you live and not be imprisoned as well. The townspeople trust me and liked my late husband. They'll listen to me, I'm sure they will."

"What about me?" asked Ludwig. "I demand a trial too, Fitch."

"Nay. There is no need to waste time on a trial for you," said Zachariah shaking his head. "You already confessed and everyone here heard it. I can tell you right now that you will end up being executed for your crimes, probably by hanging, even though that is too good for the likes of you."

"Good! Let him die. He deserves it," said Lady Lovelle, anger contorting her face. "Ludwig is an awful man and I never want to see his face again."

"And neither will you have to," said Zachariah. "Isaac, help me put them both in the dungeon until we can take further measures."

"Aye," said Isaac getting up and holding Ludwig's hands behind his back. When he passed by Vivienne, he leaned over and whispered. "Lady Vivienne, where is Morgana? Did she see me take down Ludwig?"

"I don't know where she went," said Vivienne looking around to first realize that Morgana was gone. She was a mysterious woman who seemed to come and go without anyone noticing. Vivienne still didn't know how Morgana knew what was going on or how she ended up being outside the door just when they needed her. But by the looks of Lady Lovelle and the way she was sitting up and smiling at Jerome, Vivienne realized Morgana's dragon blood potion must have worked. She supposed time would tell, but hopefully the baby would be all right and Lady Lovelle hadn't lost her unborn child. Vivienne's heart went out to her. When the men all left the room, Vivienne walked over and sat on the edge of the bed.

"Thank you for all your help, Lady Vivienne." Lady Lovelle's smile was sincere.

"It was my pleasure. But it was really Morgana's potion that stopped your baby from being aborted. She saved your life as well."

"Yes, she did. I would like to thank her. Where is she?"

"I can't answer that," said Vivienne. "However, I am sure if her help is ever needed again, she'll somehow magically appear."

The woman's smile suddenly faded. "Lady Vivienne, what do you think will happen to me now that the truth is exposed and Daniel is dead?"

"I don't know the answer to that either."

"All I want is to be able to be with Jerome and to raise our child together."

"I wish that for you as well."

"Then I ask you again, will you talk to your father? To the King? Will you put in a good word for me to make my wish happen?"

Vivienne felt bad for Lady Lovelle and truly wished she could help her, but she really didn't think she had any power to do such a thing. "I will do my best," she told her, taking Lady Lovelle's hand in hers and giving it a light squeeze. "I promise you that I will do all I can to help you in any way possible. However, I will not do it in a deceptive manner. There have been too many lies already, and the truth needs to prevail."

Chapter Sixteen

Three days later

Now that they were back at Mablethorpe and everything was cleared up and resolved regarding the murders in Grimsthorpe, things were finally starting to calm down. Vivienne felt so happy to be home. She sat with Zachariah on the dais, sharing a meal in the great hall.

"Vivienne, I don't feel right sitting up here," Zachariah told her, squirming in his chair.

"Why not? My aunt and uncle insisted," she answered with a smile. There was a feast being held in their honor. A betrothal celebration was now underway, since things didn't go as planned at Grimsthorpe. Also, because her aunt and uncle and the rest of her friends and family for the most part had not been able to attend. "Would you rather be wearing a costume and mask? Would that help?" she asked with a giggle.

"Nay, never again," he told her. "I like being who I am, not pretending to be someone else."

"Well, you know if we end up living at the castle after we are married, you'll not only be sitting up here to eat your meals every day, but you will have earned the courtesy title of being called Lord."

"Lord Fitch? Nay, that sounds weird," he told her, shaking his head. "I have always been Sheriff Fitch and that is what I'm used to. If we live in town after we're wed, I'll be able to keep being called Sheriff Fitch. Won't I?"

"I don't really know at this point," Vivienne told him. "It seems like whether we live here or in town, one of us is going to have to make a sacrifice. Our lives are really going to change, aren't they?"

"I suppose so," he said, still squirming in his chair, trying to get comfortable. "I never really gave much thought to what it would feel like to live as a noble, I suppose."

"Well, neither have I thought how it would feel to live as a commoner, either."

"What are we going to do?" he asked her. "We still haven't even decided where we want to have the wedding."

"Oh, Zachariah, look! Martin and Starah are having so much fun together. They are going to love being brother and sister." Vivienne realized she was trying to distract him and change the subject once again, but she just didn't want to have to plan the rest of their lives right in this minute. They were finally home again, and it felt good. All she wanted to do was to relax. And to spend time with the man she loved. Zachariah.

Vivienne's son Martin and the sheriff's daughter Starah were laughing and dancing around the floor to the music of a lone jester playing a small flute. The sheriff's sister Cassandra sat below the salt with his other sister, Magdalena. Magdalena had come here today from Mablethorpe Abbey to be with them. It did Vivienne's heart good to see a nun and an ex-prostitute sitting at the same table as sisters, with no barriers up between them.

"It was nice of the jury to pardon Rodger at the trial," she made small talk as they ate.

"The people of Grimsthorpe like Gunora, and she was able

to convince them of his innocence," said Zachariah. "I suppose Rodger isn't that bad, even if he doesn't really know the first thing about being a deputy."

"I hear they are both leaving Grimsthorpe to start a new life together. Isn't that nice?"

"I suppose so."

"Is Grimsthorpe going to have a new sheriff now that Ludwig has been condemned to death?" she asked.

"That is still something that King Edward has yet to decide," he told her. "Right now, the Town Watch will take over until things are finalized. However, Edward did agree that Sheriff Ludwig would be executed for the murders. Especially since Lord Daniel Lovelle was a good friend of his."

"Oh, Zachariah, did you give the King my missive? I told Lady Lovelle I'd put in a good word for her. Mayhap I should have gone with you."

"Nay, there was no need, Vivienne. He received the missive and said he'd make his decision soon regarding a new husband for Lady Lovelle. Whether he decides to assign one to her or let her choose her own."

"I hope she'll be able to marry Jerome."

"If she does, she'll no longer be able to stay at Grimsthorpe Manor, you realize."

"I know," said Vivienne. "However, I don't think Amelia really cares about that, as long as she can be with the father of her baby. Do you think the King will be giving the estate and lands to one of his wealthy barons if that happens?"

"He didn't say and I didn't ask. Don't worry, I am sure you will find out soon."

"I'd like to propose a toast to my niece, Lady Vivienne, and Sheriff Zachariah Fitch on their betrothal," called out Uncle Gilbert, raising his goblet in the air. He started to stand, but was yet to recover from his recent condition and still a bit wobbly.

So Vivienne's Aunt Ellen stood up and continued the toast for him.

"May you both find happiness together, and health of course. Oh, and lots of babies," said Ellen, followed by a giggle.

"Ellen, sit down," complained her husband. "You're embarrassing them and have had too much wine."

Everyone clapped, and the music started as the wine flowed freely.

"That's something we haven't even thought about, Vivienne." Zachariah looked up at her over the rim of his goblet.

"What's that? People embarrassing us?" she asked, giggling too.

"Nay. I'm talking about babies. Or us raising a family together."

"Oh." Vivienne lowered her goblet to the table. "That's true, we haven't discussed it. Yet. We'll do so right after we decide where we'll live."

"I'm Sheriff of Mablethorpe, sweetheart. It is important for me to be in town where I'm needed."

"I know and I understand. But your house is going to be too small for us, both our children, your sister, and any other children that might come along the way."

"Not to mention any more orphans you plan on taking in."

"Yes, that's right. I can't leave Mouse behind. And Maleine will need to be with me too."

"Zachariah groaned. "Well, what do you suggest, Vivienne?"

"My aunt and uncle have told us that we can live here at the castle. There is plenty of room. They offered to have the wedding here too."

"I see." Zachariah didn't seem pleased. "I'm sure that's where you want to live since you are a noble. It's where you belong. Not in a town." He said the words, but didn't sound as if he really believed them.

There was silence between them and Vivienne felt as if the mood was ruined. She needed to do something quickly to cheer them both up. "We haven't even discussed the wedding ceremony. Did you want to be married in town instead of here? If so, that is all right with me, I guess. As long as it is not on Rotten Row."

"Vivienne, I'm really not sure about anything right now. This is all happening so fast and it will mean a lot of changes for both of us, as well as the children and the rest of our families."

"I know. I've had a lot of questions rolling around in my mind lately too."

"You have?" He looked over to her in surprise. "Are you having second thoughts? About marrying me?"

"Nay! Never." She put her hand on his shoulder and sneaked a quick kiss to his cheek. "I think mayhap a little fresh air would do us both good. Why don't we sneak out of here and go for a ride? I saw an interesting area between here and Grimsthorpe that I'd like to check out."

"Really? What was it?"

"I couldn't tell for sure, but I saw some standing stones in a circle off in the distance. It looked so magical. Actually, I had a dream about it the other night and I feel as if it's calling to me."

"Magical," he repeated, looking at her from the side of his eye. "What do you really mean to say?"

"I mean, why don't we get out of here and go somewhere else? A place where it's quiet. In nature. Mayhap then we can both finally relax."

"All right, let's go," he told her. "I like that idea. And don't let the children or Isaac or even Grunt see us leave. I want time all alone with just you."

"Isaac's not going to notice, since he's been sitting there, nursing his drink and sulking ever since we returned."

"What's wrong with him?" asked Zachariah.

"I'm not sure, but I think he really took a liking to my sister and he's sad that she's gone."

"The fortune-teller?"

"Yes, the fortune-teller, but I wish you'd start calling her by her name. It's Morgana."

"Sorry, sweetheart. All right, let's sneak out of here and go have a magical time in this stone circle."

It didn't take them long to get to the stone circle, and when they arrived, the sun was just starting to set. The sky lit up in hues of orange and red, making the standing stones seem so majestic that it made Vivienne's heart sing.

"Oh, look, Zachariah." She slid off her horse. "The stones are so beautiful and look like they're glowing. And they're covered with vines and even some with roses." She ran into the middle of the stone circle and held out her arms and looked up at the vast, open sky.

"It is nice here, you're right." Zachariah walked up holding the reins of both the horses. "Very peaceful."

"Let's be married here instead of in town or at the castle," she said, feeling so excited that she could barely stand it.

"Here? Get married out here in nature? Inside a stone circle?"

"Sure. Why not?" she asked. "Then it is neither in town nor is it at Mablethorpe Castle. It is in between both. Neither one of us will have to compromise. And everyone can join us and it will be so perfect. This is the answer, I just know it is, Zachariah."

"Do you really think so?" Zachariah didn't seem as sure as she was about the idea.

"Yes. I do."

"Is this really want you want, Vivienne?" He took her hands in his and stared deeply into her eyes.

"It is. I want a perfect wedding with good things happening to us for a change. And I believe that right here in the stone circle is the best place for us to start our new life together."

"Then this is where we'll have it." Zachariah reached over and kissed her. "Now, the sun is going down, so let's get back before we're missed and anyone starts to worry."

"There's nothing to worry about anymore, my love. From now on, our lives as husband and wife will bring us nothing but good luck, happiness, and be our dreams come true."

"I'm sure you're right. Now come." Zachariah helped her mount her horse.

As they turned to go Vivienne thought she heard someone call out her name. *Vivienne*, she heard on the breeze. She glanced back over her shoulder and realized her eyes were playing tricks on her, because in the setting sun, in the center of the circle, for a brief second she swore she saw her mother standing there. But as fast as she'd appeared, she was gone.

"What is it, Vivienne?" asked Zachariah, as they slowly rode back to the castle.

"It's nothing." She glanced back once more but saw nothing. This time a shiver ran up her spine and she had no idea why. Her stomach clenched as well.

"Are you sure? Because right now I swear you look as if you've seen a ghost."

"A ghost?" That made her heart jump into her throat. "Why would you say that? You don't even believe in ghosts."

"Now, that's not true," he said with a deep chuckle. "After all, I have to admit I saw those two ghosts in the graveyard just like you did after we solved that murder at Maltby le Marsh. I just hope with our future cases we don't encounter that again because I really didn't like it in the least. I don't want anything to do with the spirit world."

"I agree," she told him. "However, you have to admit that seeing the ghosts wasn't half as scary as meeting that wretched rat catcher, the Pied Piper, on Rotten Row."

"Vivienne, as long as we're together, I can handle ghosts, rat catchers, pirates, or anything else that is thrown my way. I really enjoy our time together even if we are solving murders. The important part is that we're doing it together. And that is something I'll cherish forever."

"Me too," she softly answered, still wondering if she should stop investigating now that she was going to be his wife. She'd have two children to care for now, and mayhap more if they had babies together. That wasn't counting all the orphans she'd taken in, like Mouse and Maleine and Wymond and Leif. She didn't feel as if she could leave any of them behind. They were all her children in a way, and she liked filling the role of mother.

So many thoughts filled her head, but tonight she didn't want another worry. She just wanted to relax and be happy. "Let's race back to the castle, because I am so excited to tell everyone that we're going to be married in the stone circle that I can't wait any longer."

"Me too," he answered.

"Our wedding day is going to make up for all the other horrible things that have happened in our lives, Zachariah. The stone circle is a perfect place to start our new life together, and I just know we're going to be so happy. I cannot wait to get married."

"Neither can I."

With that, they raced their horses back to Mablethorpe Castle, not even knowing that they were being watched from the shadows inside the stone circle.

From the Author:

I hope you enjoyed *Murder at the Masquerade* and will take a moment to leave a review for me on Amazon, Goodreads, Book-Bub, or another social media platform.

Even though most of the time when you hear about a masquerade it takes place in the Renaissance Era, or even later, there were some masquerade balls in medieval times as well. One of the most talked about in recorded history was the Bal des Ardents or Ball of the Burning Men, which took place in Paris, France, in 1393. With everyone in costumes made from animal hair, feathers, wax, silk, velvet, and such, a burning torch was a true threat. As seen in this story, a torch was the cause of a deadly fire. At the Bal des Ardents, dancers dressed in costume were actually killed by burning to death.

The costumes were elaborate through the ages, some being of animals with antlers upon one's head and others portraying historical figures. Everyone wore masks hiding their identity which gave them the opportunity to flirt with whomever they wanted and no one would ever know. The masquerade was all about fantasy and playful deception.

Join me as Lady Vivienne Harlowe & Sheriff Zachariah

Fitch continue with their next endeavor in ***Murder at the Stone Circle***. While Vivienne is always hoping for a peaceful quiet life, trouble and murder always seem to follow her wherever she goes.

If you haven't read the rest of the books in my ***Harlowe & Fitch Historical Mystery Series***, please do so in order to find out what's happened up to this point. Each book is a standalone, but it is always best to read the series in order so surprises will not be ruined.

<u>The stories in the series are:</u>
> ***Murder at Mablethorpe Castle***
> ***Murder on Rotten Row* (my favorite)**
> ***Murder at Maltby le Marsh***
> ***Murder at the Joust***
> ***Murder on the High Seas***
> ***Murder of a Winchester Goose***
> ***Murder at the Masquerade***
> ***Murder at the Stone Circle***

If you like paperbacks and audiobooks as well as e-books, the good news is that my entire Harlowe & Fitch Historical Mystery Series will appear in all three formats.

And be sure to watch for a spin-off series with a paranormal touch, coming after the next book, the last book of the series releases.

To see more of my books (over 100 and counting), please stop by and visit my **Website** at **http://elizabethrosenovels.com.** You can also follow me on **Amazon, BookBub, Goodreads, Facebook, Bluesky, TikTok, Instagram,** and **Twitter**. I also have a **Private Readers' Group** on

Facebook that I invite you to join. And be sure to sign up for my newsletter, so you won't miss my new releases, sales, and contests. You can do so through my website at www.eliza bethrosenovels.com.

As I am sure you know by now, I like to have characters from some of my other books (mainly romances) make cameo appearances in different series. In this book you've met Vivienne's brother, Rowen the Restless, who is also a bastard of the King.

If you'd like to read his story and also about his brothers Rook and Reed, you can do so in **Legendary Bastards of the Crown**. They are triplets. Back then twins, or heaven forbid triplets, were considered spawned by the devil and bad luck. Therefore, King Edward has ordered his bastard triplets killed as babies, right after birth. Of course, someone saves them, and years later when they learn the truth, the brothers are out for revenge on dear old dad, but also find romance along the way.

Below, I'm including an excerpt from *Restless Sea Lord*, Rowen's story and the first book of the series.

Until next time,
Elizabeth Rose

Excerpt from Restless Sea Lord:

Excerpt: Restless Sea Lord

Legendary Bastards of the Crown, Book 1

SCOTLAND, WINTER 1356

From vengeance and strife, a legend is born.

Twelve-year-old Rowen Douglas looked up from his meal of eel and pottage as the door to the cottage burst open and his father limped in, being held up by their Uncle Malcolm. Rowen's brothers, Reed and Rook, looked up from their game of chess—a game they'd been taught by their father that Rowen could never win.

"Ross!" Their mother, Annalyse, gasped when she saw her injured husband. She'd been tending to Autumn, the baby of the family, while Rowen's two other sisters, Winter and Summer, sat playing on the floor by her feet. "What happened?" Annalyse put the baby down and ran to help her husband. Ross Douglas was a big man with red hair, and had a tremendous skill with the blade. But today, Rowen could see that his father had failed. Many times, Rowen's father returned from battle tired and dirty, but never had he looked so broken, bloodied, and defeated as now.

"'Tis bad, lassie. Verra bad," said Ross, shaking his head, his voice sounding low and gravelly. "Ye'd all better say a prayer." His mangled leg bled profusely and his green Douglas plaid was now black with soot. Malcolm looked no better.

Rowen's mother rushed around the room to collect water, herbs, and rags to use in aiding her husband.

"It's the English King Edward, isn't it?" she asked softly, looking over her shoulder at her triplet sons as if there was something she didn't want Rowen and his brothers to hear.

"Aye," Malcolm answered for them. "The English king has invaded with his troops and seized the castle at Berwick-upon-Tweed."

"Nay," said his mother, as she wrung out the water from a cloth and tended to her husband's wounds. "Tell me it isn't so."

"The Scots surrendered to him," said his father, with despair in his voice.

"Not only that," added Malcolm, "but Edward Balliol surrendered to the English wretch and resigned his claim to the Scottish crown."

"Oh!" shrieked Rowen's mother with her hand covering her mouth.

"The coast is on fire and Edward's troops continue to sack our lands, while his fleet of ships waits at the shore." Rowen's father gritted his teeth, holding his knee, and then half-squinted his eyes as he looked up to the ceiling. "The Scots are burnin' anythin' that could be used by the English, includin' livestock as they flee for their lives! We have no choice. We need to head for the Highlands. We're doomed, Annalyse, doomed I tell ye, and it's all because of the faither of our triplet sons." He shot the boys an angered look, fire in his eyes. Rowen felt confused as to what he meant.

"Ross, quiet!" warned Annalyse, putting down the cloth and hurrying to pick up one of the crying siblings. "We promised to keep my sister's secret—now hush."

Rowen looked over to his brothers. They didn't need to speak to know they were all wondering the same thing. Rising from the table, they headed over to their father.

"Father, what do you mean?" asked Rowen. He and Rook used the speech and mannerisms of their English mother. But Reed, who was closest to their Scottish father, mimicked the man. He talked with the Scottish burr and even wore a plaid, though Rowen and Rook wore tunics and breeches.

"We'll get that bastard," said Reed, pulling his dagger from his waistband. "Let me fight the English king."

"Nay, let me cut off his head, instead," said Rook, pulling his dagger from his waistband as well.

"You fools! We can't fight with only daggers," said Rowen. "Father, give us our swords. You've trained us as warriors, and we'll make the English king pay for what they've done to you and our land."

"Nay!" shouted his mother, trying to calm the squalling baby. "You boys will do no such thing."

"Why not?" asked Reed. "We hate the English."

"Reed, stop it," warned Rowen. "Mother is English, or did you forget?"

"Don't ever talk that way about King Edward," his mother warned them.

"Why shouldna we hate him? We're Scots," said Reed.

"Half-Scots," Rook reminded him.

"Stop the squabblin'," shouted their father, reaching for a bottle of whisky on the table. He pulled out the cork with his teeth and spit it across the room. "Yer mathair doesna want ye to hate King Edward, but I feel as if ye should. I dinna care if he's yer real faither."

"Ross!" shouted their mother, and Rowen saw the tears in her eyes.

"Our real father?" asked Rowen. "What does that mean?"

"Ye're our faither," said Reed, going to his side.

Their uncle worked at wrapping up their father's leg, shaking his head and keeping silent. Ross picked up the bottle and took a swig of whisky, his eyes never leaving his wife.

"How could you break our promise to my dead sister?" asked their mother angrily.

"I dinna care any longer and neither will I pretend the boys are mine when they are that bastard's!" Ross finished off the whisky and threw the bottle across the room. It hit the wall of the cottage and shattered upon the dirt floor.

"King Edward of England is our father?" asked Rook. Rook's hair was as black as a raven, but his eyes were clear blue just like his brothers.

"You're saying we're bastards?" asked Rowen.

"Ye're no' really our faither?" asked Reed, sounding the most disappointed of the three of them.

"It's time they ken," said Ross, shaking his head and looking down at his mangled leg. "I'll ne'er be able to stand and fight again. And because of their faither, I've lost most of my family. Now our lands are being burned to the ground."

Shouting came from outside. Their uncle ran over to the door to talk to the passersby.

"What's happenin'?" asked Malcolm.

"Berwickshire is wasted, and now the English king is headin' north to Haddingtonshire," said the man outside the door. "Ye need to get yer family to safety."

"Annalyse, take the girls to the Highlands where ye'll be safe," ordered Ross.

"I'll not leave without you," she said, sounding frightened and angry at the same time. Little Autumn started to cry again. Annalyse picked her up and went over to comfort the other two girls.

"I will just slow ye down," Ross told her. "I am too wounded to walk or even ride a horse."

"We'll take the cart," said Malcolm. "I'll go hitch up the horse." He hurried out the door. Reed looked at his brothers, able to feel their emotions and know they were just as upset as him.

"Mother, tell us the truth," said Rowen. "Are we really the English king's bastards?"

His mother's eyes interlocked with their father's. The glance they exchanged told him it was true. Finally, she answered in a soft voice.

"Yes, boys, you are. I'm sorry to have never told you, but your mother, my sister, begged me on her deathbed to not only keep it a secret, but to raise you as my own."

"Nay! It's no' true!" Reed looked over to the only father they'd ever known and the man they most admired.

"It is true, boys," said Ross, his shoulders slumping as he leaned forward on the chair. "Yer true mathair was a mistress to the English king. She died birthin' ye, and the king feared ye."

"Why would a king fear babies?" spat Rook.

"Because ye were born on the cursed day of the Holy Innocents, and ye all looked verra much alike. Ye ken the superstitions surroundin' twins." He moaned in pain and tried to wrap his leg on his own. Rowen could see the shards of broken bone sticking out from his knee.

"But we're not twins," said Rook.

"Nay, but I was," answered their mother, putting down the baby and coming to gather the boys into her arms. "I was a twin. I will tell you that you're lucky no one in Scotland has considered you evil and spawns of the devil for not being the first born. We did what was necessary to protect you boys. We love you and don't you ever forget that."

"Nay," said Rook, pushing away from her. "If you loved us, you would have told us the truth years ago."

"Would ye have wanted to ken that ye were bastards of an enemy who ordered ye all killed at birth because he was afeared of bein' cursed by ye?" shouted Ross, having no more patience for this conversation.

"Ross! That's enough." Annalyse pulled all three boys to her in a protective hug. "We've got to get to safety before it's too late."

"I don't want to hide. I want to fight the man who wanted me dead!" said Rook, always the angriest of the three. They'd been called Rowen the Restless, Rook the Ruthless, and Reed the Reckless, their entire lives. Tonight was no different because they were about to live up to their names.

"I can't just hide. I want to fight, too," said Rowen, always feeling unsettled.

"Look at your father and what the king and his army did to him," said their mother in a stern voice. "You boys are young and can't yet fight like a man. What do you think will happen to you? It's too dangerous out there."

"He's no' our faither," spat Reed, eying the broken and bloodied man on the chair. "And we ken how to handle a sword. I'm goin' to get our swords from the barn and fight!"

"Me, too," said Rook. The two boys ran from the house.

"Nay! Stop!" shouted their mother. Rowen just watched what transpired, not knowing what to do. "Rowen, go stop your brothers," begged Annalyse. "Make them come with us to the Highlands."

Rowen understood his brothers' anguish because the same vengeance now flowed through his blood. He didn't want to cower in fear from the man who'd ordered his death when he was naught but an innocent and helpless infant. He wanted to fight as well.

"Tell me about our mother," said Rowen. "Did she love King Edward?" he asked, needing to know if his mother had been used as naught but a whore.

"Aye, she did love him," said Annalyse. "And she loved you boys, too. She was the one to name you. She said someday you'd all be legends."

"How did we survive death?" he asked, his eyes going back to the man he'd thought for the last twelve years was his father.

"Rowen, you don't need to know that right now," Annalyse spoke out.

Also by Elizabeth Rose

Mystery Series:

Harlowe & Fitch Historical Mystery Series

Murder at Mablethorpe Castle

Murder on Rotten Row

Murder at Maltby le Marsh

Murder at the Joust

Murder on the High Seas

Murder of a Winchester Goose

Murder at the Masquerade

Medieval Series:

Below the Salt

Legendary Bastards of the Crown Series

Seasons of Fortitude Series

Secrets of the Heart Series

Legacy of the Blade Series

Daughters of the Dagger Series

MadMan MacKeefe Series

Barons of the Cinque Ports Series

Holiday Knights Series

Highland Chronicles Series

Pirate Lords Series

Highland Outcasts

Medieval/Paranormal Series:

Elemental Magick Series

Greek Myth Fantasy Series

Tangled Tales Series

Portals of Destiny

Contemporary Series:

Tarnished Saints Series

Working Man Series

Western Series:

Cowboys of the Old West Series

And More!

Please visit http://elizabethrosenovels.com

About Elizabeth

Elizabeth Rose is an award-winning, bestselling author of over 100 books and counting. She writes medieval, historical, contemporary, paranormal, and western romance. Her books are available as EBooks, paperbacks, and some audiobooks as well.

Her favorite characters in her works include dark, dangerous and tortured heroes, and feisty, independent heroines who know how to wield a sword. She loves writing 14th century medieval novels, and is well-known for her many series.

Elizabeth loves the outdoors. In the summertime, you can find her in her secret garden with her laptop, swinging in her hammock working on her next book. Elizabeth is a born storyteller and passionate about sharing her works with her readers.

Please be sure to visit her website at **Elizabethrosenovels.com** to read excerpts from any of her novels and get sneak peeks at covers of upcoming books. Join Elizabeth's **newsletter** so you don't miss out on new releases or upcoming events. There is also a **Private Readers' Group** on Facebook that she invites you to join.

A small press bound by the belief that every voice matters.

Sign up for our newsletter to learn about new releases and more.
https://oliver-heberbooks.com/subscribe/

Follow us on social media:

facebook.com/oliverheberbooks

instagram.com/oliverheberbooks

amazon.com/oliverheberbooks

youtube.com/@OliverHeberBooksPublisher